Murder at the Columbarium

Emily Gallo

The author may be reached at ecegallo@gmail.com

www.emilygallo.com
http://emilygallo.blogspot.com/

ISBN-13: 978-1950561087

ISBN-10: 1979821283

The first step to living the life you want is leaving the life that you don't want.

That happened. Now you get to choose what happens next.

1

JED WAS UNLOCKING THE FRONT GATE OF THE COLUMBARIUM WHEN HE THOUGHT HE HEARD A CAT IN DISTRESS. He peered around into the typical San Francisco gray misty morning but saw nothing. He pulled the key from the lock, pushed open the gate, and started walking toward the front door. The strange noise was now clearly near his feet. When he stooped to look he didn't find a cat, but an infant swaddled in a pink blanket. He froze for a moment, caught up in a fast track of repressed memory, and then he brushed the branches away to lift the baby. The tableau widened and darkened with the sweep of his arm. There was a black shoe lying on the ground and a few inches away he noticed a leg and then saw it was attached to the body of a woman. "Oh!" Jed gasped. The woman wore a long, black, embroidered dress and there was a hijab wrapped tightly around her neck. Her eyes were open but staring straight ahead, vacantly. Jed pressed the infant tightly to his chest.

Jed was a tall, sinewy African-American in his early sixties. He was one of those people who turned heads not because of his good looks, but for his aloofness and the general air of mystery about him.

Slowly he pulled himself together and started rocking the baby. The baby's mewling softened as he walked into the office and sat down at his desk. His only thought was to soothe the baby. He wished he had a rocking chair but maybe the swivel action of the office chair would work. Jed wasn't new to soothing babies in pain and he was good at it. His brain skimmed through his limited repertoire of songs to come up with an appropriate one and landed on *Amazing Grace*. Maybe that one was a little too appropriate. He started to sing.

After the baby quieted down, Jed realized he needed to call the police. He dialed 911. "I am the caretaker of the columbarium on Lorraine Court and I just got to work. I found a dead body . . . and a baby lying next to it. They were lying outside the building." He took a deep breath. It had been a long time since he needed to use his pranayama breathing. "Yes. The baby is alive. My name? Jed Gibbons." He hung up and continued to breathe and rock the baby until he heard the distant sound of sirens. Then he stood up and walked outside, cradling the now cooing baby.

An ambulance arrived first, closely followed by two police cars and a fire truck. Why did they need to send a fire truck whenever they sent an ambulance? And why did they dispatch two police cars? Isn't there enough crime in the city of San Francisco to keep the police busy enough for them to go on separate calls? A dead body hardly warranted all of that. He approached the cars and trucks just as the EMTs were stepping out of the ambulance. "You the guy who called?" one of them asked as he approached Jed.

"Yes. I'm the caretaker. It's over here." Jed led the way to the woman's body. Three policemen followed behind, sauntering and talking among themselves. Jed stepped aside after pulling the branches away to expose the body. The baby started wailing again and he sang softly while patting her back. One of the policemen approached Jed.

"The baby was with the body?"

"Yes. That's how I found the body. I heard the crying."

"When did you get here?"

"About fifteen minutes ago."

The policeman nodded and went back to his patrol car. Jed noticed him speaking into the radio. A couple of minutes later the cop returned to where Jed was waiting. "The detectives will be here shortly to ask you some more questions."

Jed nodded and turned his attention back to the EMTs. They had confirmed that the woman was dead and they were now chatting nonchalantly with the firemen and policemen. The whole scene seemed surreal. He hadn't had a PTSD episode in a long time. Each time he had one, he was brought back to the escape from Jonestown more than forty years ago: the screaming and gunshots and then the running. His heart pounded, he had difficulty swallowing, his head throbbed, and he gasped for breath. Jed resumed his pranayama breathing. After getting his emotions under control, he asked, "What about the baby?"

"We'll call Family and Children's Services. They'll bring her to the hospital and have her checked out and then find a foster home until we can locate the family. I assume it's a 'she' since the blanket is pink."

"I guess so. I haven't looked," Jed answered.

He walked away and took out his cell phone. He dialed Monica's number and told his wife what was happening. As he spoke to her, he looked down at the baby's face and saw a sweet smile. Jed smiled back and pulled her up to his chest. "How awful! Are you okay?" Monica asked.

"Yes, I'm fine."

"Do you want me to come down there?"

"No. I'll call you when I know more." He hung up and watched as two more cars pulled up, one a Ford Escape, the other a Toyota Prius. Two men in suits got out of the Escape and a young woman got out of the Prius. Jed figured out pretty quickly who was who.

The woman got there first. "Are you Jed Gibbons?"

"Yes."

"I'm Elizabeth Halifax. I'm a social worker with the city. I can take the baby." She reached for the baby and Jed handed her over.

"What hospital will you bring her to?" he asked.

"San Francisco General."

He nodded and turned toward the two detectives who had just appeared next to him. "Jed Gibbons?" the portly, balding, middle-aged, white one asked.

"Yes." Jed spent the next half hour relating how he stumbled upon the body and answered a plethora of what he considered unnecessary questions. He finally interrupted them. "I need to call the Neptune Society to let them know what's happened. They run the columbarium. I assume I won't be opening today?"

"That's correct. Go ahead and call them but don't go anywhere. We'll need to take you downtown." That was the other one, a thin Hispanic man who looked to be in his thirties.

"Why?"

"You're a witness."

"I'm not a witness. I just found the body. And I've already answered a lot of questions."

"We need to get your answers on tape. And you are the only witness so far."

"Anyway, wasn't the gate locked?" the other detective asked.

"Yes."

"Hmm. Then how did she get in?" He raised his eyebrows. "And how did the murderer get in?"

That was the moment that Jed grasped the seriousness of his situation.

2

JED CALLED THE NEPTUNE SOCIETY BOARD PRESIDENT AND GAVE A BRIEF ACCOUNT OF WHAT HAPPENED. Then he called Monica to tell her that he had to go to the police station.

"Why?" she asked.

"I wondered the same thing. I guess I'm the only witness."

"But you're not a witness. You didn't see her get killed."

"I'm the closest thing to one because I found her body. I need to cooperate." Jed paused and his voice softened. "I might still be in the system as a fugitive."

"That was a long time ago, and you were only a person of interest."

"C'mon Monica. This may be San Francisco, but I'm still a black man and this is the police." He bit his tongue on the pointed observation the detective had made. No need to worry her. "I'll call you later when I'm done," he added hastily as the detectives approached.

"Are you ready to go?" one of them asked.

"What about the columbarium? No one will be here to let people know what's going on."

"There will be plenty of people here to keep people out and there will be police tape across the gate." Jed reluctantly agreed and followed the detectives to their car. They were both silent throughout the drive to the station.

When they arrived at the police station he was taken to a small interrogation room, empty except for an old wooden table and four folding chairs. Jed glanced around, looking for the cameras he knew were probably there.

"Do you want a cup of coffee?" the older detective asked.

"No."

"I'm Inspector Goodman. My partner will be here shortly and we can start the interview. Have a seat." Goodman left the room.

It was more like half an hour before the door opened and Inspector Goodman entered followed by two people, an African-American woman in her sixties and the Hispanic male he had spoken to earlier. "Hey, Jed. I'm Inspector Diaz."

Jed turned to the woman, expecting her to introduce herself as well. She didn't. In fact, her steely expression and hostile body language made Jed think that she was playing the "bad cop" role. How appropriate that Inspector Goodman played the "good cop" one. He decided to make a stab at being in the less subordinate position by asking the woman her name. "And you are?"

The woman was taken aback, but then her expression turned quizzical. "Captain Young," she answered but didn't shake the hand he offered.

"So, Jed, tell us what happened," Diaz said.

Jed frowned. It was maddening to him that police, doctors, lawyers etc., used their last names with a title while he was always just Jed. Do they only do this to African-American men? Besides which, he was probably twice Diaz's age. "We are taping this so please speak clearly. Please start from the beginning and include the time you got to work and when you found the body."

Jed told his story to the inspectors and the sullen captain. When he finished, he watched the captain's expression. It must have been just protocol for her to be there, but it was obviously the last place she wanted to be. Maybe she was on the verge of retirement and was counting the days. At any rate, everyone was cordial enough. Maybe the television crime shows exaggerated the good cop/bad cop interviewing technique. "What's going to happen to the baby?" Jed asked.

"That's no longer in our control. Family and Children's Services is in charge."

"Can I leave now?"

"How do we get in touch with you?"

"At the columbarium."

"Outside of working hours?"

Jed gave the two inspectors his cell phone number. Before Jed left the police station, he asked the sergeant at the desk to look up the address of Family and Children's Services. It wasn't too far away so he decided to stop off there before going back to the columbarium. He called Monica while he walked. "I did the interrogation and now I'm going to check on that baby."

"You are? Why?"

"I don't know. I'm curious, I guess."

"I could call for you. I know some social workers there."

"I need to walk."

"Yeah, I know." Before he learned Pranayama breathing, he used to just walk . . . sometimes for long distances. "Keep me posted," she replied.

He got to the address given to him by the sergeant and walked inside. No one there knew what he was talking about and explained to him that there were several different offices. When he got outside and started walking back to the columbarium, he called Monica back. "I'll take you up on your offer to make those calls."

"Okay. Are you on your way back to the columbarium?"

"Yep." Jed hung up. When he arrived at the columbarium he saw a horde of news station trucks parked on the tiny, usually quiet cul de sac. The policeman guarding the gate remembered him, thank goodness, so he was able to sneak under the tape before the reporters and photographers could get to him. The last thing he wanted was to see his face on the 5 o'clock news.

3

JED ANSWERED PHONE CALLS IN HIS OFFICE MOST OF THE DAY. The family members of the columbarium occupants were worried. A few years ago there had been a bout of vandalism that had almost closed it down. The news of the murder had everyone anxious about another possible closure. The body was finally removed that afternoon and the police cleared out about four. A couple of the board members had shown up at lunchtime, but it was mostly just for appearance sake. Jed was the man in charge . . . always. He decided to go home early. There was no point opening for one hour.

Their house was only a few blocks away. Monica wasn't there when Jed got home. She worked at Glide Church as a social worker, helping the homeless and the marginalized population get the resources they needed: housing and job help, as well as a place to take a shower and some clothes and food. Sometimes they required her expertise to diffuse situations that arose, so she had to stay until the crisis was over. She finally walked in the door after seven, finding Jed sitting on the sofa in the dark.

"You okay, babe?" she asked softly.

"Yeah," he murmured as he tried to find his voice. "It kind of threw me for a loop, seeing that poor woman's body and trying to quiet her baby."

"At least the baby part was right up your alley." Monica's hand slid down his shoulder as she sat down next to him. "Why do you think she was at the columbarium?"

"I don't know." Jed turned on a lamp and sat up. "But I think I've seen her there before."

"Really? Who was she visiting?"

"I don't remember." He stood up and started to pace. "I need to think about this."

"Well can you think about it while we eat? I'm starving."

Jed got up and went towards the kitchen. "I made pasta and salad. Nothing fancy."

Monica had known Jed long enough to eat in silence when he had something to ponder. Several minutes went by before she finally spoke. "Oh, I did talk to some of my friends in Family and Children's Services. They said they'll look into it and get back to me tomorrow."

"I wonder if I could go see the body again."

Monica's fork fell to her plate, her appetite momentarily lost. "What?"

"Maybe I'll recognize her." Jed bolted from the table and found his phone in his jacket pocket. He dialed the number of the police station and was put through to Goodman's voice mail. "This is Jed Gibbons. Please call me back as soon as possible. I might have some information for you." He hung up.

"Guess it can't hurt to show them you're cooperative," Monica mused.

"Are there any alternatives?" But before Monica could answer, Jed's phone rang. He answered. "Hello? Yes, this is Jed. I was wondering if you have a picture of the victim. I may have seen her visiting a niche and maybe it would jog my memory as to which one." He glanced at Monica who nodded in approval. "Okay. Now? I guess I can be there in an hour." He hung up and looked at Monica apprehensively. "I hope I won't be sorry for this."

"You're doing the right thing. That's what's important. I can drive you."

"Nah, I'll walk." He took a bite of salad and motioned to her to continue eating.

They ate quickly and silently, both of them not exactly sure that what Jed was doing was a wise choice. Some years ago he had been a person of interest in the death of a woman in Venice. He hadn't killed her, but he had been in her motel room and he had a motive. The woman had been a nurse in Jonestown where Jed had spent several years of his childhood and where his mother and sister had died. It hadn't been easy proving his innocence.

"Are you sure I can't drive you?"

"I'll be fine." He kissed her, grabbed his jacket, and walked out the door. When he got to the station, the sergeant at the desk said that Inspector Goodman hadn't arrived yet, so Jed sat on a bench to wait. He watched two cops come in with a couple of prostitutes and then a couple more arrived with a vagrant who was obviously high on some hallucinogenic drug. It brought back memories of his nights sleeping on the Venice Beach boardwalk.

After several minutes Inspector Diaz showed up, dressed in more casual attire than the business suit he wore earlier. "Hi Jed. Inspector Goodman will be here any minute. Follow me." Jed followed him into a large room with several old metal desks. Diaz's desk was toward the back of the room. He motioned to Jed to sit on a chair alongside the desk. "Coffee?"

"No thanks."

"Well, I need some." He went to a table with a coffee maker and poured two cups and brought them back to his desk.

"I really don't want any."

"I know but I'm sure Ted will." They sat in silence as Diaz went through some papers on his desk. "Ah, here it is." He took out a packet of papers stapled together. "No name yet. She had no identification on her."

"Hey Jed," Goodman called out as he entered the room. "Thanks for your call." He approached Diaz's desk and pulled up a chair. He was still in the clothes he wore earlier minus coat and tie.

"I was just telling Jed here that she had no identification."

"Do you know her?" Goodman was blunt.

"No. But I wanted to look at her face and see if I recognized her and remember who she might have been visiting."

Goodman and Diaz glanced at each other. "Do you have the picture of the body yet?" Goodman asked Diaz.

"Not yet. Haven't got one from the lab."

Goodman turned to Jed. "Do you want to see the body?"

"Uh, I dunno." Jed faltered. "Are they open now?"

"Someone's always there." Diaz and Goodman both stood. "Let's go, buddy," Goodman said touching his shoulder.

Jed followed them out and down to the squad car. No one said a word during the drive to the medical examiner's office. When they got there, Goodman knocked on a door and a diminutive Asian woman answered. "Hey Ted. Hey Mario."

"Hey, May. That woman from the columbarium, have you finished working her up?"

"Still on the table." She opened the door wider for the men to file in. She nodded at Jed. "You a relative?"

"No. I work at the columbarium."

She gave the officers an appraising look and crooked her head to follow her. They came into a large room set up like an operating arena and walked to a covered body on one of the tables. May lifted the sheet and folded it across the chest. Jed looked at the woman's face. She was young, a pretty woman, brown-skinned or maybe multiracial like Monica. He stared for a couple of minutes and then turned to Goodman. "Yes. I do remember seeing her in the columbarium. I think it was yesterday. I don't know whose niche she was visiting though. That's not coming back to me right now."

"I should have all the results by the morning," May said. "I'll send them up when I'm done."

"Anything unusual so far?"

"Not really. Strangled with her own hijab."

"Thanks, May," Diaz said.

They all filed out and went back to the police station. "You can leave," Goodman said. "We'll be in touch tomorrow. Thanks for coming down."

Jed nodded and walked briskly out. It had started to rain so he jogged the few blocks. He felt a tightening in his chest and a knot in his stomach. He was anxious to get home and into Monica's arms.

4

JED SLEPT SOUNDLY AFTER HE AND MONICA MADE LOVE. He awoke groggy after such an unusually long sleep, and went to the kitchen to make a pot of coffee. He was on his second cup when Monica sat down to join him. "You snored last night," she laughed. "You must have been really tired."

"I guess I was."

"Did you dream about who she was visiting?"

Jed shook his head. "Nope. Two cups of coffee haven't given me any idea, either."

"So I guess it's just back to work."

"Yeah. I need to see if the cops damaged anything."

"What kind of damage?"

"I don't know. I just want to go early and check things out. It may jog my memory."

"Now you're adding 'detective' to your resume?"

"I . . . no, just . . . I don't know."

"I'm just teasing. I'll call you as soon as I hear anything about the baby." She paused and then asked warily, "You're not thinking of adding 'father' to that resume, are you?"

"Of course not." Jed snapped. "How could we take a baby? We both work . . ." he trailed off. Monica turned her gaze out the window. Jed touched her chin and brought her face around to face him. "Right?"

Monica smiled. "You know it's a crazy idea. We're too old to take care of a baby and raise a child."

"I know." Jed kissed her and left to take a shower and try to wash such thoughts out of his mind.

He got to work and found the police tape torn and flapping, but no cops there. He walked gingerly around the clump of bushes where the body had been, but found nothing unusual except for the trampled plants.

He unlocked the front door and went inside gingerly, worried that he might find some vandalism. He went on his regular early morning rounds. First he went to Rose's "apartment." He called the smaller niches "apartments" and the larger ones "condos." Rose's looked fine. Her beloved San Francisco Giants memorabilia and the mural Tony had painted were intact. He hummed a few bars of "Take Me Out to the Ball Game" and moved on.

He stopped at Frank's apartment and found his beads and vaudeville accouterments untouched as well. Jed took out the tiny horn and blew it and followed that with some of "Give my Regards to Broadway" and then turned his gaze to Goldie's, right next to him. He gasped. The glass door was broken, the mezuzah that had been nailed to the front was on the floor, and the jar of gefilte fish was broken, its jellied broth spilt all over the inside of her apartment. It brought back those awful memories from several years ago when the vandalism at the columbarium was extensive and almost shut it down.

He hurried down to Sam and Sadie's condo as rage boiled up inside him. The tomatoes on the sconces that were mounted on either side of the door were smashed on the floor along with the glass from the broken door. A swastika was spray painted across their picture displayed in a frame inside. Yet, Chloe's, right next to it, was not affected.

He checked out Sunny's and some of the other African-American apartments. Their doors were also smashed and their contents strewn about. Remembering that the murdered woman had been wearing a hijab, he started to put things together. He had not gone inside yesterday morning to see this. He needed to call Goodman. Could this be some kind of domestic terrorism? It was certainly a hate crime at the very least.

He took out his phone and made the call, left a message, and continued to check out the rest of the niches. There were almost nine thousand in total, but not all of them were filled. As he walked around all four floors and waited for Goodman to return his call, his hunch was verified over and over. Those that belonged to whites of indeterminate religion were left alone. Finally his phone rang. "Hello? Jed Gibbons speaking."

"It's Inspector Goodman. You called?"

"Yes. There's been some vandalism inside the building."

"What's the damage?"

"Many of the niches were broken into, their glass doors smashed and the contents spread around the floor. All the ones that were hit belonged to Jews and people of color." The inspector was silent for a full minute. "Are you there?" Jed finally asked.

"Yeah. People of color, huh. You mean Blacks?"

"Well . . . yes."

"Interesting."

"I thought maybe it was some kind of hate crime because the woman was wearing a hijab." Jed tried to interpret Goodman's apparent lack of interest in this news.

"Hmmm. Yes. Well, I'll come down. Please don't start cleaning up until we've had a chance to check it out and dust for fingerprints."

"Okay. Do you know when that will be? I need to be able to tell people when we'll be opening."

"Within the hour. By the way, have you remembered where you might have seen the woman?"

"No," Jed answered. "Did you get the results from the lab?"

"Not yet. I'll see you shortly, Jed." The inspector hung up.

Jed put the phone in his pocket and flopped into the nearest chair. His heart was beating way too fast, so he tried some breathing to calm himself. Before he reached any sense of serenity, however, his phone rang again. He didn't want to talk to anyone, even though he knew he had to tell the board and the visitors something. He looked and saw it was Monica so he answered. "Hi." He tried to sound nonchalant. It didn't work.

"What's wrong?" she asked.

He sighed. "When I got inside I saw that a lot of the apartments and condos had been vandalized. Swastikas on Sam's and Goldie's, KKK on Sunny's . . . lots of broken glass . . . you get the picture."

"Hate crime."

"Yep. I just got off the phone with the police. They're on their way down."

"Well that's good. Maybe this will help find the killer."

Jed started to talk but stopped. He didn't need to worry Monica with his paranoia. "So, did you have some news or just calling to check up on me?"

"Oh yeah. Sorry. I heard from my friend. The baby is in a temporary foster home."

"Is the baby going to be able to stay there?"

"Not too long. Apparently they have different levels of foster home and this is a very short term placement."

"So, what will happen if they don't find any family to take her?"

"She'll go to another more permanent one if they can find one. Fewer people are fostering because of all the budget cuts. There isn't as much money in it for them as there used to be."

"What does it take to become a foster parent?"

"Why do you want to know?"

"Well, we could do it temporarily." Monica didn't answer. "What do you think?" Jed added.

"What about our jobs?"

"I could take her to work. It wouldn't be a problem."

"You really are serious?"

"I guess I am. Are you game? I mean it wouldn't be forever. Just until they identify the body and locate her family."

Monica sighed. "I'll look into it and get back to you." She hung up as abruptly as Goodman did. He went downstairs to make a sign explaining to the public why the doors were still closed. He was angry that the police seemed disinterested in the hate crime angle and wanted to write something apropos to that, but he settled for CLOSED FOR POLICE INVESTIGATION and taped it to the door.

5

JED DIDN'T HAVE TO WAIT LONG. Goodman and Diaz arrived within fifteen minutes, trailed by a motley group of men and women. Some were in uniform, but there were others who Jed assumed had to be fingerprint technicians and investigators of some kind. It seemed to him to be a bit of overkill, but there were a lot of damaged niches to examine. Goodman stayed with the others while Diaz approached Jed. "Thanks for calling, Jed. Is there somewhere else we can go to talk?"

"Talk about what?" Jed asked warily.

"It might get pretty noisy in here," Diaz responded, ignoring Jed's question. Jed led him to his office in back of the building and sat down. Diaz took out his tape recorder and set it on the desk as he pulled up a chair to face Jed. "I need to tape this. Do you mind?"

"No." Jed had already decided to say as little as possible. He was beginning to realize that he may need a lawyer and was trying to think if he knew one.

"So, Jed, just tell me what you told Goodman this morning."

"When I opened up this morning and went inside I saw that many of the niches were vandalized. All the targeted ones were . . ." Jed hesitated.

"Yes?" Diaz prompted.

"Uh, they were all Jews and Blacks. There were swastikas and KKK letters."

"And what's your assumption, then?" Jed stared at Diaz, not sure how to answer. How would it sound to the police? Would they make their own assumptions based on how he responded? "Jed?"

"Um, that it might be related to the murder."

"In what way?"

"I don't know. What do you think?" Jed sat back and crossed his arms.

"I'll ask the questions. I'm not the one being interviewed."

Jed exhaled and shrugged. "That maybe it was a hate crime because she was wearing a hijab."

Diaz smiled and nodded. "Do you know how many niches were hit?"

"No. I didn't count them. Isn't that what the police would do?"

"I'm sure they are doing their jobs."

"I didn't say they weren't." Jed sighed. "Look, I have a lot of cleaning up to do. Any idea how long this will take?"

"The interview is essentially over unless you have more to add."

"I meant in there," Jed said as he pointed to the main building.

"Nope. You'll have to ask them." Diaz stood and put the tape recorder away. "I'm sure we'll have more questions. You aren't planning on going on a trip or anything, are you?" He smiled a bit too smugly.

"No. I'm not going anywhere. I have a lot of cleaning up to do."

"Good. We'll be in touch. And let us know if you think of anything else."

After Diaz left, Jed leaned back in his chair and closed his eyes. He practiced his breathing techniques for a few minutes and was able to get his emotions under control. He let his mind wander to daydreaming about the baby. He opened his eyes and took out a piece of paper and a pen and started to make a list of the equipment they would need if they brought a baby into their house. He was startled out of his musings when the phone rang. He saw it was Monica calling. "Hello, love."

"I found out where the baby is and what it would take for us to register as foster parents. It's usually a long procedure, but it pays to know people in high places. Or at least in the world of San Francisco social work." She laughed. "I doubt, however, that would be considered a high place."

"Are you kidding? Social work and teaching are the noblest professions there are!"

"Pass that along to the taxpayers, will you?" she laughed. "Anyway, we can skip a lot of the red tape and I've filled out the paperwork. They still need to come out to the house and look around. Can you meet them there?"

"Sure!" Jed stood up abruptly, grinning. "When?"

"I'll have them call you and set it up. I need to get back to work. Oh, how did the interview go with the inspectors?"

"Pretty quick. Nothing major. But I still don't know what they're thinking about me."

"Relax. They have no reason to suspect you. Especially in light of the damage done to the building."

"I guess you're right. A Black man would hardly be spray-painting KKK across the door to Sunny's niche. Besides I'd just be making more work for myself!"

Jed went out to the main building to see how the investigation was going. Only a handful of people were actually doing any work. Most of them were just standing around joking with each other. He made a beeline for Goodman. "Any idea when they'll be finished?"

"No I don't, Jed."

"Well, I may need to leave and run an errand."

"That's fine. You don't need to be here."

"Well, what about locking up when you're done?"

"How long do you plan to be gone?"

"I'm not sure," Jed answered.

"We'll keep a cop at the door until you get back."

"Okay. Thanks." Jed rushed out and walked briskly home. He wanted to make sure the house was immaculate and inviting.

He had been home about half an hour when his phone rang. "Is this Jed Gibbons?" The female voice was soft and pleasant-sounding.

"Yes."

"This is Elizabeth Halifax. We met briefly the other day at the columbarium."

"Oh yes. Hello."

"I spoke with your wife, Monica. She said you'd be able to meet me at your house this afternoon?"

"Can you come now? I'm home."

"I guess I can be there in about half an hour."

"Great. You have the address?"

"Yes. Monica gave it to me."

"I'll see you soon." He hung up and scurried around, stuffing things that seemed un-child-friendly into a cedar chest in the bedroom. He went into the spare bedroom and piled things up so that it would look roomy for the addition of a crib. He gave the bathroom and kitchen a cursory wipe down and finished just as the doorbell rang.

"Hi Jed."

"Come in." Jed opened the front door wider and escorted Elizabeth into the living room.

She took out a clipboard and glanced around the room. "Nice place. And the flowers out front are lovely."

"There were tomatoes growing there when I moved in, but we haven't had success in keeping them going."

"I didn't think you could grow tomatoes in San Francisco."

"Normally you can't. But the woman who lived here before us was a magician as a gardener."

"This is a lovely house." She looked at him curiously.

Jed knew that she was wondering how he and Monica could afford a house like this in this neighborhood. "The house was left to me by someone whose ashes are in a niche at the columbarium. Sam and Sadie died just days apart."

"You're the son he never had?"

"Something like that."

She nodded and toured the rest of the house, checking off items on the paper attached to the clipboard as she went. "Everything looks good. Can you get a crib for the baby? We have some to loan but if you can't afford one—"

"Of course," Jed interrupted. "No problem. When can we get the baby?"

"You know this is a temporary home, right? There is much more paperwork you have to fill out to apply as foster parents. I can zip this through as emergency fostering because Monica is who she is. But I can't do anything for you long term. It's out of my hands."

"I understand."

"What time will Monica be home?"

"Usually about 6."

"I'll bring the baby this evening then. I'd like you both to be here and that will give you time to buy the crib. Please don't get a hand-me-down or a thrift store one. They don't usually meet the legal specifications. Normally I would have to check that off. I'm trusting you won't get me into any trouble." She smiled.

"Don't worry. We'll buy a new one."

She walked toward the front door and turned around. "Do either of you have children?"

Jed hesitated. He didn't like to think about that time in his life so many years ago. He nodded. "Yes. Many years ago, now."

Elizabeth laughed. "I didn't think it was too recently. So you know what you're in for?"

"I've spent a lot of time with babies." She looked at him quizzically.

"I volunteer in the neonatal ward of the hospital a couple of times a week."

"Really? What do you do there?"

"I rock them."

"That's wonderful."

"I used to do it some years ago when I lived in Venice Beach. I helped a lady who took care of AIDS and drug-addicted babies in her home."

"I commend you. Those babies are a difficult group . . . in so much pain and then withdrawal. So far this baby has been very docile."

"It should be a breeze, then." Jed smiled.

She opened the door and called over her shoulder, "See you about six-thirty."

6

JED CALLED MONICA AS HE RUSHED BACK TO THE COLUMBARIUM. "She's bringing the baby tonight at six, but we have to buy a crib and it has to be a new one because the old ones —"

"I know, Jed," she interrupted. "I am a social worker. It's kind of my job to know this stuff."

Jed detected some annoyance in her voice. "Are you sure you're okay with this?"

"Why do you ask? We've discussed it."

"Well, you seem annoyed."

"Jed, I'm busy here at work. I have a line of people waiting to talk to me and a pile of paperwork on my desk."

"Okay. Shall I buy the crib?"

"Obviously I have to get it on my way home. I'm the one with the car."

"Maybe they would deliver?"

"I'll pick it up and meet you at home by six. I'll leave here a little early." She hung up abruptly. Jed was starting to think that she didn't want this at all and was doing it for him.

Maybe she'll change her mind after she sees the baby.

He was happy to see that the entourage of inspectors and police had left. A lone cop sat in his patrol car by the closed though unlocked gate. Jed walked over to him. "Thanks for staying here but I can take care of things now," he said.

"You Jed Gibbons?"

Jed stared at him, not particularly fond of his tone. "Yes."

"May I see some identification?"

"Are you serious?"

The cop got out of his car. "Yes sir. I am serious. I was told I could leave when Jed Gibbons gets here, but I would like to know that you are, in fact, him."

Jed was immediately sorry he had reacted so strongly. He never did well with authority figures. His childhood in Jonestown had given him a perpetual distrust of anyone in a position that might have any semblance of power over him. There was much to blame Jim Jones for, but Jed had worked hard to overcome the rage and anguish that had taken over so much of his adult life. He removed his wallet from his pocket and showed him identification. "Yes, of course."

"Thanks." The cop nodded, got into his car and drove away.

Jed opened the front door of the columbarium gingerly, not sure what to expect. Although the body had been found outside, he wasn't sure whether or not the investigators had been looking for clues inside as well and had left the inside a mess. He was pleased to find out that it wasn't that bad and he would be able to get it presentable fairly quickly. If he was going to do any cleaning today, he preferred to be doing it in his own home to prepare for the baby. He worked swiftly, then locked up and hurried out.

Monica was already home when he got there. "Wow? You're here!" Jed exclaimed when he saw her in the kitchen. "I thought you were so busy at work and then having to buy the crib."

She put her arms around him and kissed him. "I'm sorry for being so short with you today."

"Hey, I understand. Your job is tough and —"

"That's not the point," she interrupted. "I don't want you to think that I'm not excited and happy for you."

Jed stepped back and looked into her eyes. "For me? So you don't want to do this? You're doing it for me?"

Monica took a breath. "I didn't mean that the way it sounded."

"Hey, Monica. You need to be honest with me."

"Well, let's just say that I'm not into it as much as you are. I'm not against it or anything. It's going to be a huge adjustment and a lot of work. I'm not sure I'm up to it."

Now Jed felt terrible. He hadn't even considered the fact that Monica's HIV positive diagnosis might make it a hardship for her. "Oh God, Monica! I'm so sorry. I didn't even think of that!"

"It's not just about the stamina or tiredness. I mean, a little of it is the emotional toll. We're going to take this baby into our lives and love her and then have to give her up."

Jed sighed. "I guess I didn't think the whole thing through."

"And one other thing. It's a reminder of how I never had a baby of my own. It just brings up all that stuff."

Jed enveloped her with a tight hug and kissed the top of her head. "I feel terrible. I should never have —"

"Yes you should have. It's fine. We'll get used to it and it'll be a wonderful experience. And maybe we can stay in touch with the baby as she grows up." She pulled away. "Now, let's go down to the car and get the crib so we can set it up before Elizabeth gets here."

Elizabeth showed up right on time, just as Jed finished setting up the crib in the spare room. He saw her car pull up and went out to greet her. She took the baby out of the car seat and handed her to Jed. The baby smiled and cooed at him. "She's a good baby, very placid."

"Hello little one." Jed hugged the baby to his chest and walked back to the house where Monica was waiting in the doorway.

"Hi Elizabeth," Monica called out. "And hello to you, sweet girl," she said as Jed held the baby so that Monica could see her face.

"Apparently she's a quiet, sweet baby," Jed said.

"That's a bonus!"

Elizabeth went inside with Jed and Monica and they all sat down in the living room. Monica signed papers and Elizabeth gave instructions while Jed rocked the baby, the smile never leaving his face. "Did you get a crib and car seat?"

Monica and Jed glanced at each other with chagrin. "We have the crib. I'll buy a car seat tomorrow. We promise we won't take her in the car before we have it. Jed's going to bring her to work with him and he doesn't drive there." Jed and Monica looked at each other again, realizing that they didn't have a stroller either, or anything to leave the baby in at the columbarium like a carrier or backpack.

Elizabeth finally left at seven. "Well, it looks like I'm going to have to go out shopping right now and get some equipment," Monica sighed.

"Not now. You haven't eaten and you're tired. I'll carry her to work tomorrow."

"You can't just carry her around all day. Maybe I need to take the morning off and —"

"Hold everything. Let's just savor this moment with this little being. We don't have to do anything else right now. We have the crib and that's all she needs tonight."

Monica smiled and reached out her arms. Jed put the baby into them and watched as Monica brought her to her face and kissed her. "Hello my sweet princess." The baby smiled and gurgled, waving her arms and kicking her legs. Monica looked up at Jed. "I think I'm in love. I hope you don't mind me two-timing you."

Jed's smile turned abruptly into a quizzical look. "What's her name? We forgot to ask!"

Monica laughed. "How would they know? She doesn't talk yet. And remember, they haven't identified the mother."

"Well maybe they had to write something on the papers we signed and the agency gave her a name." He leafed through the papers. "They just refer to her as baby Jane Doe."

"Then I guess it's up to us to name her. At least until they identify the mother and find family members."

"This feels weird," Jed exhaled. "I mean she's not a dog we got from the humane society."

"Oh, Jed!" Monica turned to the baby. "Your daddy can be such a silly goose."

Jed stiffened at the word, daddy. It didn't seem right, at least not if they weren't going to be able to keep her. "Maybe we shouldn't call ourselves mother and father."

Monica gave him a puzzled look. "Right now that's what we are to her. Why are you acting so strangely?" she asked. He shrugged but didn't answer. "Why don't you take her and I'll go to my computer and look up some names."

"They should be Muslim names. Her mother wore a hijab," he called out to Monica as she walked into the bedroom. Then he realized they hadn't bought any formula or bottles. "Oh Jeez, little one. We forgot everything." He went to the bedroom. "Monica? We forgot to get milk for her. And what about diapers?"

"It's all in the car. Put her in the crib and go get the bag in the front seat." Jed lay the baby down in the crib, kissed the top of Monica's head and went to get the grocery bag.

After the baby drank a whole bottle, she fell fast asleep and Jed and Monica discussed names as they ate a quickly assembled dinner of scrambled eggs and salad. It was a difficult chore, not because they couldn't agree. There were just so many beautiful and appropriate names, that they couldn't narrow it down. Finally it was decided. Aja.

7

AJA SLEPT SOUNDLY THROUGH THE EVENING, BUT DECIDED TO WAKE UP JUST AS JED AND MONICA GOT INTO BED. "Welcome to parenthood," Monica sighed as she went to the kitchen to warm up some formula.

Jed sat on the sofa with Aja and took the bottle from Monica when she walked into the living room. "You go to bed. I'll take this round."

"Shall we alternate?"

"No. I'll do everything tonight. You have some shopping to do tomorrow besides work. It'll be a long day for you."

"For me? You're the one who's going to have her all day."

"I don't mind. Really. I'm not even tired. Too wound up to sleep anyway."

"You're something else, Mr. Gibbons!" She kissed him and went to bed.

Jed gazed down at Aja. "So what do you think of your new name? I'm sorry about your mother. But we will make sure that you will be loved and cherished. We will find you a wonderful home." He stopped, not even sure whether that was what he wanted. Her eyes closed and she was again, fast asleep. Jed started to get up to put her in the crib, but then sat back down and closed his own eyes. And that's where Monica found them both the next morning.

"Jed, did she keep you up all night?"

He opened his eyes and yawned. "Not at all. She woke up once and then went back to sleep in my arms. I didn't want to wake you. We were actually quite comfortable."

"Well, let me have her and you can get ready. I've already called and left a voicemail that I'll be late today. I'll shop before work and get the car seat and a stroller. Anything else?"

Jed handed Aja to Monica. "Probably a carrier of some sort. I'll want to use that when I'm at work."

"How are you going to do your work with her on your back or your front?"

"I'll figure it out."

"I'm sure you will. But what are you going to do if she starts screaming or something?"

"Why would she scream?"

Monica gave him a half smile and shook her head. "Oh, I don't know, Jed. Maybe she'd be hungry? Or need to be changed? Or be in some kind of pain? C'mon. You of all people should know about screaming babies."

"It'll be fine." He said as he went to the bathroom to shower, trying not to show Monica his actual feelings of apprehension.

Monica handed Jed a bathed, changed, fed baby in a new outfit. "She's ready for her day at the columbarium."

"Did Elizabeth give us extra clothes? I thought we would have to add that to our growing list."

"No. I bought a couple of things when I got the crib. Isn't it cute? I thought it was appropriate, the elephant on it."

Jed looked at her curiously. "Why's that? What significance does the elephant have?"

"You know. The elephant in the room?"
"Huh?"

"The discussion about whether we try to keep her ourselves."

"Oh, that one." He smiled. "Well, she should be plenty warm enough with the hood and feet. Is it flannel?"

"Yes. I just hope she doesn't get too hot. I'll buy a few other things for her this morning, and I'll bring another outfit and the Snugli to you. I put some extra diapers and bottles of formula in your backpack. You have a refrigerator in your office, don't you?"

Jed shook his head. "Nope."

"Well, I'll put an ice pack in with the formula. Jed, we really do need to think this through before we spend a fortune on things we won't need."

"I know. I know. We'll —"

"Figure it out," Monica finished his sentence. She kissed him. "I should be there by 11 with the stuff."

Jed kissed her back and held Aja close to his chest as Monica opened the front door. "See you later."

"I'll bring you some coffee and breakfast when I come, although it will probably be closer to lunch time. You haven't eaten anything."

"I'll be fine," he called over his shoulder as he started his journey.

Even though it wasn't far to the columbarium from Jed and Monica's, it was a typical cold and foggy morning in San Francisco. Jed worried that Aja wasn't warm enough. Monica hadn't bought a jacket or hat. He hoped she would think of that when she went shopping this morning. Aja smiled up at him as they walked. If she was cold, she certainly didn't let on.

As Jed turned the corner of Lorraine Court, he saw a police car at the locked gate and an unmarked car idling behind it. Two uniformed officers got out of the police car and approached him. "Are you Jed Gibbons?"

Jed immediately stiffened. He hugged Aja closer to his chest as if to protect her. "Yes?" he said warily as he unlocked the gate.

The two men in the unmarked car got out and joined them. "This is him," one of the policemen said to the men in suits.

They flashed badges as they spoke. "FBI. Is there someplace we can talk privately?"

"The columbarium doesn't open until nine. I have some things to do before I unlock the front door."

"This won't take long."

Jed sighed and brought them into his office. He sat on the edge of the desk and waved his hand toward the two chairs, indicating that they could sit there. Jed wanted to be in the higher position while being questioned. "I've already told the San Francisco police everything I know."

"The FBI is taking over the investigation." The older of the two suits spoke authoritatively.

"Why?" Jed wasn't usually one to ask questions, but it slipped out.

"Any crime that looks like there may be a terrorism connection is under our command. You gave that impression to Inspectors Diaz and Goodman. We are acting on your own interpretation of events."

Jed could feel his heart pounding and his breathing become labored. Aja picked up on his anxiety and started to whimper. He rocked her and that calmed him as much as her. He took a deep breath and then repeated everything that he had already told Diaz and Goodman. The younger agent took notes although he had already agreed to be taped. "I really need to get the building ready to open. That's everything I can think of."

"Thanks. We'll be in touch." The older agent handed Jed his card and nodded to the younger one to do the same.

Jed looked down at the cards. "You know, I didn't mean to give the impression that this was terrorism. It seemed more, uh, like racism or white supremacy."

"That would be domestic terrorism. Still under our jurisdiction."

"So which one is Mick Kelly?" Jed asked.

The older one nodded slightly. The younger one said "I'm Lenny Schultz. You can call me if you need to get a hold of us." They left and Jed plopped into one of the chairs.

"This is getting out of hand, Aja." He kissed her and hugged her tight to his chest. "Well, let's get to work. I'll show you the ropes.

Maybe you can take over for me in twenty years."

He unlocked the front door to the stately, copper-domed building and pointed out the architectural features: the stained glass windows, the carved columns and the curved walls. After explaining what neo-classical architecture was, he discussed with Aja that some people were cremated when they died, rather than buried in cemeteries. "These niches are places where these ashes could be kept if they aren't scattered at sea, or wherever they or their loved ones choose." Aja seemed to hang on every word, looking up at Jed as he spoke, her eyes glued to his face. "I hope we can bring your mother here after the autopsy so I can watch over her."

Jed looked around the large central room. He was trying to figure out a place he could set the baby down without her rolling off. "I guess most of my work is going to have to happen after Monica gets here with the stroller and the carrier." He glanced at the clock and saw it was almost nine. "Well, we will just have to open without my usual morning tasks done." He unlocked the door and started up the stairs. "Let's go meet some of my dearest friends."

Jed took Aja to visit Sam and Sadie's niche. "This is Sam and Sadie's condo. It's Sam's house you're sleeping in." Jed picked up one of the two tomatoes that had been sitting on the sconces. He squeezed it. "These will be good for another couple of days. Sam wanted me to make sure that there were always fresh tomatoes."

They continued on to some of the other niches where Jed sang their specific songs. When he got to Chloe's he opened it and took out the teddy bear and laid it on Aja's chest. "This is Chloe. She was only four when she died." He smiled as Aja laid her tiny hand on the teddy bear. He heard some voices and put the bear back in the niche. Then he went back downstairs to greet the visitors.

It didn't take long for the parade of mourners and tourists to begin. Much had been written about the beauty of the building and it had become a stop for many visitors to San Francisco, even if they had no loved ones in the building. Jed welcomed them all and did his customary singing and greeting to many of the niches. The morning went quickly, everyone oohing and aahing over the baby and some even holding her, giving Jed a break. Aja never cried, enjoying every new person's cradling arms.

Monica arrived at noon and Jed was quite ready to relinquish Aja so he could take more than a five-minute breather. "Why don't you let me take her for a half hour walk in the stroller. I already told them at work that I wouldn't be in until one," Monica said. "Anyway, she probably could use a nap and the walk will rock her to sleep. Did you feed her yet?"

"Oh jeez. No. The bottles are in the office. She's such a good baby that she didn't let me know if she needed changing either. And I just plumb forgot."

Monica laughed. "Go ahead. I'll take care of all that. But Jed —"

"I know, I know," he interrupted. "This will all just take some getting used to. I'll get it worked out."

Monica raised her eyebrows, but didn't open her mouth. Jed's first stop was the rest room. Yes, this would take some getting used to.

8

THE STROLLER AND THE SNUGLI MADE THE AFTERNOON GO MUCH MORE SMOOTHLY. Aja was asleep when Monica brought her back from their walk and she stayed that way for a good two hours. Jed then put her in the Snugli and she was quite content, although Jed wasn't able to get much work done. She was kind of in the way, bouncing against his chest every time he moved.

Jed was about to close up for the night when an agitated, young, white man burst into the columbarium. He was dressed in a black T-shirt and jeans. The number 1488 was tattooed on the back of his otherwise shaved head. He carried a large duffel bag with the number 1488 in large letters on its side. The man glanced quickly to his left and right and then bounded up the stairs. Jed followed close behind, stepping quietly, watching closely and hoping Aja wouldn't cry out or make a noise.

The man stopped on the third floor and hurried in the direction of Sam, Sadie, and Goldie. Jed decided he needed to speak before any damage was done. "We're about to close. Perhaps you can come back tomorrow."

The man stopped in his tracks and turned around. Jed instinctively shielded Aja with his arm, worried that this man was going to open his duffel bag and produce some kind of weapon. But the man glared at him, said nothing, and ran back down the stairs. Jed hustled after him and watched as he ran out the door.

Aja only started whimpering once the commotion was over. Jed wrapped his arms around her as he thought about what had just happened. What was the meaning of 1488? Maybe all the excitement made him feel paranoid, but surely the guy was up to no good.

He got home before Monica. After changing Aja's diaper, he got her bottle ready. Holding Aja in the rocking chair and feeding her would calm him down, and he needed that.

Monica arrived just as he was burping Aja who had gobbled up her formula in record time. "She likes to eat," Jed said as Monica kissed him on the top of his head.

"I've noticed that. And you?"

"And me what?"

"Would you like to eat?"

"Well, yes, but I have a couple of things to do first." Jed had already decided not to tell Monica everything right away. He didn't want her to be afraid for them. He could just see her forbidding him to take Aja to work or something and it would give her more fuel for her already skeptical opinion of this new life they were embarking on.

"Okay. I'll take this little munchkin from you. What do you need to do?"

"Just look up something on the computer." He handed the baby to Monica and went into the bedroom.

He googled 1488 and sat back in his chair, sighing loudly when the page came up. It was a white supremacist symbol. 14 stood for the fourteen-word saying that was the mantra of the White Pride movement: "We must secure the existence of our people and a future for white children." The 88 stood for "Heil Hitler," H being the eighth letter of the alphabet. Jed took his phone out. He had to call Lenny Schultz and get the FBI involved. His fears were validated. This was not paranoia. This was being realistic. He was probably who had vandalized the columbarium. He could be the murderer as well.

Monica entered the bedroom just as Schultz answered. Jed wanted to tell her everything but he didn't want her to hear it described the way he was planning to tell the FBI. He had wanted to tell her a more sugarcoated story. He turned his head and whispered into the phone. "Hello? This is Jed Gibbons. From the columbarium."

"Yes, Jed. What can I do for you?"

Jed glanced over to Monica who had finished changing clothes and was sitting on the bed, watching him. He looked into her eyes and smiled sheepishly. "We, um, had a strange visitor late this afternoon." Monica came and stood next to him. "Can you meet me at the columbarium tomorrow morning?"

"Okay."

"Maybe a little before nine?"

"What's going on Jed?" Schultz asked.

"I'll tell you tomorrow." He hung up abruptly and turned to Monica. "Let's make dinner and I'll explain."

They went to the kitchen. Jed glanced at the living room floor and noticed that Monica had put a blanket down and Aja was sleeping peacefully on it. "I'll make a salad. Why not just scramble some eggs. I think there's some cheddar you can grate in," Monica said coolly.

Jed opened the refrigerator and took out the eggs and cheese. "I just didn't want to worry you." She didn't answer but made quite a bit of noise as she tore lettuce leaves and chopped vegetables. Obviously she was not pleased.

They sat down to eat and Jed took a bite and then sat back in his chair. "Okay. Here's what happened. First of all, I had a visit from the FBI this morning."

"The FBI?"

"Yes. They are taking over the murder investigation because they think that it's terrorism, either domestic or international, so it's under their jurisdiction now."

"Why? Because you told them about the anti-Semitic and racist damage done to the niches?"

"Exactly. That's who I called just now. This agent named Schultz."

"You called him why?"

"Well, that's the second part of the story." He looked into her eyes and took her hand. "Just as I was locking up, a man rushed in and scurried up the stairs toward Goldie and Sam."

"And?"

"Well, he had 1488 carved into his scalp and on his bag."

"1488?"

"Apparently it's a symbol for white supremacy and neo-Nazi."

She shook her head. "Never heard of it."

"I hadn't either but I just looked it up."

Monica was quiet. They had both stopped eating. "You know this isn't just about your safety anymore. There's Aja too."

"I know. That's why I called them right away."

"How will that help you? It might help in their investigation, but that's all."

"I'm hoping they'll leave an agent or a policeman there to watch."

"Oh, Jed. This is way more than you should take on," Monica sighed. "Have you called the Neptune Society yet?"

"You mean after what happened today?"

"Yes. They need to be kept abreast of all this. Maybe they should shut it down until this is over."

"They're not going to do that. This could take a long time to solve." Jed stood and came around the table. He put his arms around her. "Please don't worry. I can take care of myself and Aja."

"I think we need to figure out something else for babysitting. I'll take off some time —"

"You can't use up your sick days. What if you need them again? Just because you haven't had a flare-up lately . . ."

Monica sighed. She picked up her fork. "Let's just eat dinner and try to save this evening from being a total disaster. Let's try to enjoy the food, each other's company, and that adorable little darling in the next room."

"Good idea." And that is how they spent their evening, although the recent events were never far from their minds.

9

SLEEP ELUDED ALL THREE OF THEM THAT NIGHT. Aja whimpered, Monica tossed and turned, and Jed lay on his back with his eyes wide open, staring at the ceiling. This went on for about an hour until Monica finally spoke. "Maybe she's hungry."

"I'll feed her. I'm not sleeping anyway."

"Did you think I was?"

"You have been a bit restless."

Monica sat up. "This is frightening me."

"I know. I should have just kept my mouth shut." Jed got up. "It's too late now."

"Can't you just tell them you don't know anything and just stay out of it from now on?"

Jed shrugged his shoulders and went to the kitchen to warm up a bottle. He settled in to the rocking chair with Aja, but she was not interested and soon started wailing. Jed got up and changed her diaper, but that did nothing to soothe her. He held her close and paced, singing softly. It worked and he was able to set her back down and climb back into bed. Monica had fallen asleep by then, so Jed lay awake by himself and pondered his predicament. He finally closed his eyes and joined the rest of the family in sleep mode, but it wasn't for long. Aja started screaming again within minutes. He got up and took her to the couch, realizing that this was probably where he would be sleeping for the rest of the night. And he was right.

What seemed like a few moments later, Monica shook him awake as she lifted the sleeping baby off his chest. "Good morning," Jed said, smiling at her. "Did you get any sleep?"

"Probably a lot more than you did," she answered. "What time did you finally get her quiet and fall asleep?"

"I have no idea. What time is it now?"

"Time for you to hustle to work if you want to get there by nine."

"Damn! I told that Agent Schultz I'd be there before nine." He bolted off the couch and looked at the clock. "I'll jump in the shower. Will you get Aja ready to go?"

"You go ahead. I've already called work and told them I'd be late again this morning. I have a car seat. I'll bring her in a couple of hours."

He kissed Monica and was at the columbarium by 8:45. Kelly and Schultz were waiting at the gate in their black sedan. They nodded at Jed while he unlocked the gate and then drove in and parked in front of the door.

"So what's up, Jed?"

"Late yesterday afternoon a man rushed into the columbarium and ran up the stairs."

Kelly and Schultz looked at each other and then back to Jed. "Go on," Schultz said.

"He had 1488 on his duffel bag and tattooed on the back of his head."

They both nodded. "Do you know who he was going to see?"

"I followed him up the stairs, but he ran away when he saw me."

"So you think this has to do with the murder?"

Jed shrugged. "I don't know."

"Do you have any thoughts on what niche he might have wanted to visit?" That was Kelly, much to Jed's surprise. He usually let Schultz do all the talking.

"He was near Sam's and Goldie's. They were two that had been damaged."

"Would you bring us up there?" Schultz asked.

Jed led the way. It didn't take any great sleuthing to put two and two together, when they saw the names on the niches. Sam and Sadie Cohen and Goldie Klein were about as Jewish as any names could be. "They were ones that had swastikas on them, as well as being smashed."

"While we're here, could you show us the others that had been damaged?"

Jed showed them Sunny's and some of the others that had been affected. He took out his phone and checked the time. "I need to go downstairs and open up."

"Well, we need a better description of the individual."

"He was white with a shaved head, maybe in his twenties. He was dressed in a black T-shirt and black jeans. I don't think I noticed much else other than the 1488 on his head."

"Clean-shaven?"

"Yes." Jed started down the stairs and the agents followed him.

"I'm going to call Diaz and Goodman. Would you go down to the police station and check out some photos and see if you can identify him?"

Jed exhaled. He wished he had never called them. "Not until after work."

"That's fine. Give them some time to pull the pictures together."

Jed opened the front door and they walked out as a group of visitors stepped inside. Among them was Jed's friend, Tony, who always took over for him as columbarium caretaker on the few days that Jed would take off. "Jed!" Tony hugged him.

"Hey man, haven't seen you in ages!"

"I've been traveling."

"That's wonderful. Where did you go?"

"The Caribbean." Jed's eyebrows went up. "Not what you think. Anyway, we don't need to go there anymore to buy it. Remember, it's legal in California now."

"Just checking." Jed grinned. Tony had spent most of his life as a pot courier and dealer helping his friend, Goldie Klein, run her business.

"Why were those two Feds here?"

"How'd you know they were FBI agents?"

"C'mon, Jed. I had to be able to spot the cops. I learned how very quickly."

"The columbarium has been the center of attention lately. A woman was murdered here a few days ago."

"What?" Jesus! Are you okay? What happened?"

Jed proceeded to tell Tony the whole story. "Monica will be bringing Aja by soon. Do you want to meet her?"

Tony grinned. "Sure. I can stay."

"Why are you grinning?"

"Thinking of you taking care of a tiny baby."

Jed grinned back. "What? You don't think I can do it?"

"No. In fact, quite the opposite. I think you are probably loving it and really good at it. After all, you've had a lot of practice."

Jed wasn't sure how to answer. In one sense he loved it. But there was the reality that he and Monica were in their sixties. And Monica's HIV positive status was a concern. "I have had practice, for sure."

"Are you still going to the hospital to rock the babies?" Tony asked.

"I think I'll have to put that aside. I won't have time."

"And now you have your own baby to rock." Tony laughed. He went upstairs to visit Goldie's apartment while Jed greeted some more visitors and made his singing rounds to some of the residents.

Monica and Aja finally arrived about ten. "Tony's here. He wants to meet Aja." Jed took the smiling baby out of the stroller and kissed her forehead.

"Oh, good. We haven't seen Tony in a long time."

"He's been traveling."

"Well, she is fed and changed and hopefully will be ready for a nap soon. Do you want to leave her in the stroller or put her in the Snugli?"

"The stroller is easier."

"What happened with the FBI? Did they show up?"

"I told them about the guy who was here yesterday. But I have to go down to the police station after work and look at some photos. I guess Diaz and Goodman are involved after all."

Monica sighed. "So are you planning to bring Aja with you or do I need to come and get her?"

"I'll just bring her."

"I need to get to work so I can't wait for Tony. Give him my love." Monica kissed Jed and started to leave.

"Hey Monica!" Tony called from the stairs. They hugged.

"You two work out a night when you can come to dinner. I want to hear about your latest escapades," Monica said as she left.

Tony turned to Jed and held out his arms. "May I?" Jed handed Aja to Tony and watched as she melted into his cradling arms with a smile and a soft murmur. Tony hugged her to his chest. "I can see how easy it is to fall for this little bundle."

Jed smiled. "You can put her in the stroller and maybe she'll fall asleep while I'm walking around doing my work."

"I'll take care of her for a while. You just go ahead and do what you need to do. I have nowhere I need to be."

"Are you sure?"

"Yep."

"Okay." Jed turned to go back to his office and then stopped. "Tony? Have you ever, um, you know, taken care of an infant?"

"What do you think? Just because I'm an old, gay, ex-pot dealer, I don't know how? Is it rocket science?"

"Well, no."

"I can cuddle her and push a stroller. I assume there's a bottle in the bag hanging on the back of the stroller. I can probably figure that one out too. If she screams and needs a diaper changed, then maybe you can do the honors."

Jed smiled. "Okay. Thanks, Tony."

"We'll be fine."

Jed walked toward the back door and left the incongruous pair cooing at each other.

10

TONY STAYED THROUGH THE LUNCH HOUR, GIVING JED PLENTY OF TIME TO GET HIS WORK DONE. He watched Jed change Aja's diaper and give her a bottle and exclaimed, "I can do that."

Jed laughed as he put Aja into the Snugli. "As you said, it's not rocket science."

"I'll come help you tomorrow too if you want."

"That would be great."

Tony started to hug Jed and let go when Aja yelped. "Oh, sorry. Forgot you had her on your chest." He kissed Aja. "I'll see you tomorrow little one."

Aja started to fuss. "Are you ready for a nap? Anyway, it's time for a walk. Let's go say hello to some friends." But before he got into any of the anterooms, he noticed 1488, dressed in the same black clothes and carrying the same black duffel bag, slinking through the front door. This time Jed would not confront him. He would just follow him to see whose niche he was visiting. The man raced up the two flights again and Jed followed him in the direction of Goldie's apartment.

Instead, he found the man lingering in front of an empty niche. Jed watched from behind a column as he opened his duffel bag. He held his breath, waiting to see what he pulled from the bag. But at that moment Aja stirred and startled the man. He quickly zipped up his duffel, so Jed decided to make his presence known in a friendly fashion and stepped away from the column. "Hello again. Are you looking for someone's niche? Perhaps I can help you."

The man gave Jed a furtive glance and snarled, "No." Jed stared at him as he hurried by, making mental notes of his facial features so he could identify him in the pictures he'd be looking through. The man ran back down the stairs. There was nothing to learn in following him this time, and Aja had picked up on his nervous energy and started whimpering. He brushed his hand over her head to soothe her as he stared at the empty niche, wondering why it would interest the man. It was as if he had something in the duffel bag he was trying to unload. He thought of Aja's mother and bent down to kiss the baby. He felt there were connections, but none of it made sense.

The rest of the day went quickly. Many people came to visit loved ones and several people were looking to buy niches. By the time five o'clock came, he realized that he had forgotten to call Schultz with the information that the man had returned and with the more detailed description of him. It wasn't until he locked the gate and started to walk home that he remembered he had to go to the police station to look at pictures. And on top of that, he had to bring Aja with him. He groaned. He should have told Monica to pick her up, but she had already missed two mornings in a row of work. He couldn't really ask her to take off early too. He was starting to realize that perhaps Monica had been right. This may be way too much for them to take on.

He got to the police station just as it started to drizzle. Oh great. Now he'd have to walk home in the rain. "What do you need?" The officer behind the counter asked him as he approached.

"I'm supposed to meet Inspectors Diaz and Goodman."

"Name?"

"Jed Gibbons."

"Hold on." The officer left and returned with Diaz.

"How ya' doing' Jed. Who you got with you?"

Jed didn't want to tell him it was the baby from the murdered woman. He was afraid he'd take her away. "Oh, just a baby I'm taking care of." That wasn't a lie.

"She yours?"

"No." And neither was that a lie.

Diaz brought Jed into a room with a computer. "I have the pages up for you with people who are known members of the white supremacy movement here. See if anyone looks familiar."

Jed sat down at the computer and saw that there were a ton of pictures he was going to have to look through. "This guy had 1488 tattooed on his head. Can't we pare this list down that way?"

"He could have just done that recently."

"I didn't realize there would be so many photos," Jed grumbled.

"Do what you can."

"He came again today."

"Did you call the FBI and tell them?"

"No. I didn't have time. But I did get a better look at him."

"Any scars? How about eye color? That would help narrow it down."

"I'm afraid I didn't see any scars. But I think his eye color was blue."

"You think?"

"They were definitely blue."

Diaz went to the computer and hit some keys. "Okay. A white guy with blue eyes. Anything else?"

"He was about my height."

"Which is?"

"Six feet."

Diaz punched more keys. "How about weight?"

"Medium. Not thin and not stocky."

"Take a look, Jed. Maybe you'll get lucky and find him on the first page."

Jed glanced over at Aja who was contentedly sucking her fingers and started his search. After about half an hour she started to fuss and Jed was tired of looking. He really hadn't gotten that good a look at the man's face and the picture only showed people's faces so he couldn't see if 1488 was tattooed on the back of anyone's head. He walked to the door and peered out, looking for Diaz or Goodman. It was almost six and this section of the police station was deserted. "Let's go home, Aja. We don't have to stay and do this." He pushed her out the door and stopped at the front desk. "We have to go. Please let Diaz know that I didn't find anyone who resembled the guy I saw."

The policeman at the desk nodded and answered the ringing phone. Jed left and walked home briskly, calling Monica as he passed a

Chinese restaurant to ask if she wanted him to pick up some dinner. She was all for some moo goo gai pan and won ton soup and no cooking.

When they finally got home Monica took Aja to change her while Jed set the food out on the table. Just as they sat down to eat, his phone rang. He looked at it and smiled at Monica. "It's Malcolm!"

"Why don't you answer it and tell him you'll call him back after dinner."

Jed nodded. "Malcolm, my man! How are you?"

"Not bad but I do have some news. They want to close the senior residence and sell the building. They could make much more money selling apartments on the Venice Beach boardwalk as condos rather than renting them out to low income seniors."

"Oh no! What will all those people do who live there now?"

"That's the major problem of course. Those who have family members, like Finn, will go live with them, either for good or until they find another place. There are a few who don't have anywhere to go."

"Oh man, that's terrible. "How many are there?"

"Not too many, but one of them has Parkinson's and really needs to go into assisted living. You know, we're just a low income senior residence."

"I remember you telling me about him. What's his name again?"

"Homer. His tremors are getting worse and he has trouble walking but he's so stubborn. All the people here help as much as they can, but he really needs more than this."

"I'm really sorry, Malcolm."

"Yeah. Well, I gotta go. I'll talk to you later."

"Thanks for calling, Malcolm." Jed hung up and turned to Monica. "They are selling the senior residence and now Malcolm and Savali will both be out of jobs."

"What will they do?" Monica asked.

"I didn't ask. I guess Malcolm is still waiting tables so he has that job. But Savali . . . I don't know."

"Did she — or does Savali prefer to be called they?"

"I'm not sure. Malcolm always refers to Savali as she. It's less confusing for him and I think he prefers it."

"Has Savali had the surgery?"

Jed shrugged his shoulders. "The way Malcolm explained it to me, there are a lot of different ways that trans people identify. It's a spectrum or a continuum. Savali is gender fluid.

Sometimes she feels male and sometimes she feels female."

"She could get into social work. The transgender community could really use someone who understands so many aspects of the experience."

"I think she's too much of an activist to do a desk job."

"Well, being an activist is also important."

Jed took the baby and put her in the crib. He came back into the dining room and fell into his chair. He smiled at Monica and said, "I think we need to go to bed. I'm exhausted and it looks like you are too."

"You should be. You hardly slept last night and you spent the day working and taking care of a tiny baby. I slept last night so I'll do the dishes." She went into the kitchen and Jed thought about Malcolm's dilemma. Malcolm had been a fourteen-year-old homeless, motherless child Jed had befriended on the Venice Beach boardwalk about fifteen years ago. Jed had found him a wonderful foster home with Miss Ruthie who had eventually adopted him. Jed also worried a little about Finn, an Irish author who had perennial bouts with the bottle. He was probably the best friend Jed had ever had. Finn had been living with his daughter, Kate, at that time and the scenario

had not always worked that well. He wondered
if they could survive living together again,
especially since she was now married. Jed smiled
thinking of how difficult Finn could be. He
went to the kitchen, kissed Monica on the top
of the head and went to bed. He was asleep the
minute his head touched the pillow.

11

MONICA WAS ALREADY IN THE KITCHEN, DRESSED FOR WORK AND DRINKING COFFEE, WHEN JED GOT UP. "I guess I didn't realize how exhausted I was," he said as he entered.

"You slept a long time. You obviously needed it. We're no spring chickens, you know."

"What are you saying?"

"I'm saying that you and I are going to be tired . . . a lot."

Jed frowned. "I'm taking a shower." He left the kitchen.

Monica sighed and took Aja into the living room to get her changed and dressed and to pack the diaper bag. When Jed entered she kissed him and said, "I have meetings all morning, but call me at lunch, okay?"

Jed called Malcolm while walking to work. "Hey, can you talk?"

"Sure," Malcolm replied. "What's up?"

Jed looked down at Aja in the stroller and smiled. "Well, I guess I have some interesting news."

"Oh yeah. What's that?"

Jed told Malcolm the whole story. "I don't know what's going to happen to Aja. If they ever identify the victim, I guess they would try to find her family and see if they would take the baby. Monica and I talked about adopting her ourselves, but—"

"You?" Malcolm interrupted. "Wow. That's a huge thing for you to take on at your age."

"I know."

"Well, you do love babies."

But there's so much more to it than that, Jed thought. Then he asked, "So how are you and Savali?"

"We have a lot of decisions to make. We will both be without jobs when the senior residence is sold, but maybe now we can start doing more of what we want to do. I'm going to keep making documentaries and Savali wants to do more activist stuff with the LGBTQ community. But it does mean we have to make some changes."

"Well, you guys are young, yet."

"We'll be fine. I still have my waiter job at Café Gratitude and it certainly helps that Miss Ruthie left us her house."

"Yeah, we were both so lucky. I wouldn't be living here if Sam hadn't left me his." Jed arrived at the gate of the columbarium. "Gotta go, Malcolm. If you guys have some time off, come on up and visit."

"You bet."

They hung up and Jed unlocked the gate. Just as he was opening the front door, a car drove up. He turned around to see a black limo pull up and a man get out of the back. He wore a shiny, expensive suit and his shoes were patent leather. His dyed black hair was slicked back and his face was so tanned that it looked like he was wearing makeup. A man, straight out of a film stereotype for a bodyguard, followed him out of the car. He was huge and muscular with a large scar running down his cheek. Jed instinctively took Aja out of the stroller and held her tightly to his chest.

"Are you open, yet?" the well-dressed man asked.

"In a couple of minutes," Jed answered. The man nodded and started walking around the grounds of the building with his crony one step behind him. Jed watched them warily as he went inside and turned on the lights, locking the door behind him. He went back to the office and left the diaper bag and stroller, putting Aja in the Snugli so he could do his opening chores more easily. Anyway, she liked being close to his chest and often fell back asleep.

He decided to let the men inside before finishing all his pre-opening chores. When he unlocked the door to inform them that the columbarium was now open, he saw them poking around the bushes. They noticed Jed staring at them and smiled. "Is this where the body was?" the snappily dressed man asked. "You oughta put some new bushes in."

"We are open. You can come in." Jed replied, ignoring his comment. He turned around and went back inside. Jed watched as the two men climbed the stairs. He took a rag and went upstairs as well. He started wiping down the front of the niches as he tracked the pair. They stopped in front of Francesca Balducci's apartment and the better-dressed man crossed himself while the larger man stood to the side. Jed decided to move away at that point. He didn't know much about Francesca Balducci. Her niche was one of the more traditional ones: a picture of an old woman, a brass urn, a crucifix, and a vase with some withered flowers. He would look her up to see when she had been put in her apartment. He doubted it had been more than a year ago. She hadn't had any visitors that Jed remembered. He was pretty sure that this man had not been here before. Jed watched them as they walked around, looking at other apartments and condos. Maybe they wanted to put more items in Francesca's niche and were looking for ideas. He went back to his cleanup chores and after a few minutes he saw the two men leave the building.

Jed returned to his morning routine and decided to check the restrooms next. He opened one of them and noticed a need for toilet paper in one of the stalls. He went to the storage closet to get a roll and opened the door. Shoved into a corner of one of the shelves was a large canvas bag. He took it out and unzipped the top. Inside was a baby bottle, a couple of disposable diapers, a knitted baby hat and sweater, and a stuffed faceless felt doll. Jed checked to see if Aja was awake yet but her eyes were closed and she was snoring softly.

He left the bag on the shelf and replaced the toilet paper roll as quickly as possible. He took out his cellphone to call Schultz, but hesitated. He wanted to check for identification first.

He went back into the storage closet and took out the bag. He took out the baby items to see what else was in the bag. There was a packet of tissues, a water bottle, but no wallet and no cellphone. There was a folded piece of paper. He opened it up and saw the address of the columbarium written down, as well as the name Laila.

He heard his name being called and hurriedly put the piece of paper back in the bag. He carried the bag to the foyer and saw Tony waving at him. "There you are. I came to babysit my godchild."

Jed laughed. "Your godchild?"

"Why not? Did you have anyone else in mind to be the godparent?"

"Actually, I hadn't given it much thought."

Aja gurgled and moved her head back and forth. Her head was about the only thing she could move, the Snugli swathed her so tightly. Jed took her out and handed her to Tony. "Is the diaper bag in the office?"

Jed's eyes widened. "You're going to change her?"

"I watched you yesterday. I'll call you if I have any problems. Is she hungry?"

"I don't know. What time is it?"

"I'll just see if she takes the bottle."

Jed shook his head. "You're so well-versed in baby speak. Did you do some homework last night?"

"Maybe a little."

Tony took Aja to the office while Jed went to the front counter to look up the name Laila in the computerized listings. But his intentions were thwarted by the arrival of a large group of visitors who had come not to visit anyone specific, but to admire the gorgeous building. Jed stepped up to give them the tour, another task he had begun doing even though it was not in his job description.

12

IT WAS A BUSY MORNING AT THE COLUMBARIUM AND JED WAS GRATEFUL FOR TONY'S PRESENCE. It was becoming clear to Jed that Monica had been right about whether he could handle his job and Aja at the same time. Too bad he couldn't hire Tony as a nanny. He then chuckled to himself. It seemed Tony had already made it his job.

Tony had taken Aja for a walk in the stroller around the columbarium grounds and brought her back to Jed at noon. "I have an appointment at one but I'll be back tomorrow."

"I can't thank you enough, Tony. I mean that. I —"

"Oh, shush. I enjoy it." He rolled the stroller over to Jed and left.

Just then, Jed's phone rang. He took out his phone and recognized the number as belonging to Schultz. He had never called to report finding the bag or the mysterious visitor to Francesca Balducci. He had also forgotten to look up the name Laila and see if there was any connection to the columbarium. And that was more important to him, so he let the call go to voicemail. Sure enough, when he checked his records, he found that there was a niche for a woman named Laila Aziz and that a person named Dutch Bogart from Garberville, California had paid for her niche. He walked over to the apartment that was in one of the alcoves on the third floor. He was curious to see what items had been placed inside it. There was only a classic pewter urn, not even inscribed. No photograph, no flowers, no mementoes. It wasn't surprising that Jed hadn't remembered her. With all of the baby stuff inside, the bag must have belonged to the dead woman. And she must have been at the columbarium to visit Laila Aziz.

Jed took out his phone to call Schultz who answered on the first ring. "I've got some important news. Can you come out?"

"What is it, Jed?"

"I found a bag in the restroom. It has baby items in it."

"Leave it where you found it. I'll be right there."

Jed hung up. He tried to organize his thoughts. A part of him wanted to do his own sleuthing. He wanted to contact this Dutch Bogart, but he felt like he was constantly under suspicion, and there were obvious risks in contacting possible suspects. He turned to the computer anyway, but Aja started to fuss. He frowned and decided to wait until he got home so he could gauge Schultz's latest reactions first.

Schultz arrived fifteen minutes later. Jed was in the office giving Aja a bottle when he heard his name. "Jed? Are you in here?"

Jed started to get up but decided he was not going to cut Aja's feeding short. She was changed and would probably sleep after she ate. He didn't want to disrupt that order of things. He could get some work done this afternoon if she slept. "I'll be there in a minute," he answered.

Aja finished sucking and Jed burped her and put her in the Snugli. He walked across the walkway to the main building and found Schultz, Kelly, Diaz, and Goodman all waiting for him. "There you are." Shultz was still in charge, apparently, although Jed found it odd that the SFPD had been brought back in.

"It's over here," Jed motioned toward the restroom.

Jed opened the storage closet in the restroom and gestured to the shelf. Schultz snapped a picture, put on a pair of gloves, and removed the bag. He put it in the large plastic bag that Diaz held open for him. "You just found this today?" Schultz asked Jed.

"Yes."

"You don't come in these restrooms every day?"

"I do. But I don't check the storage closets. I just go in them when I need supplies."

Schultz nodded. Diaz spoke next. He was still holding the evidence bag. "Do you remember the last time you were in the closet?"

"Not really. A few days."

Diaz turned to Schultz. "I'll take this to the lab and let you know as soon as I've heard."

Now Jed got it. SFPD was involved because the FBI needed their lab. "There's a piece of paper in it with the name Laila. I looked it up. Her last name was Aziz."

"She's in here?" Goodman asked.

"Yes. I'll show you her apartment."

"Apartment?"

"That's what I call the niches." Jed brought the group over to Laila's niche. "Unfortunately there isn't anything in here to help you."

"How about the urn?" Goodman asked. "Anything on it to show where it was bought?"

"It's a very common urn. It could come from any number of suppliers." Jed held his breath, waiting for more questions. He wouldn't mention the records, not until he had done his own investigating that evening.

"Thanks, Jed," Goodman said. "Keep in touch." They left, but Goodman came back a minute later by himself. He handed Jed a card. "Do me a favor, would you? Call me at the number on the back. I'd like to talk to you. Privately."

Jed's heart skipped a beat as he glanced down at the card. It was a normal police business card, but scribbled on the back was a phone number, different from the one printed on the front of the card. He glanced back up at the detective and gave a slight nod. Goodman turned and left again.

Aja slept for most of the afternoon, so Jed was able to get quite a bit done. At five he locked up and hurried home, anxious to see if he could find out any information on this Dutch Bogart. Garberville is a pretty small town about two hundred miles north of San Francisco. Its major claim to fame is being known as the marijuana heartland of the United States. Pot growing drives its economy. There is even a cannabis college there. And of course, the fact that the guy's first name was Dutch . . . and his last name, Bogart . . .

Monica wasn't home yet so he put Aja on a blanket on the floor and gave her a couple of toys to play with. He booted up the computer and Googled Dutch Bogart. Several sites came up. Apparently he was a musician. Or there was another person named Dutch Bogart and that seemed rather unlikely. He played in some bands in the sixties, seventies and eighties. He tried going solo and wrote some music for other people, but his music career seemed to have come to a standstill by the mid-nineties.

Jed tried looking up a phone number for him, but of course that was a dead end. Not a surprise. Few people had landlines anymore. The only information given about the payment for Laila Aziz's niche was a post office box in Garberville. He sat back in his chair and crossed his arms, trying to decide whether or not to give this information to the Feds and/or the SFPD. That was when he remembered that Inspector Goodman had asked him to call his personal phone. He had just decided to ask Monica's opinion on what to do when she walked in the door.

"Hey little lovey!" she exclaimed, dropping her bag and packages and picking up Aja.

"And I thought you were talking to me!" Jed teased.

"Since when are you little?"

"Hey, I need some advice."

"Can we get some dinner going first? I'm starving."

Jed realized that not only had he not eaten lunch, he hadn't given dinner a thought. And it was an unwritten understanding that whoever got home first would make dinner. "I'm sorry. I forgot. I didn't make anything."

Monica shot him a scowl, but then smiled. "You're forgiven. You do have an excuse. Did you just get home?"

"Well, not exactly. I needed to use the computer."

"I guess I can find something in the freezer to heat up." Monica put Aja in Jed's arms and walked toward the kitchen. "How about Aja? Has she eaten?"

"Not recently." Jed shrugged and smiled sheepishly.

"I'll get a bottle ready and make dinner. You can finish what you were doing on the computer, but I also need to use it this evening."

Jed stared at the screen, trying to think of any other way he could locate this Dutch Bogart. Then he thought about Facebook. He didn't use it, but he figured Malcolm did. He took out his phone and dialed. "Malcolm?" But it was voicemail. Jed waited for the message to finish. "It's Jed. Could you give me a call as soon as possible? Thanks."

"Dinner's ready!" Monica called from the kitchen.

He went into the kitchen, took the bottle Monica handed him, and sat down with Aja on his lap. He fed Aja her bottle while eating his own dinner and talking to Monica. He was good at multi-tasking. He told her all about finding the bag and the paper inside, looking up the paperwork on Laila Aziz's niche, and then searching for Dutch Bogart on the internet. "All I could find out was that he was a musician forty years ago."

"Did you call the Feds?"

"Yeah. They came with those detectives from the police department. I figured they needed to use the SFPD lab for fingerprints and DNA."

"Aren't you the expert," Monica laughed.

Jed didn't join her amusement. "Here's the thing. I didn't tell them about Dutch Bogart."

"Why not?"

"I'm not sure. I think because I don't want them to find Aja's family."

"Jed," she said firmly. "You can't keep this from the police if it can help them solve the murder of this poor young woman."

"I guess."

"Anyway, you don't even know if this Laila Aziz is related to the murdered woman. You're jumping to all kinds of conclusions. And I'm sure the police as well as the Family and Children's Services are trying to locate Aja's family. You have to accept that, Jed."

He sighed. "Well, I can wait until they ask."

Monica raised her eyebrows. "It's your choice. But if it's advice you're looking for, I think you should tell them everything."

"Well, that's not the only thing I wanted to ask you. After they all left, Inspector Goodman came back alone and handed me his card. He had written his personal phone number on it and he asked me to call him. He said he wanted to talk to me privately."

"That's weird. I wonder what that's about."

"Me too. Any thoughts?"

"Well, the easy way to find out is to call him. Why wouldn't you?"

"You know why," Jed answered.

"You really think he's out to get you? You really think you're a suspect?" Jed exhaled and shook his head. "So if you are a suspect, you are one whether or not you call him. You don't have to answer any questions or offer any information if it makes you uncomfortable. Just see what he wants. I'll take care of putting Aja to bed and doing the dishes. Go ahead and call."

Jed kissed the top of her head and went to the bedroom. He dialed the number on Inspector Goodman's card. "Hello? This is Jed Gibbons. You asked me to call?"

"Thanks for calling. Yes. I hope you understand that this is between you and me."

"Okay," Jed answered tentatively.

"You know why we were brought to the columbarium today?"

"I assume because the FBI needed to use your labs."

"Right. We have been shut out of the investigation because you brought up the terrorism angle."

"I didn't mean to —"

"No Jed. I'm not saying you did anything wrong. It's just that the FBI and the San Francisco Police Department are at odds sometimes over whose jurisdiction takes precedence. And this time we were not in agreement that they should take over. The columbarium is in the city of San Francisco and we don't know that this was, in fact, a terrorist incident. Meanwhile, we had to turn over everything to them. I'm asking you to keep me in the loop. And I repeat, this is between us."

Jed thought this very odd. Why in the world would this police inspector trust him over other law enforcement officials? He doesn't know him at all. "Uh, am I at any risk for doing this?"

"Absolutely not. I am."

Jed took awhile to answer. "I guess I can."

Goodman picked up on Jed's hesitation. "You're wondering why I'm trusting you?"

"Kind of."

"Abe Levy was my wife's uncle. He spoke highly of you when he was alive. My wife and I knew Sam and Sadie."

Jed smiled, remembering Abe, the owner of the deli where he used to hang out with Sam and Irving. They were a wonderful group. "Abe was a great guy."

"So anything to report that you haven't told Schultz and Kelly?"

For a moment, Jed thought he should tell Goodman about Dutch Bogart, but just as quickly dismissed the idea. "Nope nothing more."

13

JED COULDN'T SLEEP THAT NIGHT EVEN THOUGH AJA DIDN'T WAKE UP ONCE. So many things were running through his mind. In all the hoopla over the bag found in the restroom, he had completely forgotten about the visitors to Francesca Balducci's apartment. Who were they and was there any significance to their visit that might have to do with the murder? He had not looked up the paperwork. He wouldn't have thought that much of it if it hadn't been for the presence of the bodyguard and the stereotypical mob-like appearance of the nattily dressed man.

Jed's imagination was probably getting away from him, but he wondered if he should have shared the information with Schultz. It was just as important as the 1488 visitor. More and more, he wanted to seek out this Dutch Bogart.

Jed finally gave up trying to sleep and decided to try to find an online presence for Dutch. How hard could this Facebook stuff be? He looked at the clock and saw that it was already five thirty. Aja and Monica would be up soon, so he decided he'd call Malcolm back later and ask him to research that angle for him. Jed was still paranoid about social media. He liked being anonymous.

He made coffee, warmed a bottle for Aja, had some eggs mixed in a bowl ready to scramble and pieces of bread in the toaster. At least he would get something accomplished while he waited for his family to wake up. It made him smile to think that at this moment in time, he actually had a family. A real one.

Aja started to cry, so Jed went to change her and bring her into the kitchen. He wanted to be on his way early so he could call Malcolm and give him enough time to do some online searching. He and Aja were on their way to the columbarium by eighty thirty. He tried Malcolm, but it again went to voicemail. He started to leave a message when Malcolm's name popped up on the screen. Jed switched the call over. "Hey Malcolm!"

"Sorry I missed your call. I was in the shower. I was planning on calling you back after I got to work."

"Well, I'm anxious to have you do something for me and I'm hoping you'll have time to do it this morning. I know you often have some time to be on the computer in the morning while those classes are being held at the residence."

"Yeah. Today's a good day to do that. What do you need?"

"Could you see if you can find a guy named Dutch Bogart on Facebook or any of those other sites? He's an old musician, lives in Garberville California."

"Sure. But who is he?"

"He paid for the apartment of a woman whose name was found in the bag that probably belonged to the murdered woman."

Malcolm laughed. "Hey Sherlock! Are you trying to solve this crime yourself?" Jed was silent. "Hey man, I don't mean to tease you."

"It's okay. I'm just tired. Not much sleep last night."

"That baby keeping you up?"

"No. I managed to stay awake all by myself."

"I'll get back to you later this morning. I need to get dressed and on my way."

"Thanks, man." Jed hung up just as he arrived at the front gate of the columbarium. He opened it up and walked around the perimeter. Ever since the murder, he had made that his first order of business. He would do the same inside the building, vigilant about any new vandalism, checking all the floors, restrooms and storage closets. It was only after being satisfied that all was well both inside and outside the beautiful rotunda that he would go to the small building in the back that housed his office. Luckily, Aja had not napped on the walk to work, so he put her in the Snugli, certain that she would soon be asleep and he could get some work done. Tony said he would come again today, but Jed didn't know when.

Tony showed up just before lunch with sandwiches and fruit. "Thanks, Tony. You're a life saver."

"Well, that may be a bit dramatic, but I know you often forget to eat, or just don't make it a priority, shall we say."

"Speaking of priorities, Aja probably needs changing and a bottle."

"Hand her over. You take what I'm sure is a much-needed break."

Jed smiled appreciatively and found a quiet corner to eat and call Malcolm. "Hello? It's Jed."

"Hey, man. I need to finish helping Homer back to his apartment. Call you back in five?"

"That's fine." Jed hung up and gobbled down his sandwich. He had just bitten into the apple when Malcolm called back.

"So I did find out a little bit. He posted on a couple of 420 forums, so I'm thinking he's in the pot business." Malcolm started laughing.

"I posted on the same forum that I was looking for a job. Apparently the building sold quickly. The management wants to meet Savali and me this afternoon, probably to give us our walking papers."

"Oh, I'm sorry, Malcolm. Will you guys be okay?"

"Sure. It's probably a good thing. It'll give us more time to work on our own stuff."

"Yeah, but what about financially?"

"We don't spend a lot of money as long as we don't eat out all the time. It'll just mean a change in our priorities. Anyway, I'll let you know if I get an email back from this guy. What do you want me to tell him if he answers me?"

"I don't know. Maybe the truth? Or probably I should talk to him. Do you think he's skittish because of his, um, occupation?"

"I don't know. Now that it's all been legitimized with the laws passing about recreational use, people don't have to be under the radar as much as they used to."

"Well, why not ask him if he would call me or for his number so I could call him?"

"He may not even answer me. I replied to his post, but it doesn't mean he's looking for workers. But maybe someone else will answer and I can ask if he knows him."

"Maybe you should have asked him if he's Dutch Bogart the musician. He might be more inclined to answer you," Jed said.

"How many Dutch's from Garberville could there be?"

"One, I guess. I just don't want to make him suspicious. What about Facebook?"

"Yeah, Dutch Bogart has a Facebook page and I sent him a message there as well. But if he's a fairly famous musician, he probably doesn't monitor his own page."

"I don't think he's that famous any longer. That was years ago."

"Old groupies don't die, they just hang out on the Internet."

Jed laughed. "Hey, thanks for helping me out, Malcolm. Let me know what happens with your meeting this afternoon, as well as what happens with this guy, Dutch."

"Sure thing. Gotta go." Malcolm hung up.

Jed tried to make sense of it all but realized quickly that there were way too many unknowns for him to be able to figure out anything. Dutch Bogart was his only definitive lead. The 1488 guy and Francesca Balducci were possibilities, but he decided to leave those to the FBI to work on. But he hadn't even shared any information on the visitors to her apartment with any of the investigators. Then he had an idea. He would share that with Goodman, thinking by giving him a crumb, Goodman might stay off his back. He found Goodman's number in his recent calls and dialed.

"Yes, Jed."

Jed was still surprised when people answered their phone, knowing who it was. He was new to owning a smartphone. "I, uh, had a thought about visitors I had here yesterday morning. One looked like a mobster and he had a bodyguard with him. They visited a woman named Francesca Balducci."

"Did you let the Feds know?"

"Not yet."

"Well, you should."

Jed was puzzled. He thought Goodman wanted to one up the Feds and would appreciate the information. "Uh, okay."

"But thanks for letting me know." Goodman hung up and Jed decided to wait to call Schultz. If Goodman wasn't that interested, then maybe there wasn't any significance and he would rather not get any unneeded attention. Maybe they'd stop questioning him and leave him out of the rest of the investigation. That would leave him free to do his own exploring, such as taking a road trip to Garberville. The idea popped into his head, just like that.

He found Tony in the office, feeding Aja her bottle. "Hey, could you sub for me for the next few days?"

Tony looked a bit surprised but was his usual accommodating self. "Sure. I just need to rearrange a couple of appointments. You going somewhere?"

"I'm not sure yet. I need to talk to Monica. I just wanted to know if you were available first."

"What about Aja?" The look on Jed's face was priceless. " Are you going to take her with you?" Tony chuckled. "Or what?"

"I guess I'll have to figure that out, too," Jed grimaced.

"Just let me know as soon as you can."

"Thanks, Tony." Jed left the office and went back to the main building. He hoped it would be a slow afternoon. He had a lot to think about. He had already decided he would definitely pay Dutch a visit. It was convincing Monica and figuring out how to get there and what to do about Aja that he had to plan for, and that wouldn't be easy.

14

JED RUSHED HOME AT FIVE SO HE COULD MAKE A SPECIAL DINNER. They hadn't eaten a regular meal since the arrival of Aja and he wanted Monica to be relaxed when he broached the subject. He knew she would be supportive. She always was. But he wanted her to be onboard with it . . . not just tell him he was free to do whatever he wanted and silently not approve. But he wondered how much shopping and cooking he could do and still deal with Aja's needs. Oh well, it was a nice thought. He ended up stopping at the Japanese restaurant that Monica liked and brought home a couple of ramen bowls and some sushi. One of these days they'd actually have a home cooked meal again.

He had Aja fed and changed before Monica got home. "I'm so damn sick of some of these bureaucrats!" she exclaimed as she walked in the door.

"Uh oh. Bad day?" Jed asked.

"Staff meeting and the powers that be in City Hall are putting the brakes on an important project we want to start. I don't really want to talk about it. I just spent two and a half hours talking about it."

"Well, come on and have dinner. I went to Ginza."

"Sounds great. I could use a glass of wine first, though."

"Just sit down and say hello to Aja while I get your wine. She's all clean and fed." He handed Aja to Monica after she got her coat off and flopped onto the sofa. "Hello sweetheart," she said as she kissed the baby.

Jed brought the wine and put a blanket down on the floor. He took Aja and put her on the blanket and then sat next to Monica and poured the wine. He took off her shoes and massaged her feet. "Maybe you'd rather I did your shoulders?" he asked.

"Okay. What's going on? I mean I certainly appreciate your attention, but this isn't exactly normal."

Jed smiled. "It's been a long time since I've given you a massage."

"Yes, Jed. The arrival of Aja has certainly changed things. But I have a feeling more is going on."

He took a breath. "I want to go up to Garberville and see if I can find this Dutch Bogart guy. I need to find out whether there's any connection to the murdered woman."

"You *need* to? Why are you doing this, Jed? Why not just let the police and the FBI do their jobs? Do you honestly think you can find out more than they can?"

"I want to know about Aja's past and whether or not she has a family." He stopped rubbing her feet and reached for Monica's face. She drew back. "I just want to know if we are going to be able to keep her."

"We don't know that we can keep her even if they don't find her family. We still have to apply to adopt her. And frankly Jed, because of our age, we may not have a good shot at it."

"But at least we could know even if we should try."

"Are we sure that it's in her best interests to have such old parents?"

Jed sighed. "I know. But whoever adopts her might not love her and provide for her and —"

"That's enough. Let's not make assumptions. Everything is still up in the air. One day at a time and all that. Anyway, how would you get up there? You don't drive . . . remember? And what about Aja?"

Jed smiled. "Always the voice of reason."

"Are you being sarcastic?"

"Not at all," he replied. "Shall we eat dinner?"

"Sure." They got up and went to the table. Jed microwaved the ramen and they ate in silence.

Just as Jed finished washing the dishes and Monica had put Aja in her crib, Jed's phone rang. It was Malcolm. "Things are going to happen quickly, I'm afraid. They're being a bunch of bullheaded assholes. No regard for the residents. Some of these people are going to be up shit's creek. I don't know what Homer's going to do. He doesn't have kids or money. And he's getting worse." Malcolm drew a long breath." I didn't hear back from that guy, either."

"Oh, I didn't expect you to. I think I'm going to go up there and see if I can find him."

"Huh? You are?"

"Well, I want to. I haven't figured out all the logistics yet."

Malcolm laughed. "Like how you're going to get there?"

"I know. I have to think it through. Anyway, how are you and Savali?"

"Oh, man. Savali's going to be real busy the next week or two finding homes for everyone. They gave everyone thirty days notice. Can you believe it?"

"Is that legal? Only thirty days notice?"

"They are required to give at least sixty, but they had already done that."

At that moment Aja woke up crying. "I think she's starting to teethe," Jed explained. "I need to go. I'll be in touch."

"Yeah, let me know what you decide." They hung up and Jed and Monica met next to the crib.

"You've dealt with her all day. I'll take her," Monica said as she lifted the whimpering baby.

"Thanks." Jed smiled. He went to the computer and sat down to do a Craigslist or Google search but stopped when he realized he didn't know what he was searching for. A driver? A babysitter? He sat back in his chair and sighed. Maybe he just needed to get a driver's license again. It had been so many years that he probably had to start all over with a written test. He didn't even remember what state his last one had been from. He had lived in enough different ones, but as long as he'd been in California, he had been in cities and not needed one. Anyway, it had been even longer since he owned a car.

His phone rang and he saw it was Malcolm again. "Hey, Jed. Savali and I just finished talking. I'm going to take her van and come up and bring you to Garberville."

"What? Are you sure?"

"No one is coming to classes anymore, Jed. They're all frantic about finding a place to live. I have a few days before things start lining up for them. If they're so lucky."

"Don't you need to work at the restaurant? You'll be without a job in a month."

Malcolm laughed. "Jed, you worry too much about everyone else."

"I've heard that said about you, too, Malcolm."

"We're quite a pair, then. You know, it'll be fun. I'm looking forward to it. It'll be a little vacation. And who better to spend a few days with."

"Wow. I don't know what to say. Thanks, man. And thanks to Savali."

"I'll need to do a couple of things tomorrow morning. Get the van ready and all. I can be there tomorrow evening. Then we can set out early the next day. Does that work?"

"That would be great. Thanks again." They hung up and Jed sat back in his chair, grinning. The prospect of spending a couple of days with Malcolm filled his heart. But his elation didn't last when he remembered that he had to figure out what to do with Aja. Tony couldn't watch her and the columbarium by himself. Monica couldn't bring her to work. Or wouldn't. And that was certainly fair and understandable. But the thought of leaving her with a babysitter when they were already the foster parents seemed neither plausible nor affordable, and was probably frowned upon by Family and Children's Services.

"She's sleeping. I gave her a cold washcloth to suck on," Monica said as she sat down next to him.

"Well, aren't you the clever mama," Jed said as he kissed her.

"I read it somewhere but I'll take the compliment."

"Malcolm said he can drive me to Garberville in Savali's van."

"What?"

Jed shrugged and smiled. "He said he could miss a few days of work. He'll be here tomorrow night and then we'll take off day after tomorrow early."

"That'll be nice for you to spend a couple of days alone with Malcolm."

"Yes it will. Tony already said he could sub for me at work."

"I'd like to see Malcolm, too. He means a lot to you and I don't know him very well."

"Yep. Hopefully he'll be here early enough to have dinner and spend the evening."

"So who's going to bring up the elephant in the room?" Monica asked.

"Haven't figured that part out yet, but I'm working on it."

"I really can't bring her to work. I just don't have that kind of job."

"I know that." Jed took her hand.

"You realize then that there's only one alternative."

"It's becoming clearer and clearer. Well, it is what it is." Jed stood up. "Let's go to bed and take advantage of a sleeping baby."

"Sounds like a plan." Monica took his hand and they walked into the bedroom.

15

THE NEXT DAY WAS UNEVENTFUL UNTIL JUST BEFORE CLOSING. 1488 rushed in, just as before, and ran upstairs. This time Jed grabbed Aja out of the stroller and hurried after him. He needed to know who this man was visiting. He crept up the stairs noiselessly, praying that Aja would be quiet, and watched from behind a pillar. 1488 was again on the third floor and had stopped in front of Goldie's and Frank's niches. Jed held his breath, waiting to see what would happen.

1488 opened his duffle bag and Jed pulled Aja closer to his chest, watching silently. The man pulled out a tape measure and measured the width of the empty niche just under Frank's. Jed breathed a sigh of relief. His behavior was sneaky, but at least he wasn't destroying property. Perhaps he was just looking to get a niche for someone. Jed reluctantly started toward him with the pretext of offering information, but the man then pulled out a knife in a sheath and a replica of the Nazi flag, small enough to fit across the back of a niche. Jed stepped back behind the pillar. He was disgusted but unsure what to do. No one had ever put items in their apartment that were unsavory or insensitive.

"Can I help you?" Jed said forcefully. "We are about to close."

The man jumped and stuffed the items back in his bag. A can of spray paint fell out of the bag and started to roll away. The man made a grab for it and quickly stuffed it back into his bag. He focused a hard sneer at Jed as he shot by and flew down the stairs two at a time. Jed didn't follow. This time he felt like he'd gotten a good look at the man's face.

He took out his phone and called Schultz and related what happened. Schultz asked Jed to go back down to the police department to look through images again, but Jed was adamant that he was leaving early the next morning on a trip and didn't have time. He agreed to call Diaz when he got back to look again.

Jed made the rounds, checking out the restrooms and closets and was about to lock up the office when he realized he had forgotten to call Tony and tell him what was happening. He dialed him immediately. "Tony? I forgot to call you. I'm leaving in the morning. I'm so sorry. Will there be a problem?"

"No problem. I figured it was a go so I already changed my plans. How many days?"

"I don't know for sure. Two maybe three."

"Okay. I still have a key so no worries. How's Aja? I couldn't make it in today with all the rearranging."

"She's fine."

"Are you taking her with you or is she staying with Monica?"

"I'm taking her. My friend Malcolm is driving up from Los Angeles and taking me to Garberville. I have some business to attend to up there."

"Garberville?" Tony laughed. "Hey, you don't have to travel all the way up there to score. I still have plenty of connections."

"Not what you're thinking, but thanks. I have to get home and get stuff ready before Malcolm gets here. Oh, but there is one thing. Please make sure to check the bathrooms and closets carefully before leaving at night. I found a bag in one the other day and it dawned on me that people might be hiding there overnight."

"Sure. I'll do that."

"Thanks." Jed appreciated that Tony had not pushed on why he was going to Garberville. "I'll explain later."

"Maybe I can meet Malcolm sometime." Tony had other ways of getting information.

"Oh, well — hey, I'm making dinner tonight. Care to join us?"

"Sorry but I'm busy tonight. I do want to meet him, though. Maybe on your return?"

"Yeah, I'll keep you posted. I'm not sure when that will be. Is that okay to leave everything so up in the air?"

"It's cool, Jed."

"Thanks."

Monica called as he walked home. "What's the plan for dinner?"

Jed had also forgotten to update Monica. "Malcolm will be here around seven and I was just trying to decide what to do about dinner. Any ideas?"

"I'll bring it. You go home and get Aja changed and fed."

"Do you think we'll ever cook a meal again?"

Monica laughed. "What's this 'we' stuff? I'll see you in about an hour."

Jed got Aja changed and fed and then realized he needed to pack a bag for her. Did he even have enough clothes for her? Were they clean or did he need to do some laundry? He calmed down when he realized that they'd probably only be gone one night. He could wash something out in a sink if he had to. He would not be in the wilderness. They had stores in Garberville if all else failed.

Monica arrived with a pizza and an apology. "I just had no idea what Malcolm ate or if he was vegetarian. I figured this was best. I got one with meat and one without. And I got three salads. I'm sorry, but obsessing about it wasn't getting me anywhere."

"It's fine." Jed kissed her. "It's the company, not the food." And as if on cue, there was a knock on the door. Jed grinned as he opened the door and gave Malcolm an exuberant, loving hug.

"Hi Monica," Malcolm said as they finally pulled away from each other. He hugged her too, although they had only met once. "And this is Aja." Malcolm smiled at Aja who grinned back and gurgled.

"Come in, Malcolm. Dinner's on the table," Monica said.

They sat down with Monica holding Aja with one hand and trying to eat pizza with the other. It wasn't easy. "Hey, I got quite used to this at Miss Ruthie's. Let me have her," Malcolm said as he reached out to Aja. She went happily into Malcolm's arms.

Malcolm's adolescence had been spent taking care of the same babies Jed had so often rocked at Miss Ruthie's. He was definitely an old hand and was quite adept at eating his dinner and keeping Aja happily quiet.

After dinner, Aja was put to bed and Monica, Jed and Malcolm spent the next couple of hours drinking beer, laughing, reminiscing, and planning the trip. "It should take about four hours," Malcolm said. "It's 200 miles but getting out of the city always takes a while."

"I'm sorry I never got my license again to help with the driving," Jed said.

"No worries. I don't mind. You'll have your hands full with Aja. Oh shit!" Malcolm exclaimed.

"What's wrong?" Jed asked.

"I just realized. There's no back seat in Savali's van. What are we going to do about Aja? Nowhere to put the car seat."

Monica and Jed looked at each other with alarm. Now what? Jed started to speak, albeit slowly, not exactly sure if this was a good idea. "Well, I guess I could sit in the back and Aja's car seat could go on the passenger seat."

"That may be the only solution." Malcolm answered.

"I've ridden in worse situations. I can sit on the floor of the van."

"Oh, there's a futon in the back. It's actually kind of cozy. Savali used to live in it."

"I suppose I could switch cars for a few days," Monica offered halfheartedly. "You guys could take my car and I could drive the van to work."

Malcolm waited for Jed to answer. It was up to him. Jed seemed hesitant to have Monica driving the van or he had picked up on her reluctance. "No, it's okay. We will fit into the Garberville culture a lot easier with the van. And we need people to trust us if we are going to find this guy."

Monica laughed. "Culture! A Sasquatch sighting would cause less of a sensation. Rural northern California is not exactly overflowing with African-Americans."

Jed and Malcolm looked at each other wryly. "She's right. We will definitely stand out," Malcolm said.

"Well, we will stand out even more if we have a nice car."

"It's a Corolla, not a Cadillac," Monica snorted.

"Great," Malcolm laughed. "They'll think we're two Black dudes who can't even steal a decent car!"

"Let's just keep the plan we started with," Jed cut in. "I'll ride in the back. It'll be fine." Jed looked at the clock and stood. "I'm going to bed. It's getting late."

Monica picked up immediately on Jed's discomfort and need for time alone. "I'll get Malcolm the bedding for the couch. You go on."

"What time did you want to leave in the morning?" Malcolm asked.

Jed shrugged and turned towards their bedroom. "Whenever we're up and ready."

Malcolm looked at Monica apprehensively, but her slight nod and smile reassured him that he'd be his old self in the morning.

16

THANKFULLY AJA SLEPT THROUGH THE NIGHT AND DIDN'T WAKE THEM UP UNTIL SIX. After a hearty breakfast and quick showers, they were on the road by seven-thirty. Aja seemed to like her perch in the passenger seat. Jed, on the other hand, was not thrilled being relegated to the back with only a view of the inside of the van. Malcolm tried to soften the tension in the air by relating stories of a trip taken by Malcolm, Savali, Finn and Nick, another resident from the senior home. They had traveled from Los Angeles to San Francisco in this van. Nick and Finn, quite the pair of curmudgeons, complained loudly and continually about being stuck in the back on the same futon. This trip had been the last time Jed and Malcolm had seen each other, and Jed had not heard about its culmination. It was an interesting story that made the time go more quickly. "Sorry you don't have anyone to play cards with, but there's always solitaire on your phone," Malcolm said when he had finished telling the story.

"My phone is a phone. I don't use it for anything else besides calling and texting. Where are we, anyway? I can't see a thing back here."

"Santa Rosa area."

"So how far to Garberville, you think?"

"At least two and a half hours."

Jed groaned. "That long, huh."

"You don't travel well, do you?"

"Listen. Malcolm. I've done plenty in my time, but it was usually without a particular destination in mind. And I had nobody caring one way or the other where I was from or where I was going. I'm in a whole different place, now."

"I get you," Malcolm nodded. "Do you have any idea what we're going to do when we get there?"

"Not really. Just try to find Dutch Bogart. Maybe try City Hall or something. Maybe start with the post office since I have his box number. Maybe they'll help, even though they shouldn't be giving out any information."

"Here's where Nick would come in handy."

"How so?"

"I told you about his past. I'm sure he would know how to wring the truth out of someone."

"Well, I hope friendly persuasion is enough to get a lead on Dutch."

"Jeez, Jed. I was only kidding."

"Yeah, well, I've got to think this out. Ask the wrong questions of the wrong people and the whole town could clam up." At that moment, the usually placid baby decided she was getting sick of driving as well and started to whimper and move around restlessly in the car seat. "Maybe we should stop for a break."

Malcolm shook his head. "You really are turning into Finn! Not only cantankerous but needing to use the restroom every hour."

"I didn't say I needed the bathroom!"

"Okay, dude, okay!" Malcolm laughed. "I'm just teasing." He pulled off at the next exit and went to a gas station. "Do you want anything? I think I'll get some coffee."

"No. I'll just deal with Aja." Jed moved to the front and took the baby out of her car seat, checked her diaper and took her to the back of the van to let her lie on her stomach. He had noticed that she had started to do what looked like push-ups, as if she was getting ready to roll over. He found some toys in the diaper bag and dangled them in front of her.

After a few half-hearted games of peek-a-boo, Malcolm was back and Jed put her back in the car seat. "Are you sure you don't want to at least get out and walk around?" Malcolm asked.

"I'm fine. Let's go."

Malcolm accelerated and the only sound for the next hour was Aja's breathing. "Is it okay if I put on the radio?" Malcolm asked. "Or would it wake her up?"

"Probably best not. We should take advantage of the fact that she's asleep."

"Okay." More silence. "Can I ask you something, Jed?"

"What?"

"Are you really going to keep Aja if you can?"

"I'm not sure. It's a big commitment."

"Of course. But you must have had some reason to have wanted to foster her."

Jed sighed. "It was impulsive." He cleared his throat. "I don't think I ever told you. I had a daughter once . . . many years ago."

"You did? No, you never told me."

"Only Finn and Monica know. And now you."

"Do you know where she is?"

"She died when she was five."

"Oh, Jed. I'm sorry. That must have been awful."

"She had a good mother who took care of her. I wasn't as present as I should have been. Maybe that's part of what's going on here. But the reality is, of course, that Monica and I are no spring chickens and I'm not sure it's the best thing for Aja."

"Being loved as a child is what matters. We both had strong mothers that died young. But we know they loved us and took care of us and set us on the right path."

Jed smiled. "I'm not so sure."

"What do you mean?"

"If she hadn't been under the spell of Jim Jones and followed him to Guyana . . ." Jed trailed off. "Anyway, I guess the answer to your question is that my heart says I want to keep her, but my head is not so sure."

"I'd like to have kids."

"And Savali?"

"She said she would, but we haven't talked about it seriously." As if on cue, Aja woke up and gave Malcolm a big smile. "Hey little one." Malcolm tickled her chin and was surprised to hear what sounded like giggling. "Did you hear that Jed? Aja laughed out loud!"

"I did."

Malcolm pulled off the highway again after a while. "We're in Willits. Probably the last big town before we hit Garberville. I should get gas. Do you want to use the bathroom first while I pump?"

"Sure." Jed tried to open the back door, but it wouldn't budge.

"Oh, sorry. I forgot. I have to open it from the outside."

Malcolm walked around and opened the door and Jed climbed out. He stretched a bit. "I guess I am a little sore. I'll pay when I go inside. What's the pump number?"

"Three."

Jed paid, used the bathroom, and returned. Malcolm had taken Aja out of her car seat and was walking her around the gas station. He handed her to Jed and used the restroom. They were back on the road and finally reached Garberville an hour and a half later.

It was close to lunchtime and they decided that they would stop in a restaurant to eat and decide their first move. Jed put Aja in her stroller and looked around for a café. It was then that he noticed that most of the main street was taken up with homeless hippie types, and Monica was absolutely right. They were all white. Malcolm and Jed stood out like sore thumbs.

"I always thought the Venice Beach boardwalk was a homeless mecca, but this is unbelievable," Malcolm said. "I think they're here for a purpose. Check out the signs they're holding."

"You mean those pictures of scissors on top of marijuana leaves?" Jed asked.

"It's harvest time. They're looking for work."

"There's good money in it." Jed smiled. "And what a great place to start our search. Perhaps we can find Dutch through the people looking for work. But let's get lunch and I need to give Aja a bottle."

They found a café and took turns eating and feeding Aja. "Should we just ask until we find someone who knows him?" Malcolm asked after a few minutes of trying to resist Jed's insistence on paying and giving up when Jed grabbed the check.

"That sounds like as good a plan as any."

They each took a side of Redwood Highway, the main thoroughfare, and started asking. It didn't take long for them to get what they needed. They came back together after one block and both shared the same information. Dutch Bogart was indeed a famous icon in Garberville, both as a musician and a pot grower. However, the directions were not easy to follow. They set off with at least a vague idea of where his farm was located and hoped that they would get more information as they neared it.

"This is some beautiful scenery, Jed," Malcolm called out to the back. "Maybe Savali and I should see about moving up here now that we're both out of a job."

"You're not serious, are you?"

Malcolm laughed. "No, Jed, I'm not serious. I've got a pretty good thing going in Venice. A house that's paid for and I work at a restaurant that gives me total flexibility so I can make films."

Jed crawled up to the front of the van and peeked out the window. "It is very pretty."

"So where do you think this guy lives?"

"What did those people say? Something about a barn being the only thing you can see from the road? About a half-mile from an apple orchard with a roadside stand. Did we pass the stand?"

"I think I see it up ahead." Malcolm pointed to a sign touting apples, pears, cider and pies and an arrow.

"Okay so look at the odometer and we can count the half mile."

"Jed, I think I know that."

"Sorry, man."

They were silent until they saw an old, weather-beaten barn next to a driveway. Malcolm turned into the driveway, but before they reached the barn they arrived at a locked gate. A wire fence surrounded the property with barbed wire across the top. "I guess they have to worry about theft too."

"I'm sure they do. How are we going to get in? Any ideas?" Jed asked.

"Do you see an intercom or anything?"

"Let me get out and see." Jed climbed out the passenger door and went up to the gate. There was nothing there except a keypad to put a code in. He walked to the left and right to see if there were any holes in the fence to climb through, but found none. He came back to the van. "I guess we just wait and hope someone comes in or out."

"I doubt Aja's going to like sitting in that car seat for hours."

"Well, the only thing I can think of is to walk further around the perimeter and see if we can find someone within shouting distance."

"And what is it exactly that you're going to shout to this person?"

"Good point. But it's all we got." Jed took Aja out of the car seat and laid her down on a blanket on the grass to change her diaper. He put her in the Snugli and they were off.

They walked about half a mile or so until they finally saw someone riding a horse on the property. "Look, Jed, over there. Is it a woman or a man? I can't tell."

"Excuse me!" Jed shouted. "We are looking for Dutch Bogart."

The woman on the horse looked at them suspiciously and rode over. "Why?"

"It has to do with Laila Aziz. I need to speak to him."

"Laila isn't here."

"I know. I'm from the columbarium in San Francisco where her ashes are." Jed and Malcolm smiled at each other. They had a lead.

"Didn't Dutch pay?" she asked.

"He did. Could you just get him for us? Or give us the code to get in?"

She hesitated and finally said, "I'll see if I can find him." She started to turn the horse around, but then turned her face back to Jed. "What's your name?"

"Jed Gibbons."

She kicked the horse and it cantered off.

"So should we stay here or go back to the gate?" Malcolm asked.

Jed shrugged. "Beats me. I guess stay here. Maybe this is closer to the house or wherever he is."

They sat down on the grass, but didn't have to wait long. The lady came trotting back within a few minutes. "Nineteen forty-nine," she called to them and then pushed the horse into a gallop.

"Let's go," Malcolm got up. "Want me to take Aja for a bit?"

"I'm fine. You can deal with her when we finally get to talk to Dutch." They walked briskly back to the van. Malcolm was excited to find out more about Dutch and his growing operation. Jed was apprehensive, unsure what he was going to ask and how he was going to be received. He wished he'd done some more research on the kind of music Dutch had played, thinking that would break the ice. Jed hadn't ever been much of a pot smoker, so they wouldn't have that in common either. All Jed had was his engaging, honorable personality. He hoped that would be enough.

17

THEY HIKED BACK TO THE VAN PARKED IN THE DRIVEWAY. Jed walked up to the keypad and punched in the code. After Malcolm drove through the gate, Jed opened the passenger door, unstrapped the car seat and threw it into the back of the van. "I'll just sit here with her," Jed said as he plopped onto the passenger seat, Aja still in the Snugli.

Malcolm drove slowly up the driveway until a sprawling Frank Lloyd Wright-style house loomed in front of them. It was a house of lots of wood and glass with many smaller windows of stained glass. "Wow. He must be doing pretty well to afford this," Malcolm said.

"Maybe it's the royalties from his music."

"More likely his pot-growing." A man in overalls and a flannel shirt, with a wild, white beard and a long, white ponytail down his back, stood in front of the house with a rifle in his hand. "Whoa, what's with the gun?" Malcolm asked.

"Two Black dudes in a dilapidated van on a probably illegal marijuana farm," Jed replied.

"Yeah, but a gun? Come on."

"The sheriff's not exactly at his beck and call."

"I guess. Well, hopefully Aja will soften the tension." Malcolm stopped the van and got out. "Hey man, don't shoot."

"Oh for God's sake, Malcolm," Jed said as he got out. He did, however, subconsciously shield Aja with his arm.

"What do you want?" the man asked, still holding the gun but at least not pointing it at them.

"We just want to talk to you about Laila Aziz." Jed walked carefully toward him with his hand outstretched. "My name is Jed Gibbons. This is Malcolm Washington. And this is Aja." He took the baby out of the Snugli. That was a good move. The sight of the baby made the man change the angle of the gun toward the ground.

"What about Laila?" he asked.

"Well, first of all, are you Dutch Bogart, the man who paid for her niche at the San Francisco Columbarium?"

"Yes." Dutch placed the gun on the ground. That Jed knew he had paid for the niche was apparently enough for him to decide that these visitors were safe. "Is that A-s-i-a like the continent or A-j-a like the Steely Dan song?"

"It's A-j-a but not after the song. It's an Indian or African name. My wife and I just liked it."

"She yours?"

"For now."

Dutch gave him a wary look, but didn't ask the obvious question. Instead he asked, "What do you want to know about Laila?"

"As I told the woman on the horse, I work at the columbarium. That's how I got your name. Did she live here with you?"

"Off and on."

Jed waited for Dutch to say more, but after a couple of moments, he realized nothing more was forthcoming without being questioned. "Was she a friend of yours? Or a worker?"

Dutch hesitated and looked them over. "Come on inside. Let's have a beer."

Jed and Malcolm followed Dutch inside the house. They glanced at each other when they looked around, appreciating the stunning architecture. The walls and floors were covered with pieces of art of all kinds. Dutch brought them into a room in back of the house with a breathtaking, expansive view out the huge window that was the whole back wall: hills, orchards, a creek and several outbuildings.

"Wow!" Malcolm couldn't keep his wonderment to himself. The room was large with a sofa and two chairs in the middle and musical instruments and recording equipment taking up the other three walls. Malcolm went up to one of the walls to check out some of the framed gold records. "You played with a lot of different bands?"

"Those are mostly for songwriting." Dutch opened a refrigerator in the corner. "You like Stout or porter? Or do you like a lighter one?"

Malcolm and Jed glanced at each other, waiting for the other to answer. Finally Jed said, "Probably on the lighter side for me."

"I'll have whatever you're having, Dutch," Malcolm said as casually as possible.

Dutch took out a couple of local double IPAs and a pale ale. He opened them and handed them out. "These are organic. They come from a brewery up in Fortuna."

Malcolm and Jed took sips and sat down on the sofa. Jed took Aja out of the Snugli and placed her on her stomach on the rug. "Really nice place you have here," Malcolm said.

"Thanks." Dutch sat on a chair and faced them. "Laila was the trim mama here. She came for harvest every year. She'd been coming here for about ten years."

"Trim Mama?" Malcolm asked.

"She started out as a trimmer and then kind of made up a position for herself. She took care of the seasonal workers. Cooked for them. Showed them the ropes. Organized the trimming. She was a big help."

"How old was she?" Jed asked.

"I don't know. About my age."

"How'd she die?"

"I don't know. I just heard about the death and that she wanted to be put in your place, there, the columbarium so I paid for the niche."

"Who brought the urn with the ashes to the columbarium?" Jed was getting more and more curious.

Dutch shrugged. "I'm not sure. She was a quiet type. She never shared much."

Jed couldn't mask his disappointment. "Did you know if she had a daughter?"

"I don't recall her ever mentioning a daughter. We talked about music, mostly. She was a Dead Head. Oh, sometimes we'd talk about religion. I was curious about the Muslim religion."

Jed perked up. Finally something he could use to connect some of the dots. "Did she wear a hijab?"

"Not here, but I think she did other times." Dutch picked up a guitar that had been leaning against the wall and started to play.

Jed and Malcolm glanced at each other, both of them thinking this was some kind of signal that the interview was over. Jed figured he should hurry up and ask some questions. "Can you tell me anything else about Laila?"

Dutch continued strumming but seemed engaged with Jed and Malcolm. "Why are you asking all these questions about her, anyway?"

"A young woman was found dead on the grounds of the columbarium. She had a piece of paper in her bag with Laila's name on it. Aja was found next to the body so we are trying to find out who the woman was and if the baby has any relatives." The mention of Aja's kin caused Jed to end with a sigh.

"Why are you here? Aren't the police looking for that woman's murderer?"

"The police and the FBI are investigating. The murdered woman was wearing a hijab and the niches that belonged to Blacks and Jews were vandalized."

Dutch shook his head and then started singing, "All caught up in a landslide, bad luck pressing in on all sides . . ."

"Did you write that? Isn't that "Buried Alive in the Blues?" Malcolm asked.

"Nah, a friend of mine did. Nick Gravenites. He wrote it for Janis Joplin."

At that moment Jed realized that he didn't want to know more about Laila Aziz. Just leave it up to the police and FBI. "Thanks, Dutch. We really appreciate giving us your time." Jed picked up Aja and put her in the Snugli.

"Thanks for the beer," Malcolm said. "Can I talk to you about something totally different?"

"What's that?" Dutch answered. He started playing a more upbeat tune.

"I make documentaries. I'd like to look into doing a film about pot farming. Could I come back and interview you and maybe get some leads of others that might be interested in being interviewed? I mean now that it's legal and all in California, do you think people would mind?"

Dutch laughed. "Of course they would mind. Just because it's legal in California doesn't mean the Feds wouldn't just love to find us, as well as some of the lovely criminals who prey at harvest time to steal our finished products. Sorry."

Jed rolled his eyes toward the door to show Malcolm it was time to go. "Thanks for your time."

Malcolm and Jed left Dutch playing his guitar and saw themselves out. They got in the van silently and started to drive down the driveway. The gate opened automatically as they approached and they continued towards the road. "Are you going to put Aja in the car seat?" Malcolm asked.

"Let's get to the road. Then pull over and we can get settled for the drive home."

Malcolm knew that Jed needed time to organize his thoughts. Malcolm tapped the steering wheel in time to the song in his head, "Buried Alive in the Blues."

Malcolm pulled over when they got to the road and Jed put Aja back in her car seat. Jed stayed on the floor near the front, however, instead of sitting on the futon in the back. Malcolm pulled out onto the road. "Did you really think he was going to let you film his farm?" Jed asked.

"You miss 100% of the shots you don't take. It doesn't matter anyway. I've got plenty of ideas for other films. I want to do one on Homer and Parkinson's disease."

"That would be good."

"Homer has a lot of people looking out for him. Finn taught a writers workshop at the residence, and Homer went, but I don't know if he really wrote anything."

"Well, he's probably given it some thought anyway. Enough for you to build a documentary on," Jed said.

"There were actually a lot of writers at the residence. That guy Nick I was telling you about earlier? He was a poet. He's the guy Savali, Finn and I took to see his mother in the hospital in San Francisco. Then he disappeared."

"The one whose family were the big time drug dealers?"

"Yep. But Nick sure came through at the end for me. He financed my transgender documentary."

"I remember, now. His mother died didn't she?"

"Yes."

"Do you remember her name?"

"Francesca Balducci."

"No way," Jed shot back. "Really?"

"What about her?"

"Oh, this mobster-looking guy came to visit her in the columbarium. I wonder if it was Nick."

"Did he have shiny black hair and a tan face?" Malcolm asked.

"Yeah."

"That was probably Nick's brother, Anthony."

"Hmmm. He was looking around the bushes where the body was found. I wondered if there was a connection."

"Did you tell the cops or the FBI?"

"Yeah, but they didn't seem that interested."

"What have you told them?"

"More than I should, I think. I really don't want to be involved. I hate being in the middle of all this."

"You kind of brought it on yourself by taking in Aja and playing detective."

"I know."

They were silent for a few minutes. Finally Malcolm spoke. "So are you and Monica really wanting to take on the responsibility of raising a child?"

"I'm not sure. You said you and Savali have had a similar conversation?"

"Not lately, but we have."

Jed wondered just how they would work that out since they were both anatomically male, but instead changed the subject. "What ideas do you have for a Parkinson's documentary?"

"There are some incredible new ways they've found to deal with the symptoms using music and movement."

"Interesting. Is Homer willing to be the star?"

"Yes. He has such a great attitude. You know how he refers to it? He calls it just a hitch in his giddy-up."

Jed laughed loudly. "I haven't heard that expression in years!"

Malcolm laughed with him. "I'd never heard it before. I assume it means that it's just part of getting old. Something like that?"

"Yeah," Jed chuckled. "Something like that."

18

JED AND MALCOLM MANAGED TO DRIVE BACK TO SAN FRANCISCO STOPPING ONLY ONCE. Aja was a little fussy, but Jed took her out of the car seat a bit and that helped. Their conversation was light and unrevealing. Jed was too focused on figuring out what to do next with what little Dutch had told him. Malcolm's mind was also somewhere else. He hadn't thought much about filmmaking lately and telling Jed about Homer had awakened that side of him.

They got home after seven. Monica had actually cooked a meal: lasagna, salad and bread. It wasn't fancy but Jed and Malcolm ate heartily while Monica took over the parenting duties. Jed had entered the house proclaiming that it had not been a particular fruitful visit. That was enough to signal to Monica that she should wait for any explanations from Jed. Malcolm was obviously tired from all the driving and seemed pensive besides, so she didn't talk to him much either. Aja seemed the only one in a happy, playful mood.

After the dinner dishes were done and Aja was down, hopefully for the night, the three sat in the living room with a bottle of wine. After a little small talk between Monica and Malcolm, Jed finally sighed and spoke. "I think I'm going to stop this detective stuff. I'll answer direct questions from the cops but I'm not going to offer anything. We have enough uncertainty with Aja. Let's just concentrate on parenting her well while we have her."

"While we have her?" Monica asked.

"I'm just being realistic."

Malcolm and Monica exchanged looks. Jed stared out the window. Finally Monica said, "Did something specific happen? It sounds like you've reached some kind of decision."

"I haven't reached a decision. As I said, I'm just being realistic. We don't have that much control. I'm going to bed," Jed said as he rose. His phone rang. He looked at it and answered. "Hi Tony. Everything go okay today?"

"Yeah, fine. I'm just wondering if you want me to work again tomorrow."

Jed looked at Malcolm. "What time are you planning to leave in the morning?"

"As soon as I get up. Why? Did you need to go to some other faraway place?" Malcolm grinned.

"No, I just wondered if I should ask Tony to work for me in the morning."

"I'll leave pretty early, but we could have breakfast first. I don't mind waiting until rush hour is over before attacking the freeways. But it's up to you."

Jed turned back to the phone. "Could you open up for me? I'll get there around ten or so. Thanks, Tony." He hung up and walked to the bedroom. Monica busied herself getting the couch made up for Malcolm and then followed Jed to the bedroom. He was still awake after Monica got ready and climbed into bed. She kissed him and turned over, knowing when it was best to leave him alone.

Jed finally fell asleep, but slept fitfully. He awoke for the last time at five and decided to get up. He tiptoed into the kitchen, trying not to wake Malcolm, but Aja heard him and decided that it was time for the whole household to start their day. She didn't cry, but giggled and cooed and yelled, so that neither Monica nor Malcolm had much of a choice. Soon the whole group had assembled in the kitchen, leaning against the counters with cups of coffee in hand. Malcolm had decided to try his hand at the parenting duties so he had changed the diaper and held the bottle and the baby.

"You're quite a natural at this parenting thing," Monica smiled at Malcolm.

"Lots of practice."

"Do you like it?" Jed asked.

Malcolm looked at him, surprised by the question. It seemed like a strange thing to ask, especially from Jed. "Uh, I guess. I don't really know what you mean."

"Would you like being a parent?"

Monica gave Jed a quizzical look. "What are you getting at?"

"I'm just trying to help Malcolm see if he wants to have kids."

"I already told you that I did," Malcolm answered with a trace of irritation in his voice.

Jed grinned at Malcolm. "Yes, that's right. You did." He turned toward the door. "I'm going to take a shower."

Monica and Malcolm shrugged at each other. "He loves you, Malcolm. It's his way of showing it."

"I guess so," Malcolm answered.

"Do you want to use the bathroom after Jed?" Monica changed the subject.

"Is that okay or do you need to get ready for work?"

"That's fine. It's still early so I have plenty of time. Let me take the munchkin."

Malcolm handed Aja over to Monica and went into the living room. He started to take the sheets off the couch. Monica followed him in and placed Aja on a blanket on the floor. "What would you like me to do with the linens?" Malcolm asked.

"Just leave them. I'll take care of it."

At that moment Jed walked in. "The bathroom's available for anyone who wants it."

"I'm next." Malcolm left.

"I'll go make some breakfast," Monica said.

Jed watched Monica go into the kitchen and then gazed at Aja. He was confused but he knew he was falling hard for this baby and it wouldn't be easy letting her go. Malcolm returned to the living room after his shower, but Jed didn't notice. Malcolm watched him for a full minute before saying softly, "It's complicated, isn't it?"

"Yeah."

"Breakfast is ready," Monica called from the kitchen. They all sat down at the table and Monica brought in some French toast and fruit.

"You must have gone to the store yesterday," Jed said.

"It's amazing how much you can get accomplished when there's no husband or baby around."

"Oh, man, speaking of husband, I have to call Savali. I told her I would call last night and I forgot."

"Have you also forgotten to tell us something?" Monica asked.

"What do you mean?"

"Husband?"

"Oh, we wouldn't get married without telling you. It just reminded me of, you know, my significant other."

"Are you planning to?"

Malcolm shrugged. "You know there was a new law enacted in California so people can declare themselves a third or non-binary gender. Savali wants to register as that first and then get married. She always wants to make a political statement, you know." Malcolm grinned.

"Well good for her. I hope she'll come up here to visit one day soon so I can get to know her," Monica said.

"That would be nice," Malcolm smiled. "Well, I better hit the road." He gave both Jed and Monica hugs and kissed Aja on the head.

19

IT WAS A BUSY DAY AT THE COLUMBARIUM. There was a memorial service scheduled for the afternoon, so Jed had extra cleaning and chair set-up to do. Aja stole everyone's heart and those that were there to weep and reminisce, found that they were laughing and playing with Aja instead. Everyone wanted to hold the baby, so he was able to do many of his chores unhindered. He was relieved that he discovered nothing new about the murder as he worked.

When the service was over and the main atrium was cleaned up, Jed put Aja in the stroller and started to turn off the lights. It was after five and he was tired and hungry, having forgotten to eat lunch. Just as he stepped out the front door and had turned around to lock it, a voice called out to him. "Hey Jed! Wait up!"

Jed turned around and saw Agents Schultz and Kelly coming up the driveway. "Oh, crap," he said to himself.

"We need to talk." Schultz came up next to him and steered him back inside the building.

Jed brushed Schultz's hands off his arm and went back inside. "I need to go. What is it?"

"We need to look at your records on a certain woman named Laila Aziz."

Jed swallowed hard. "What records do you mean?" He wasn't going to make it easy.

"Who paid for her niche and anything else you have on her. We were here yesterday, but the guy here said he doesn't have access to that information."

Jed took them to the back office. He worried that he might incriminate Dutch somehow and would compromise his pot-growing situation, but he didn't know what else he could do. Jed went through the motions of pretending he hadn't already looked it up. "Here it is. A guy named Dutch Bogart."

"Where's he from?" Schultz asked.

Jed feigned looking through the paperwork. "Uh, Garberville. It's just a post office box. No phone number or anything."

"Any other information there about Laila? Or this Dutch character?"

"Nope. He just sent the money."

"Who sent the urn and ashes?"

Jed looked down at the paperwork again. "A Santa Rosa funeral home. Are we done? I need to leave."

Schultz smiled at him sarcastically. "Not quite. We need the name of the funeral home."

"Oh, yeah . . . um . . . The Golden Crescent."

"Thanks. And remember, you need to give us any information you get. Or discover." He stared hard into Jed's eyes.

Jed led them out the door and locked it. He watched them go down the driveway and out the gate before pushing the stroller ahead of him. He didn't want any more conversation with them. He was tired of the questioning, and the innuendos. After locking the gate, he called Monica. "Hey. We're just leaving and we had visitors that kept us here late."

"The FBI or Goodman?"

"Schultz and Kelly. I had to tell them Dutch's name and who sent the ashes and urn. I need to walk. Aja and I are going through the park so we'll be even later. I'm sorry. I'm kind of shook up and worried."

"We've discussed this again and again. They're just doing their job. You can't expect to beat them to it."

"But Aja —"

Monica cut him off. "And why do you need to take Aja on this roundabout walk home? What's on your mind?"

"Can't it wait? I need to walk now. I need to think."

"Okay. I'll have dinner ready? Or are you planning to eat out?"

"Hadn't even thought about eating."

"That's what I was afraid of. You didn't eat lunch either, did you? You remembered to feed Aja, I hope."

"Yes. I fed her. See you in a little bit." He hung up. He hated to be so short with Monica, but he would be no good to anyone until he cleared his head. Luckily, Aja loved to walk. And walk they did. Before he knew it, he had gotten to Crissy Field and almost an hour had passed. It was getting foggy and cold and although Aja had slept through most of the walk, he knew that he had gone too far with her.

He called Monica back. "I'm sorry, Monica. It might be too cold for her. I think you had better come and get us."

She sighed. "Where are you?"

"Crissy Field."

"I'll be there in about fifteen minutes."

"Did you make dinner yet?"

"Yes."

"Oh, I thought maybe I'd take you out."

"Not tonight. It's late and Aja needs to go home." She hung up.

"I'm sorry, baby." Jed took Aja out of the stroller and held her close to his chest to warm her. She snuggled next to him but whimpered.

Monica drove up about twenty minutes later and Jed put Aja in the car seat and got into the passenger side. She drove away from the curb. "What do you have up your sleeve?"

"What do you mean?"

"I know when you have to walk that badly, it's to work something out."

"I haven't worked anything out." He shrugged. "Maybe I need to get away."

Monica pulled into an empty space in front of a hydrant and stopped the car. She turned to look at him. "Get away alone and leave Aja with me?"

He sighed. "No. I'll take her."

"Oh Jed! I've put up with a lot, but I'm getting pretty angry now."

"I'm sorry, Monica. Maybe I'm thinking the worst."

"I was going to wait until a better time to tell you, but I think it's better to give you some perspective. Elizabeth called. There is a good chance that they won't okay us as adoptive parents. We're just too old. She said it's very rare that they approve people over sixty, especially if they're not relatives. Also, they do an exhaustive search for relatives so there wouldn't be an answer for quite a while."

"But don't you have some kind of pull or anything?"

"Some, but if I were in Elizabeth's shoes, I would probably come to the same decision."

Jed was silent. Monica heard him start to breathe rhythmically, his way of calming himself when he was afraid he'd explode. She turned the car back on and pulled out. They drove the rest of the way with the sound of Jed's breathing and the hungry, tired cries of Aja coming from the back seat. It was not a pleasant drive.

Monica took Aja out of the car seat and took her inside. Jed told her that he wanted to walk some more and would be home in an hour. By the time he walked in the house, Aja was asleep, Monica was in bed and the dining room table was set with a plate of food. Jed ate the cold food and climbed into bed next to Monica. He turned on his side and lay with his eyes open, knowing that sleep would be eluding him. He wanted to stay in bed, though, to show Monica that he was still there for her in body, if not in mind.

20

MONICA AND AJA WERE UP, DRESSED AND FED BY THE TIME JED GOT TO THE KITCHEN. "Good morning." Jed kissed Monica and Aja and then poured a cup of coffee. "What time is it?"

"Eight."

"I'd better shower then." He gulped down half his coffee and set the mug on the counter.

"It's Sunday. You don't have to be there until 10."

"Jeez, I haven't been keeping track of the days." He leaned against the counter.

"So what decisions did you come to on your walk and your sleepless night?" Monica asked.

He took a breath. "None."

"So you're not going to run away from home?"

"Monica, I was never going to leave you."

"I know."

Jed's phone rang at that moment and he looked at the screen. "It's Malcolm." He answered it. "Hi."

"I've got a favor to ask."

"What's that?"

"Well, actually it's probably more for Monica. You know Homer? The guy with Parkinson's?"

"Yeah. I remember. The one you and Savali are trying to find housing for."

"Well, time is closing in on Homer. He has nowhere to go. It seems he grew up in some rural area up north and wants to go back there."

"Where's that?"

"A place called Honeydew. I think it's somewhere between Mendocino and Eureka, but more inland, not far from Garberville. Homer said he wants to get out of the city and live his last days in fresh air."

"So what's the favor?"

"I thought Monica might have some insight into how to find Homer a place. Maybe she only knows about places in San Francisco, but at least she knows how to navigate the system."

"I'll ask her. When does Homer have to be out?"

"Soon. Next couple of days."

"It sounds like things are going fast in closing down the residence."

"Much too fast for everyone. We're packing everyone's stuff. It's kind of overwhelming for most of them. They moved in here thinking they would be here for the rest of their lives."

"You and Savali are good people," Jed said.

"I learned how to be a good person from the best: you and Miss Ruthie."

Jed walked back into the bedroom and found Monica playing with Aja on the bed. "Malcolm wanted me to ask you for help finding a nursing home or something for Homer, but not in the city. He wants to live somewhere up north in a rural area. Do you have any connections or any ideas who to contact?"

"I'll see what I can do. And I'll keep Aja home today since I don't have to go to work."

"It's up to you."

"I don't have anything special planned. You'll only be there half day today, so maybe we can actually have a nice family evening together."

Jed sat on the bed and took her in his arms. "We will figure this out somehow. And do what's best for Aja."

"Yes, but sometimes in your quest to do what's best for others, you don't do what's best for you."

"Well, I'll keep that in mind." He kissed her. "I'm going to shower." He left.

Monica picked up Aja and looked into her eyes. "No one could ever love you more than that man. I just hope he doesn't do anything foolish." She sighed and took Aja to the living room. She put her on the floor and logged on to her computer to start searching for places for Homer. There were never many choices in rural areas. She'd start with Ukiah and work up to Crescent City and see what she could turn up.

Jed spent his four hours at work doing a thorough cleaning. People came and went but he wanted to take advantage of not having to care for Aja, so he wasn't especially gregarious. He wasn't feeling that friendly, anyway. There was way too much on his mind. He had called Malcolm on his way to work asking him to contact Dutch on Facebook or on one of those cannabis forums and warn him that the FBI was going to try to talk to him.

A few minutes before closing time, Jed noticed a man standing by Laila's apartment. He looked Middle-Eastern, so Jed thought perhaps he was a relative. He approached the man, not sure what he would say. "Hello. Just want to let you know that we'll be closing in a few minutes."

The man smiled warmly. "Oh, thank you."

"Is Laila a relative?" Jed asked.

"No. I was just looking around. This is a beautiful building."

Jed didn't believe him. He hadn't been looking around at all. "Yes. Another time I can tell you some of the history behind it, but I need to lock up pretty soon."

"Oh, that's fine." The man started down the stairs with Jed. "I heard there was a murder recently." He shook his head and frowned. "Terrible. Must have been awful for you."

"Yes. It was a shock."

"Were you the one who discovered the body?"

"I'm afraid so."

They reached the front door and the man smiled at Jed. "Maybe I'll see you again soon and I can hear all about this place."

Jed watched him leave, not sure what to make of him. He certainly was a friendly guy, but Jed was wary. There was no doubt that he had been standing in front of Laila's apartment for a while. And her niche was probably one of the least interesting ones in the whole building. It held one simple urn and nothing else.

Tony appeared just as Jed was locking up. "Just thought I'd check in. Hey, where's my girl?"

"She stayed home with Monica today."

"How was the trip? Fruitful?"

"Not particularly."

"That's too bad. Well, let me know if you need my services as caretaker for the building or the baby." Tony smiled. "I'm happy to do either . . . or both."

"I really appreciate it. How much do I owe you?"

"Nothing. Really. I don't need it. Goldie left me plenty and I don't spend much." They walked out together to Tony's car. "Can I give you a ride home?"

"Nah, I need the walk. Thanks again for helping me out." Jed watched Tony drive out of the parking lot and then locked the gate. He turned toward Golden Gate Park instead of toward his house. He glanced at his phone and noted the time and promised himself he would only go as far as Strawberry Hill. He would be home early enough for Monica to have some time to herself.

He kept his promise and was home by four. Monica, however, was not there. He was secretly pleased because he wanted some time on the computer. He wanted to figure out how to get to Garberville himself without having to rely on anyone driving him. He also looked at the Department of Motor Vehicles page to see about getting another driver's license. It had been a long time since he had driven a car.

Monica walked in the door about half an hour later with a bag of tacos from the local Mexican restaurant. Aja was wide-awake and crying. "I don't know what's wrong. She's been crying for the last couple of hours. I finally took her for a walk, hoping that would soothe her."

Jed took Aja out of the stroller and tried pacing back and forth, rocking her. "Do you think it's teething?"

"I rubbed her gums, but it didn't help. I've tried everything."

"Maybe it's a stomachache?"

"I don't know. But I'm pretty exhausted trying to get her to stop."

"I'll take over."

"Thanks. And when she's finally quiet, we need to talk." Monica went into the bedroom before Jed could ask any questions.

He started to follow her, but he heard the shower go on. Monica would not be sharing any news until Aja was asleep and they could talk. It was probably about Aja. Either Elizabeth had called with news about the possible adoption, or Monica had come to some decision. Jed picked up Aja. He knew that his tolerance for screaming babies was more than most people's and that he had an innate ability

to calm them quickly. Within a few minutes Aja
was asleep in his arms.

21

MONICA WAITED UNTIL THEY HAD FINISHED DINNER BEFORE BRINGING ANYTHING UP. "Elizabeth called again." She looked into his eyes. "She said a letter would be coming in the mail about adopting Aja."

Jed smiled brightly. "That's good news then."

"It's just a formal invitation for us to fill out the forms and get things rolling. It doesn't mean we would get her. And of course, they still might find family members."

"Is there a deadline for how long they wait for family members to step in?"

"I don't know." She took his hand. "The thing is, Jed, what it means is that we have to make a decision. And besides that, it means that if she goes up for adoption, they could choose someone else." She looked away for a minute and then turned to him again. "I don't necessarily see it as good news."

"I don't understand why you're reacting this way," Jed said. "We'll just fill out the papers and see what happens."

Monica took a breath. "Jed, I don't really think I'm up to this. I know you want to adopt her and I do want to be a part of her life. I'm sorry." She bit her lip.

"I know what you mean. But if she's adopted by someone else, we would never see her."

"Jed, I've fallen for her too, but . . ." She pulled Jed to her and started to cry.

"Monica, it's okay. I understand. I do. I think we could get help. Maybe we could hire a nanny . . . a young person." He smiled. "Or Tony. He loves taking care of her."

Monica laughed. "Tony's older than you are."

"Yeah, it would be quite a sight watching us all chase her around once she's walking." His face became serious again. "Did Elizabeth say anything about the fostering part? I mean can we keep fostering until the adoption process is finished?"

"I asked her and she said she didn't know. It isn't up to her. There's no guarantee."

"Well, let's just fill out the adoption papers and see what happens. We still have time to decide."

"Jed," Monica's voice became quiet. "Have you really thought this through? I mean, not just about us, but whether this would be the best thing for Aja."

"What's best for Aja is to be raised by people who love her. She won't care how old we are."

"I'm not sure that's true. Maybe a young family . . . parents that will be around for her for many years."

"There's never a guarantee. You and I know that as well as anyone."

"I know, Jed, but there's certainly a better chance with younger parents."

Jed stood up, a bit exasperated. "Enough of this. Let's enjoy her while we have her, fill out the papers, and see."

Monica nodded without a word and watched him go into the bedroom. She followed him in and they both fell asleep. They awoke with a start to the ringing of Jed's phone. Monica looked at the clock. "What in the world? It's two in the morning!"

He looked at the screen of his phone. "It's Malcolm! Hello?"

"Jed, I'm really sorry to wake you. But I just got home from the restaurant and turned on my computer. I had a Facebook message from Dutch."

"What?" He glanced at Monica.

"What's wrong?" she asked.

"What did he say?"

"He was visited by a couple of FBI agents who asked a lot of questions."

"I hope you told him that I had no choice but to share the information about who paid for the niche."

"He's not blaming you. He wanted to warn you."

"What do you mean warn me?"

"Warn you about what?" Monica grabbed Jed's arm and asked with alarm.

"Most of their questions had to do with you," Malcolm said.

"Me? Why would they ask about me?

"That's what he said."

"They don't even know we went there."

"Apparently they do."

"What? How would they know?" Jed asked.

"They're the FBI. They probably have some surveillance on you."

"Know what?" Monica asked sharply. Jed put up his finger, telling her to wait.

"Dutch seemed to think they are looking at you as a suspect," Malcolm said. Jed stayed quiet. "Jed, are you still there?"

"Yeah. Thanks Malcolm."

"What are you going to do?" Malcolm asked.

"I don't know yet," Jed answered.

"Please let me know. I don't know how much help I can be right now. We are so busy moving everybody into their new places."

"That's okay. I'll figure something out."

"I'll try to come up north again as soon as I can. We have to figure out what to do about Homer. Savali and I are taking him to our house until he has a place to go."

"Hold on. Let me ask Monica if she found anything out." Jed turned to her. "Any news about a place for Homer?"

"Nothing yet. Tell him I'm working on it."

"Did you hear that, Malcolm?"

"Yes. Tell her thanks. Call me later. Okay?"

"I will. Thanks Malcolm. Oh wait. Did you by any chance get a phone number for Dutch?"

"No. But I'll message him and see if he'll give it to me." Jed hung up.

"Will you please tell me what's going on?"

Jed started to pace. "Schultz and Kelly paid Dutch a visit in Garberville."

"They did?"

"And apparently they know that I visited him and asked him all kinds of questions."

"So why does that warrant a middle of the night phone call from Malcolm?"

"Their questions were all about me."

"You? Why? What questions about you?"

"I don't know. But whatever they were, Dutch seemed to think there was a need to warn me."

"They think you killed her?" Monica jumped out of bed and grabbed his arm.

Jed stared at her and then took her in his arms. "I need to go back to Garberville."

"Why?"

He pulled away from her and stared into her eyes. "I'm not going to jail."

"Jed! You're not going to jail. You didn't kill anybody! You didn't even know this woman. This is absurd."

"Why, then, are they asking Dutch questions about me? And how did they know I went to Garberville unless they were tailing me, or something? And why would they tail me unless they suspected me?"

"But why would they suspect you?"

"I'm sure they can find reasons. For one thing, how did her body get inside the locked gate of the columbarium? And why did I go to Garberville and ask questions about Laila Aziz, the woman whose name on that piece of paper is about the only clue they have?"

"Now I'm scared, Jed."

"Join the club."

"Maybe you should talk to Goodman and plead your good standing with Abe."

"I think I need to go for a walk and figure this out." Monica nodded. She kissed him and watched as he put on some clothes and left.

Jed walked through the empty, dark streets of his quiet, residential neighborhood. He was a fast walker and it wasn't long before he reached Golden Gate Park. It was probably not safe for him to walk through the park in the wee hours of the morning, but Jed had lived on the streets for many years. He was used to defending himself when necessary.

He knew he was running away. But now there was Aja and Monica to think of, and he wanted to talk to Dutch again. What had the Feds asked specifically? He turned toward the ocean and continued walking for more than an hour and then walked north on the sand. It was almost seven when he checked the time on his phone and turned around to head home.

He was startled out of his daydreaming by the ringing of his phone. He took it out of his pocket and saw that it was Monica. "Hello?"

"Kelly and Schultz are here."

"At the house?"

"Yes."

"Do they know you're calling me?"

"No. I told them you weren't here and they said they would wait. I'm in the bedroom. I told them I needed to change Aja."

"Did you tell them when I'd be back?"

"Of course not. I said I didn't know when you'd be back. That it might be a long time."

"Did they ask where I went?"

"Of course they did. I said I didn't know. And that's not a lie."

"Certainly they can't stay when you leave for work."

"I can't bring Aja to my job, Jed."

"I'll get her from you at Glide. I'll call Tony to work for me."

"Where are you going to go?"

"I don't know, Monica. I'll think of something and I'll let you know."

"Okay. I'll text you when I get to work."

"Wait. No. They may follow you. Or someone might be there waiting to see if I show up."

"Jed, this is crazy. I'm sure the Feds have better things to do."

"Go to the McDonald's on Haight by the park. I'll be inside. Just park and bring her in and order something so they'll think you just stopped for a coffee. I'll leave with her out the back."

Monica hung up and Jed continued walking away from the ocean. He strode with angry purposefulness and reached Haight Street long before Monica would get there. He needed to talk to Dutch and find the murderer himself before the FBI could pin anything on him. He hoped if he got up there today, he might be able to get enough information to point the Feds in some other direction.

22

JED AND MONICA MADE THE SWITCH EASILY. He took Aja out the back door of the restaurant, still unsure where he was headed. He had called Tony and explained everything, and Tony was happy to take over the columbarium for as long as was needed.

Jed headed down Haight Street to an ATM and took as much cash as he could out of his bank account. He wouldn't use a credit card so he hoped it would be enough until he could hit another ATM the next day. He knew the FBI could track him that way also, but he hoped he could elude them. His next stop was a phone store to get a prepaid burner. The first thing he did, though, was ask the clerk if he could use her phone to call Monica and give her the number. "Don't call me unless it's an absolute emergency. I will throw the phone away right after the call if you do."

"I thought those burner phones were untraceable."

"We are talking about the FBI and the San Francisco Police. They can trace it, I'm sure, and especially through your phone."

'I'm petrified. And what about Aja? Aren't you putting her in danger?"

"I promise you that I will never put her in danger. I'll go to jail before that. I just have to resolve this and the only way I can do this is through the Garberville farm."

"Well, just don't resume the life you led before we met."

Jed detected the anger and hurt in her voice. "I love you, Monica. I'm doing this for us and for Aja. I will try to use strangers' phones and call you but I can't use this one. I've thrown away my old phone."

"What if Tony needs you?"

"He'll have to deal with it himself. He'll know what to do. And I don't expect there to be any problems."

Monica sighed. "I hate this."

"So do I." Jed hung up and handed the phone back to the clerk. "Thanks."

The clerk had been playing peekaboo with Aja. "Oh no problem. That's a cute baby you have there."

Jed smiled and finished the transaction as quickly as possible. When he got outside he looked furtively around but saw nothing that looked out of the ordinary. Now that he had gotten the cash and the phone, he had to figure out how to get to Garberville before Schultz and Kelly paid another visit to Dutch. None of this would ever be cleared up unless Dutch opened up. Jed was sure that he knew more than he was sharing.

Of course, there was only one way for Jed to get there: Greyhound. He started walking. He would just go to the terminal and wait for the next bus, hoping the police or FBI hadn't caught on yet. He might be making more of this than was necessary, but he couldn't be too cautious. He had learned that lesson only too well after a childhood in Jonestown and most of the rest of his life on the road.

Luckily, Aja slept peacefully in the Snugli until he got to the bus station. The clerk there was very helpful. A baby made everyone much more pleasant and accommodating than they would have been otherwise. The next bus to Garberville wasn't for several hours, but there were other options by transferring. The clerk found a way to do it so that Jed would get there before dark. This clerk was so helpful, that Jed pressed his luck and asked to use his phone. Once again, Aja's engaging personality kept the clerk busy while Jed called Malcolm.

"Hello?" Malcolm answered tentatively. "Oh, Jed. I tried calling you but your phone just went to voicemail."

"That phone is history. I'm on my way to Garberville. Did Dutch give you his phone number?"

"How are you getting there? Is Monica driving?"

"No. Bus. Do you have the number?"

"Yes." Malcolm gave him the number.

"Wait, hold on." Jed turned to the clerk. "Do you have a pen?" The clerk handed him a pen and Jed wrote the number on his hand. "Thanks Malcolm. I'll call you when I can."

"Good luck, Jed. Hey, do you have Aja with you?"

"Yes."

"Oh man! Well, give her a kiss and hug from Uncle Malcolm."

"I will." Jed hung up and handed the phone and the pen back to the clerk. "Thanks a lot. What was that gate number again?"

"Four."

Jed stopped in the restroom and changed Aja's diaper. He figured he'd feed her on the bus. Monica had packed plenty of bottles and diapers to make it through the day.

He went to Gate Four and stood in line, looking to see who might be willing to lend him their phone. He noticed an older woman and started baby talking with Aja to get her attention. She looked over and smiled. Aja made it easy to ask favors. He called the number Malcolm had given him for Dutch, fearing that it would go straight to voicemail, but Dutch answered.

"Dutch?"

"Yeah."

"This is Jed."

"I figured. I don't normally answer numbers I don't recognize, but I spoke to Malcolm. I know what's going on. What time will you be in?"

"Five thirty."

"Okay. Someone will be there to pick you up." Dutch hung up.

Jed handed the phone back to the woman and thanked her. The bus arrived and he watched some people get off as he waited to board. He was anxious to get on the bus, still worried that the FBI was on his tail. The bus had arrived from points south and was on its way to Portland. Jed would have to transfer twice before getting back on the 101 toward Garberville. He hoped Aja could wait to eat until they changed buses in Vallejo. She usually slept soon after eating, and Jed would love to close his eyes for a bit too. She accommodated him and waited until they were on the bus from Vallejo to Garberville before starting to fuss. Jed gave her a bottle, held her close to his chest, and let the bus do the rocking. She fell asleep and so did Jed.

23

JED AWOKE WHEN THE BUS JERKED TO A STOP IN WILLITS. He had slept through the stops in Santa Rosa and Ukiah. He was still a couple of hours from Garberville. Aja was asleep on his chest, giving him time to think about what he was going to do when he got there. He hoped Dutch was open to their staying the night. Maybe he could offer to trim the pot plants. He thought back to times in his life when he did those kinds of jobs, just to make enough money to move on to the next place. Much of his life had been spent running away from something. He had hoped never to be in that position again. And yet, here he was.

For the rest of the bus ride he focused on Aja. He played with her, changed her, fed her, and hugged her. They arrived in Garberville at dusk. Jed stepped down off the bus and looked around. He saw some motels and cafes, a gas station and as he peered down the street he saw a grocery store and decided to make that his next stop. He needed to get some baby supplies before going to Dutch's. And if no one was there to pick them up, he could check into one of the motels. He started to walk toward the grocery store when a woman appeared next to him. It was the woman who had been riding the horse the last time he was here with Malcolm.

"You're Jed, right?" the woman said.

"Yes."

"Come on." The woman walked toward a very old Chevy pickup. Jed followed tentatively. She climbed in and opened the passenger door from the inside. "No door handle."

Jed got in. "Nice truck. What year?"

The woman shrugged. "It belongs to Dutch. A fifty-something. I think."

Jed glanced around at the torn seats and at the dashboard, empty in the places where a glove compartment and a radio would ordinarily be. "I remember you from the last time I was here, but I didn't get your name."

"Juniper." She pushed the shifter into gear and punched the gas pedal, causing Jed and Aja to hit the back of the seat with enough force to make Aja cry out. "Sorry. It's hard to get this thing to move. It's fine once we get going."

"I need to stop at a market before we leave town. I have to get some supplies for the baby."

Juniper made a sharp U-turn into the parking lot of the store Jed had been headed to originally. He wished he had just walked there. She pulled up in front of the door. "I'll stay in the truck. You won't be long will you?"

"No. I just need some diapers and formula."

He climbed out and headed for the door. He quickly returned with a box of diapers and a can of powdered formula. Juniper seemed lost in thought and didn't jump out to help him as he struggled with carrying both items and Aja. He put his purchases down and knocked on the window for her to open the door.

They settled back inside the truck and this time Jed was prepared for the jerky acceleration. Finally they were out of town and on the road toward the farm. Jed wanted to ask Juniper about Laila, but decided to wait until he talked to Dutch first. The drive was a quiet one, only broken by an occasional babble out of Aja. Jed tried to judge Juniper's age and her relationship to Dutch. She looked to be much younger, but that didn't surprise him. Maybe she was his daughter. But who was he to talk. He was holding a tiny baby and he was old enough to be her great grandfather!

It was dark when they arrived at the farm, but Juniper was quite adept with the old truck and maneuvered through the gate easily.

Dutch came out of the house to greet them. Unlike Juniper, he picked up the package of diapers without being asked. Juniper got out of the truck and went in the house without a word. She was definitely an odd duck. "So you're wanted by the FBI?" Dutch asked dryly.

Jed was a little annoyed that he thought it funny but answered politely. "Apparently."

Dutch laughed. "Well, you have lots of company, I'm sure."

Jed wasn't sure what Dutch meant by that. Was he talking about himself or just making a general statement about the whole country or at least the world he lived in. "Thanks for letting me come and talk to you. And I hope I can stay here tonight since there are no buses back until tomorrow."

"Stay as long as you want. Are you hungry?" Dutch asked as he got two beers out of the refrigerator and handed one to Jed. "I remember that you like it lighter. This is a nice pilsner."

"Thanks. And yes. I'm hungry."

"Juniper is fixing some dinner. I'll show you where you can sleep." Jed followed Dutch down the hall and into a bedroom with a futon on the floor and a table with a Buddha statue and a small fountain on top. "Make yourself comfortable. I don't have a crib or anything so I figured this would be a good room with the mattress on the floor. That way the baby won't roll off the bed."

"You know your way around babies, I see."

Dutch smiled. "I'll meet you in the music room when you're ready. Do you remember where it is?"

"Yes. Thanks." Dutch left the room and Jed put Aja down on the futon. He unpacked the diaper bag and took out one of the clean bottles. He took out a water bottle Monica had thoughtfully packed and poured it into the baby bottle along with a scoopful of formula. It certainly wasn't the ideal way to give her a bottle, but he didn't want to go in the kitchen and warm it up.

As he thought about the short life Aja has led, he wondered if she had ever slept outside on the street. It reminded him of Mother, the stray cat he had found on the Venice Beach boardwalk when he lived there. He had always wondered where Mother had come from and what hardships she had endured. He hoped his worst fears for Aja's past life weren't true.

He left Aja on the futon and found a bathroom. He was apprehensive about leaving her at all. He trusted Dutch and maybe Juniper. But who else was staying there? His impression of the trimmers he and Malcolm had seen standing around downtown Garberville were that they were a shady-looking group. He hurriedly finished and flushed the toilet, then rushed back only to find Aja exactly where he'd left her. He breathed a sigh of relief, then softly laughed at himself and took Aja to the music room.

Dutch was strumming his guitar, sipping his beer, and taking periodic tokes from a joint resting in the ashtray. He held the joint out to Jed, but Jed shook his head. He started feeding Aja her bottle, waiting for Dutch to stop playing the guitar. He wanted to ask him questions without Juniper. "You want to tell me why I had a visit from the Feds?" Dutch finally asked.

"Malcolm didn't tell you what's going on?"

"A little. I want to hear it from you. All of it."

"From the beginning? I already told you some."

"Let's start over. Dinner won't be ready for a while. Tell it to me straight. I'm pretty involved at this point. I think I have a right to know."

"Yes. You do. And I apologize." Jed decided to be totally upfront with Dutch. He needed Dutch to be truthful, so Jed thought it only fair to do the same. Dutch didn't say a word while Jed related the whole story. He didn't even look at him. He just played his guitar and kept his eyes on his fingers.

Dutch looked up when it was obvious that Jed was finished. Aja's bottle was done and Jed had her over his shoulder, patting her gently. "Quite a story. And what's yours?"

"Mine? Why is that relevant?"

"Just interested. I like you. Believe me, I wouldn't be putting myself in this situation if I didn't."

"And I appreciate it." Jed was about to say he liked him too but thought it sounded trite. He gave him a brief version of his time in San Francisco at the columbarium. He didn't touch on his growing up and ultimate escape from Jonestown or his years on the road.

"And before that?"

"I lived on Venice Beach for several years."

"On," Dutch smiled. "Okay. I get it."

Jed smiled back. "Anyway, I'm here to find out about Laila's past and more about your relationship to her. I want to solve this crime for a lot of reasons. For one, to get the FBI and the San Francisco cops off my back. As well as yours, I might add. And for Aja."

Dutch took another toke and swigged down the rest of his beer. "Let's wait until after dinner. Okay with you?"

"Yes, but I'd like to talk to you alone."

"Juniper might have something to add. She knew her too."

"I want to talk to her. But I think it would be better if I talked to everyone alone."

"Who else are you going to talk to?"

"I thought maybe some of the trimmers who knew her. They might have a different perspective than you two."

"I doubt they'd know anything that could help you. But suit yourself." Dutch went back to playing his guitar while Jed and Aja enjoyed the music.

24

AFTER DINNER WAS OVER DUTCH AND JED WENT BACK TO THE MUSIC ROOM. Juniper walked in and Dutch turned to her, "Jed wants to talk to each of us separately. You cool with that?" Juniper shrugged. "Want to take the baby so Jed here gets a little break?"

Jed was torn. He didn't want to say that he wasn't sure he trusted Juniper with the baby, but he didn't want to offend his host. There was, however, a part of him who wanted a little break. Actually, he thought Juniper would say no so he wouldn't have to decide. She didn't appear to be the mothering, nurturing type. But he was wrong.

"Sure. She can come with me." Juniper swooped Aja up into her arms and was out of the room before Jed could protest.

Dutch turned to Jed. "Laila was a bit of a mystery to me. She came during harvest every year and stayed for a couple of months. Apparently she made enough money to travel the rest of the year."

"Was she American?"

Dutch shook his head. "Pakistani. She was a good worker. She managed a lot of things when she was here." Dutch picked up his guitar and resumed his picking.

"Did Laila talk about having a daughter?"

"I told you that last time. She never spoke about it."

"Was she your, um . . . partner?"

"We hooked up when she was here. But no, she wasn't my old lady. She was a — what do they call it now? Friend with benefits?"

"I think so," Jed smiled.

"She was pretty mum on what she did when she wasn't here. Maybe she talked more to Juniper about that."

"Where did she die?"

"I don't know."

"So she wasn't here?"

"Nope."

"Who told you she had died?" Jed thought he was beginning to be onto something.

"One of the trimmers."

"Is he here now?"

"Who?"

"The trimmer who told you about Laila. I'd like to talk to him."

"I don't know. Juniper keeps track of all that. She does what Laila did." Jed wondered if that included the friends with benefits role.

"Maybe I should talk to Juniper now. Where can I find her?"

"I'll get her." Left alone, Jed got up and nervously wandered the room, looking at the framed gold records and other tributes that lined the walls and shelves. Jed wasn't sure whether it was the royalties or the pot that provided Dutch with all the acreage and impressive house. Maybe it was both.

Dutch returned with Juniper and Aja and then left them alone. Aja seemed perfectly content in Juniper's arms, but Jed took her and held her while he asked Juniper questions. "You knew Laila pretty well?"

"Not well. No one knew her well."

"What about this trimmer who told Dutch she had died? Did he know her well?"

"Better than anyone else. She got him the job here."

"Is he here now?"

"Haji?"

"Is that his name?"

"Yeah, Haji's here."

"I'd like to talk to him also. But first, I have just a couple more questions for you. Do you know if Laila had a daughter?"

"I don't know. She didn't mention one to me."

"Do you know what she did when she wasn't here?"

"Not really. I know she went back and forth to Pakistan. I doubt it was to see a daughter though. Why are you asking all these questions, anyway?"

Jed knew he needed to say something about why. He knew that Kelly and Schultz wouldn't be too far behind him in asking her some of these same questions. "A woman was murdered at the columbarium in San Francisco where I work. Aja was found near the body. I am trying to locate any family of the murdered woman and Laila's name was found on a piece of paper in the woman's bag."

"Isn't that what the police are supposed to do?"

"The FBI and the San Francisco police are investigating."

"And you?"

"I'm fostering Aja. I want to get to the bottom of this — to find the best outcome for Aja."

"You think the Feds will be back here?"

"Probably. They're looking at this as some kind of terrorism because the murdered woman was wearing a hijab."

That got Juniper's attention, but she tried to hide her concern with an annoyed sigh. "I'll go get Haji." She opened the door but stopped and turned around. A faint smile flickered across her face. "I hope you get to keep Aja." She turned away and left.

How did she know he wanted to keep Aja? Before he had time to ponder that, she returned with a man who looked to be in his early twenties. He, too, may have been Pakistani.

"I could take Aja again if you want," Juniper said.

"Okay." Jed replied only a little reluctantly. Juniper took Aja from him and left. Jed turned to Haji. "Did Juniper tell you why I'm here?"

"A little. Some chick was killed and you think she might be Laila's daughter. Well, she's not. Laila didn't have a daughter."

"Do you have any idea why she would have Laila's name in her bag, then?"

Haji glanced around and then kept his gaze on one of Dutch's gold records on the wall. "I don't know, man."

"Are you Pakistani also?"

"Yeah. But I was born here. My parents were from Pakistan."

"How did you know Laila? Juniper said she got you the job here."

"I don't know. Just met her in the city."

"San Francisco?"

"Yeah."

"Your families knew each other?"

"Man, I don't like being in the middle of all this." Haji sighed. "No, not through our families."

Jed knew he was keeping something big from him. Haji was obviously afraid. He tried to figure out a way to get Haji to talk without incriminating himself. "Laila's dead so you're not going to get her into any trouble. Just tell me what you know about her. You don't have to tell me anything about yourself."

"I don't want to."

"I'm not the police or the FBI. You're not going to get in trouble with me."

Haji stared hard at Jed as he mentally worked out the pros and cons. Finally he blurted out, "She was a mule."

"You mean a drug runner?" Haji nodded. "That's why she went to Pakistan when she wasn't here?" Haji nodded again. "Do you think that's how the murdered woman knew her?"

"I got a call from some woman not too long ago asking me about Laila. Laila had given her my phone number as a way to get in touch with her."

Jed's heart started racing. "You did? What did she say?"

"She just asked if I knew where Laila was."

"Did she say her name? Or give you her phone number?"

"I don't remember any name and I know she didn't give me any phone number."

"Did she say anything that would help me find out who she was?"

"Why are you so interested?"

"For Aja, the baby they found." Jed hoped Haji would share more if he knew it was for Aja's sake.

Haji shrugged. "Yasmin, I think."

Jed was elated. Finally some concrete information. "Any last name?"

"No."

"Is there anything else you can tell me?"

Haji hesitated a minute and looked away. "No."

Jed knew that wasn't the truth, but he also knew that Haji had already told him more than he had wanted to. Jed wouldn't push him. He would try tomorrow. Haji made a pretext of leaving but glanced back at Jed as if he had suddenly thought of something. He breathed in, but the thought died on his lips. He turned and walked out the door.

Jed called out after him, "If you think of anything, please tell me. I'm staying here tonight."

Juniper entered at that moment with a fussy Aja. "I think she's tired." She handed the baby to Jed and left as quickly as she had come in.

"Let's go to bed. It's been quite a day." Jed put Aja close to his chest, felt her breathing, and immediately relaxed. Babies calmed him. It wasn't the rocking. It was the babies.

25

JED WOKE UP BEFORE IT WAS LIGHT. He lay there awhile, thinking of what Haji was keeping from him, let alone Juniper. He wasn't sure about Dutch. Maybe Laila had been just a friend with benefits, an arrangement too many questions can ruin. Dutch seemed to be someone who kept things to himself just like Laila . . . and Jed.

Aja stirred from a deep, nightlong sleep. She had a lot of stimulation the day before and was exhausted. Jed went into the bathroom to get some water for her formula, and after feeding and changing her, took her along as he went looking for coffee and company. There was an assortment of twenty-somethings in the kitchen, standing around with mugs of coffee or tea. Juniper was at the stove, scrambling eggs and singling out individuals for daily duties. They mumbled responses and took plates to fill with food that was spread out on the counter. Her authoritative manner caught Jed by surprise, but he could see that someone definitely needed to take control.

Jed took a cup of coffee but decided to wait for the crowd to thin before helping himself to a plate of food. Haji wasn't in the kitchen, so he decided to wander around the house, hoping he'd bump into him. But he found the rest of the house deserted. Maybe the trimmers were only allowed in the kitchen. He tried to open the door to Dutch's music room, but it was locked. That was probably not a bad idea with all those expensive guitars and gold records.

By the time Jed got back to the kitchen, the crowd had thinned and he was able to talk to Juniper and grab a bite. He stood at the sink and ate a bowl of yogurt and granola while Juniper did dishes. "Is Haji around?" he asked.

"I don't keep tabs," she grunted as she scrubbed egg out of a pan. "He knows what time breakfast is. If he doesn't show up, that's his problem."

"Could you point me toward the trimmers' area so I could see if he's there?"

Juniper stopped scrubbing. "I thought you talked to him last night." She was clearly not pleased.

"He was very helpful, but I thought of a couple more questions. Did you know that Laila was a drug runner?"

Juniper turned off the faucet. "Not really."

"You mean you suspected it?"

"It crossed my mind."

"Did she ever mention a woman named Yasmin?"

Juniper shrugged. "Maybe."

"Someone she knew in Pakistan?"

"I guess."

"I'm not the police. I'm just trying to help Aja. You can tell me anything you know."

"Laila just told me about a poor woman in Pakistan who was in an arranged marriage. Maybe her name was Yasmin."

Aja started to fuss and Jed tried to shush her. Juniper was finally opening up and he didn't want to lose momentum. He reached for a bagel and broke off a piece that was large enough for Aja to gnaw on, but not swallow. He remembered that Miss Ruthie used to do it for teething babies. "Do you think Yasmin might be the woman who was murdered?"

"No. She lived in Pakistan. Laila told me how difficult it was for women in those countries to do anything on their own. She had no money. How could she get here?"

Jed decided it was time to let up on Juniper and look for Haji. "Thanks for breakfast. Could you tell me where the trimmers work?"

She sighed. "I don't know how Dutch would feel about that."

"Can we ask him? I need to see about getting a ride back to town anyway."

"I'll go see if he's up." Juniper left the kitchen.

As Jed waited he thought about calling Monica, but he didn't want to use his burner phone. He could ask Dutch to use his but it would be better to use someone who had no ties to him at all. Maybe he'd ask Haji.

Juniper returned and said, "Dutch is waiting for you in the music room." She went back to washing the dishes.

Dutch sat in his chair sipping a smoothie and talking on the phone. He hung up abruptly when Jed entered. "Juniper tells me you want to talk to Haji?"

"Yes. I think he knows a lot more than he's letting on."

"Didn't you already talk to him last night?" Dutch asked.

"Yeah, and he was very helpful, but —"

Dutch cut him off. "Look, Jed, I've been accommodating. You're a nice guy, but I don't want to get in the middle of all this. I'm sure you can understand that."

"I appreciate that. I also don't want to be in the middle of this. I am doing this for Aja."

Dutch finished his smoothie and picked up his guitar. He started playing and Jed grew uncomfortable, not knowing if this was Dutch's way of saying he was done with him. "I, uh, also need a ride back to town to catch the bus. Do you have a phone or computer I could use to check the schedule?"

"There's a bus around noon. Juniper will take you." Dutch stood up and put his guitar back on its stand. "C'mon. Let's find Haji."

Jed smiled. "Thanks." He followed Dutch out of the music room and through the back door. They walked in silence to a large barn. Dutch opened the door. Inside were several large tables. Jed recognized most of the people sitting at the tables from the group who had been in the kitchen. Music blared and the walls were covered with hanging branches of marijuana. Each trimmer had a plastic bin next to them on the floor and a bowl in front of them. Haji looked up and scowled when he saw Jed.

Dutch walked over to Haji and beckoned him to follow. Haji got up reluctantly, but he knew who paid his salary. He followed them outside. Dutch led them to another small building and unlocked the door. Inside were some other chairs and tables, but they were empty. There were, however, several stacks of large plastic bins, piled high to the ceiling. Jed figured that during the height of harvest, this room was also filled with trimmers. Dutch sat down and pointed to a chair across from him. "Sit down, Haji. Jed has some more questions."

Haji sat down reluctantly and looked down at the table. Jed sat next to Dutch and put Aja on his lap and said, "I'm not trying to get either of you in trouble. I'm trying to help. The Feds are probably on their way here, so if we can get to the bottom of this ourselves, maybe you won't have to answer to them."

"What else do you know about Laila, Haji," Dutch said. "I have told Jed everything I know about her. You are the one who told me she had died, but you never told me how." Dutch turned to Jed. "I'm being straight with you, man. She came here every year but she spent most of her time with the trimmers or by herself."

"I believe you, Dutch." Jed looked at Haji. "How did you find out she had died? What was your relationship with her?"

Haji sighed. "What are you going to tell the cops?"

"About you? Nothing. I will only share what you tell me about Laila."

"What about if they ask you who told you all this?'

"I'll just say it was some guy I met in Garberville and I don't know who he is."

"I don't want to talk to the cops."

"If nobody points you out, you should be safe."

"Well, what if they ask Juniper or one of the other trimmers? They know that I knew Laila in the city."

Jed turned to Dutch. "Maybe he should leave for now . . . before the Feds get here."

"Do you know the Feds will be back?"

"I'm pretty sure they'll want to ask you more questions. Especially after they find out I've been back," Jed answered.

"Why do they think it's you?"

"Probably because they have nothing to go on right now. But if they come back here and take a closer look, Haji is going to look like a suspect or a witness to them. We need to keep ahead of them, and to do that I need answers."

"Haji can get on the bus with you. Juniper will take you both."

Haji frowned at Dutch. "How long will I have to be gone? I want to work, man."

"I'll contact you as soon as the Feds leave. Just tell Jed what you know."

Haji glowered at Jed, obviously not happy about this turn of events. "She was afraid Interpol was after her. She found out that they were tracking her source in Pakistan."

Dutch stood and started pacing. "Man!"

Jed wanted to ask Haji how he knew this, but thought it might be best if he didn't ask. That way Jed wouldn't have to lie to the police and possibly get Haji in trouble or perjure himself. It seemed pretty clear, though, that Haji was probably part of this drug ring in some way, thus his reluctance to share. "What do you think might be the murdered woman's connection to Laila, then?" he asked instead. "And how did Laila die?"

Haji shrugged. "I don't know how that woman knew her. Maybe from Pakistan. And I don't know how Laila died." He glanced at Dutch who was still pacing.

Jed tried to connect the dots with what Haji told him about Laila and what Juniper had said. "Do you know anything about a woman Laila talked about who was trying to escape an arranged marriage?"

"We didn't talk about stuff like that," Dutch answered. He shook his head in disbelief. "Wow! Laila was a mule!"

Jed then realized that Dutch hadn't known about Laila's other life. Growing marijuana and the international drug trade were definitely not the same thing. He would have liked to ask more questions, but like Haji, he didn't want to be there when the Feds came. "Maybe we need to get going," he finally said.

Dutch nodded and locked the door behind him after the three exited the building. "Be at the front door in fifteen minutes. I'll tell

Juniper to be ready," he told Haji. Jed and Dutch walked back to the house in silence. When they got inside Jed went back to his bedroom to change Aja and fill a bottle for the bus ride. She had started to fuss so he knew she was ready for sleep. He put the Snugli on and placed her inside. She was asleep before they got to the front of the house. Haji and Juniper were waiting for him. Jed wanted to thank Dutch but he wasn't there. They piled into the pick up. The trip was silent, everyone lost in thought.

When they got to town, Jed turned to Juniper. "Could I borrow your phone for a minute? I just want to let my wife know that we're on our way home."

She handed Jed the phone. He dialed and waited for Monica to pick up. Meanwhile Haji got out and Jed overheard him say to Juniper, "I'm not going to the city. I'll hang around town. Could you let me know when the Feds have left so I can come back?"

"Yeah."

Haji started to walk away just as Monica picked up. "One second, Monica," Jed said in the phone. "Hey Haji, can I get your phone number?" He kept walking without answering.

"I'm on my way home, Monica," he said into the phone. "I'll tell you everything when I get home. Are they still watching the house?"

"I don't think so. They know you aren't here," she answered.

"Good. I'm not going to run." He hung up and handed the phone back to Juniper. "Can I have your number?" he asked.

"Okay."

"Do you have paper and pen?"

Juniper rummaged through a pile of crap on the floor and managed to come up with an old receipt and a pen. She scribbled her number on the paper and handed it to Jed. "Dutch told me about Laila. I want to know what you find out."

"I'll call. And if you can help —"

"I will," she interrupted. "How will I get in touch if you have a burner?"

Jed gave her Monica's number. "Thanks, Juniper."

She leaned over and patted Aja's head. "She's very special."

"Yes. She is."

26

AJA AND JED BOTH SLEPT THROUGH THE FIRST LEG OF THE BUS RIDE. They had a half hour layover in Willits, so Jed bought some fruit and crackers and made another bottle of formula for Aja. He marveled at her. She was such a young baby and yet so compliant. He thought of what her short life had been like up until now. She was probably used to sleeping in unfamiliar places with unfamiliar people, so perhaps that's why she was so adaptable. He could certainly relate. It had been the story of his life too. He smiled down at her and, as always, she smiled back with adoration.

The next leg of the ride was another two hours to Santa Rosa. They had a twenty-minute break and he took the opportunity to walk around the block several times. They both needed it. Aja slept after that, so Jed was able to organize his thoughts and plan his next step. Or try to, anyway. He didn't know what Schultz and Kelly would do. He thought about calling Goodman to tell him everything. He needed advice and he wanted to trust him. After all, he was Abe's nephew-in-law.

The layover in Oakland was brief, and it wasn't long before they got to San Francisco. Monica would help him figure out what he should do next. He would be home for dinner and he hoped that visitors with badges would not interrupt his reunion with Monica.

Rush hour was in full force when the bus pulled into San Francisco, so it was slow-going. He finally walked in the front door at seven pm. Monica rushed to greet them. "Oh my goodness! How's my baby?" she cooed as she pulled Aja out of the Snugli and hugged her. Jed grinned as he watched, thrilled that she called Aja her baby.

"It's been an eye-opening trip," Jed said.

"Let's sit down to dinner and you can tell me, but first I'd better change this girl."

"I'll get a bottle ready." Jed went into the kitchen. Monica came back in and settled Aja on the couch surrounded by pillows. Jed placed the bottle in such a way that Aja could drink from it. "We'll see if this will work so we can have a peaceful dinner."

They sat down at the table. Jed had barely taken a mouthful of food when Monica's phone rang. "It's probably for you," she said coolly. "Your friends in the FBI have been bugging me, trying to find you. I'd rather not answer it."

"Maybe it's Tony or Malcolm."

"They're just waiting to hear from you. They know better than to call."

"By the way, I gave your number to Juniper, the woman who works at the farm with Dutch." Monica sighed. "Are you angry with me?" Jed asked.

"I'll get over it. Why don't you tell me what's going on."

Jed nodded and gave Monica the rundown of all that he had learned from Haji, Juniper and Dutch. "Haji knows more than he's telling, but for obvious reasons, he is reluctant to talk to me. Juniper is my only chance of learning anymore. I'm hoping Haji will open up to her."

"I thought you just said he's not at the farm any longer."

"He says he'll be back. He just left because Schultz and Kelly were coming. Juniper will let him know when they've left and then he'll return."

"What do you think he knows that he's not telling?"

Jed shrugged. "I have some suspicions that he's more involved with the San Francisco end of the drug transactions. How else would he know what happened to Laila?"

At that moment there was a pounding on the door. Aja let out a frightened cry. Monica rushed over to soothe her. She and Jed exchanged a look of alarm. "Jed? It's Goodman. Are you there?"

Jed breathed a sigh of relief. All of a sudden, Goodman had become the good guy. Jed answered the door and let Goodman in. "What's up?"

"I've been trying to reach you but your phone's out of service and your wife's not answering hers. We need to talk."

"What about?"

"Schultz and Kelly are up in Garberville. I guess you just missed them."

Jed looked surprised. "You knew I was there?"

Goodman smiled. "I'm a detective, remember?"

"Well, then, I guess if you know everything, we don't have much to talk about."

"I only know you were there. Not about anything you found out. Jed, we can help each other, you know."

"Will you be straight with me about why you want to do this sleuthing behind the back of the FBI?" Jed asked.

"That's fair. I'll explain if you'll share your end."

Jed looked at Monica and she gave him a barely visible nod. He turned to Goodman. "How can you help me?"

"I have pull around here. I can help if the Feds take you in for questioning."

Monica gasped. "What do you mean? Are you saying they want to arrest Jed?" she blurted out.

"I'm not saying that's what's going to happen. But if you are withholding information from the FBI, it is perjury. If you've shared it with me, then you have an out. I guarantee it. I can take the blame. I'm not the only one in my department who feels that this should be under the jurisdiction of the SFPD."

Jed wanted nothing more than to get all of this off him and let the police take over. But he was also afraid that it would jeopardize Dutch and his farm and that he would lose his chance to keep Aja. Whether Laila was a link or not, Jed wanted to help find some resolution to the murder. "Nothing I found out really helps in figuring out who the murdered woman was except for the possibility that her first name is Yasmin. As far as anyone up at the farm knows, Laila didn't have any children, so I don't know why her name was in the woman's bag."

Goodman nodded. "What did you find out about Laila?"

"She was Pakistani and she was a drug runner."

"Well, that's interesting. How did you find that out?"

"No one at the farm knew that. I mean not Dutch or the woman who lives there with him." Jed had decided not to bring up Juniper's name. No need to include her if it wasn't necessary. "All the others are just itinerant workers."

"So how did you find out?"

"One of the workers, but he left the farm after he told me."

"Do you know his name?"

"I promised not to get him in any trouble."

"Jed, you don't have the power to do that. I can make a promise to that kid, but you can't. And you can get in trouble with the FBI so tell me and then get yourself off the hook."

Jed sighed. He tried to weigh all the consequences. This was beyond being the nice guy. His life was not just about him anymore. He had Monica and Aja to think about now. "Is there some way you can use the information and not arrest him?"

"Sure. Anyway, you don't know where he is, right? You're merely telling me what he told you."

"I guess that's true. But I don't really know much more than that."

"So did this guy tell you that Laila was murdered or how she died?"

"No. I had hoped he would. But he wouldn't."

"So he knows?"

Jed nodded. "I think he does."

"He's part of this drug cartel?"

"Obviously he wouldn't say that. It's just what I think. How else would he know all this?"

Goodman's face took on a pensive, brooding look. "So let's see if I have this straight. Laila is a drug courier between Pakistan and San Francisco?"

Jed nodded. "That's all I really know."

"And this person . . . this trimmer . . . he found out she was dead and told this fellow, Dutch, who then paid for her funeral?"

"I don't know about a funeral. He paid for her niche in the columbarium. But Dutch didn't know anything about her other life."

"And again . . . how does the murder victim fit into all this?"

Jed exhaled. "I don't know if she fits in at all. I only know that the, uh, trimmer guy told me that he had gotten a phone call from a woman looking for Laila and he thought her name was Yasmin."

Again, Goodman was silent and contemplative. "And this Dutch character or his girlfriend never heard of Yasmin?"

"I had thought maybe she was Laila's daughter, but they didn't think Laila had any children."

"That they knew of," Goodman added.

"Well, yeah."

"Apparently there was a lot about Laila they didn't know."

Jed looked away, deciding whether or not to share the last bit of information he had with Goodman. He wanted this investigation off him so he chose to tell him. "One more thing I found out."

"Oh yeah? What's that?" Goodman asked.

"Laila had talked about a woman in Pakistan who wanted to be out of an arranged marriage. Maybe that's who the murdered woman was."

"You mean Laila might have been helping to get her out of Pakistan?"

"It's just a thought."

Goodman didn't want Jed to shut down on him so he stood to leave. "Thanks Jed. You still have my number?"

Jed nodded. "But I don't have my phone anymore."

Goodman smiled. "Probably a good idea. So how do I reach you?"

"I guess by pounding on my door."

Goodman laughed. "Okay or at the columbarium? You are going back to work?"

Jed had forgotten all about getting in touch with Tony. "Uh, yes."

Goodman stuck out his hand and Jed shook it. "I appreciate your help. And I'll keep this under the radar for now but I'll need that trimmer's name."

"Let me talk to him first. Then I'll give it to you."

"Okay, Jed. But you're not doing yourself any favors by keeping it to yourself." Goodman turned to Monica who had sat silently through the whole conversation. "I can see myself out." He left.

Jed turned to Monica. "Where's your phone? I need to call Tony."

"In my purse."

Jed found her phone and looked at the missed call. It was from Malcolm. He decided to call him back first. He pressed the button and Malcolm answered after one ring. "Malcolm, I'm sorry. I just got back and so much is going on. I need to call Tony and —"

"No problem, man. I didn't even expect to talk to you. I was just concerned and wanted to see if Monica had heard from you."

"Okay. I'll call you tomorrow if that's alright with you."

"Sure."

"Thanks. Talk to you tomorrow." Jed hung up and called Tony, but it went to voicemail. "I'm home and will work tomorrow. I'll call you in the morning and tell you what's going on. Thanks a bunch, man." Jed hung up, went back to Monica and Aja and took them both in his arms.

27

THE NEXT MORNING WAS A FLURRY OF ACTIVITY AS JED PREPARED TO GO BACK TO WORK WITH AJA IN TOW. He tried to push his apprehension aside. He had told Goodman just about everything he knew and it felt like a weight was off his shoulders. He and Monica had talked into the wee hours about letting go of his paranoia and to forget about investigating the crime. He would give up Haji's name and let Goodman and the FBI take over. They both had confidence that Goodman would protect Jed. They would concentrate on giving Aja the best life they could, even if they would only have her for a short time.

He called Malcolm as soon as he got to the office and updated him on everything. Malcolm did the same. The residence had closed and Homer had already moved in with them. Jed planned to call Tony but he didn't need to. Tony showed up anyway. Jed shared the latest updates and Tony took Aja for a long walk, giving Jed time to get his mind back into his job and off the murder. It felt good to get his priorities straight.

He made his rounds, singing to Chloe, Frank, Goldie and Rose. He replaced the tomatoes on Sam and Sadie's sconces. By the afternoon, Aja was asleep in the Snugli and all seemed right with the world until the door opened and the same two men who had visited Francesca Balducci's niche barreled in. They went in a different direction this time, not toward Francesca Balducci's niche. Jed watched as they took the stairs two at a time. He tiptoed up the stairs and hid behind a pillar. They stopped at Laila's niche and opened the glass door. Jed's first inclination was to stop them. It was, after all, not theirs to tamper with. But he wanted to see what they were up to. Unfortunately, he was thwarted from that by Tony's arrival. "Jed? Are you upstairs?"

The two men closed the door of the niche quickly as Jed stepped away from the pillar and answered, "I'll be right down." The men noticed him and made a beeline for the stairs. The well dressed one smiled at Jed while his bodyguard gave Jed a piercing look. They left and Jed went downstairs to greet Tony and Aja.

"Aja was perfect," Tony beamed. "I took her to the antique store and gave her an education on different periods of furniture style."

"I didn't realize you knew about that."

"Goldie liked antiques. I probably made up half of what I was saying, but Aja didn't know any better."

Jed laughed. "Thanks, Tony." Jed wanted to call Goodman and tell him what just happened. "Hey, could I use your phone a minute? I know you have to leave, but it'll be quick." Tony handed Jed his phone and Jed dialed Goodman. It went to voicemail so Jed left a message telling him to come to the columbarium. Jed gave Tony back his phone and Tony left.

Goodman walked into the atrium of the columbarium a couple of hours later. He found Jed giving a tour to a group of high school students. Jed liked that teachers used the architecture of the columbarium as well as the choices people made to decorate their niches as a way to have a conversation about death and grief with teenagers. They were always lively, thoughtful discussions.

Goodman stood to the side and waited for Jed to finish his tour. After the teachers managed to corral all the teenagers out the door, Jed walked over to Goodman. "Thanks for waiting."

"I enjoyed it. So what did you want to tell me?"

"Remember those two men who came a couple of days after the murder victim was found. One of them was dressed up, I don't know, like a dapper mobster type and the other one looked to be his bodyguard or something?"

"Yes. What was the name of the woman they visited?"

"Francesca Balducci."

"Let's go look at her, uh, apartment," Goodman smiled.

"It's pretty nondescript. And anyway, they didn't visit her this time. They went to Laila's."

"Oh yeah?" Goodman's eyes widened.

"I hid behind a pillar and watched them open her door. Ordinarily I would have stopped someone from doing that. It's obviously not okay. But I wanted to see what they'd do."

"And?"

"Unfortunately my friend came just at that moment and called my name. They closed the door quickly and left."

"Did they see you?"

"Yes. The well-dressed one smiled, but his buddy glared at me as they walked by."

Goodman was quiet for a minute. "This is important. We'll need to share this information with Schultz and Kelly."

"I was afraid of that."

Goodman patted Jed on the back. "I know they are a couple of pricks, but this could be a big break in the case. You'll have to take a look at those mug books and see if you can identify them."

Jed's heart sank. This was exactly what he wanted to avoid by talking to Goodman. "I thought you wanted to investigate yourself."

"I have to include them and they would want to interview you."

Jed sighed. "When will I have to come in and look through the books?"

"Today?"

"I guess."

"Listen, you just come in after work and I'll tell Schultz and they can meet you there. Just answer their questions. I'll have told them the whole story."

"Are they going to wonder why I told you and not them?" Jed asked.

"Play dumb. Say you didn't realize it mattered who you told."

Jed nodded and Aja decided she was hungry and started to fuss. "I need to take care of her."

"I'll see you later." Goodman patted Jed on the back again and left. Jed took Aja to the office and got her bottle.

There wasn't much left of the afternoon and Jed arrived at the police station by five thirty. He immediately called Monica from Diaz's phone to tell her what was going on.

"Well I guess you can stop hiding now and you can get your own phone. Everything's out in the open." Monica sighed with relief.

"And I'll probably have to answer questions about the Garberville group as well."

"You have nothing to hide. And you do not have any power to stop whatever may happen with Aja, so stop trying to play detective."

"Yeah, I guess you're right. I'll see you later."

"I'll come there and get Aja on my way home."

"Good idea. I don't know how long I'll be." He hung up and walked slowly over to the table where the Feds waited for him.

"Nice to see you again, Jed," Schultz said with a sardonic smile.

"Where's the book I have to look through?"

"First we need you to answer some questions. Please sit down."

Jed sat and crossed his arms. "I have to get home so let's make this quick."

"Why the animosity, Jed?"

"Let's just get on with it," Jed replied.

Just then Goodman appeared with the mug book and bellowed, "I want him to look through this first. I've already told you what he told me. It might save us a lot of time if he recognizes someone right away."

"Sure," Jed blurted out with relief as he took the book. He started to leaf through it and found a picture of the bodyguard in a matter of minutes. "Here's one of them."

Goodman took the picture out of the mug book and nodded to Diaz who had just approached the table. "Schultz and Kelly, follow me. Jed, please stay and look through the photos. See if you can find the other guy." The four investigators left and Jed continued to look through the book.

Diaz came out of the office after several minutes. "Any luck, Jed?"

"No."

"We were able to convince the Feds that you're not a flight risk and that we have enough to go on for now. The man you identified is known to us."

Jed stood. "So I can go?"

Diaz nodded. "We'll be in touch."

Just as Jed and Aja walked out the door of the police station, Monica appeared. "You can leave?" she asked.

"Yes. Let's go." Jed took Monica's hand and the family of three walked down the street to Monica's car.

Jed, Monica and Aja spent the evening quietly and as soon as Aja was asleep, Jed and Monica got into bed. Monica's voicemail had several messages, but they chose not to listen to them. They made love with a passion that had eluded them lately and slept soundly.

28

JED AWOKE, REJUVENATED AND AT PEACE, READY TO LISTEN TO HIS MESSAGES. Tony wanted to know if he was needed at the columbarium today. Malcolm reported that although he and Savali were fine with their houseguest, Homer was antsy to get into a permanent living situation. But the first call Jed returned was to Juniper.

"Hello?" she answered on the first ring.

"It's Jed."

"Oh, yeah. Dutch wanted me to call you. He didn't have your number. Hold on a minute."

He heard a swishing as she walked. "Juniper?" He wanted to talk to her as well, but she didn't have the phone to her ear. He heard muffled voices and eventually Dutch came on.

"Jed?"

"Hi, Dutch."

"I wanted to report on the visit from the FBI."

"Thanks. I appreciate it."

"Watch your back."

"What do you mean?" Jed asked.

"They had more questions about you than about Laila."

Jed froze. Just when he thought he was in the clear. "Like what?"

"I think they just find it odd that you are going through all this trouble to make it look like someone else murdered that woman. Coming up here twice and then reporting to them about all the vandalism. They said there's been vandalism at the columbarium before."

"I saw them today. And Laila's very much back in the picture."

"I told them that she was a drug runner and they chalked that up to another one of your deflections."

"What else did you tell them?" Jed asked.

"Just what you had told me. And I said that you had just found that out too from Haji."

"Did you give them Haji's name?" Jed asked.

"No. I said it was one of the itinerant trimmers and I didn't know his name. I said that I didn't handle that part of the business."

"So you didn't try to hide what you do?"

"Jed, I've been farming for a lot of years and most of the agents and police don't care. I usually give out samples to anyone who seems overly zealous and that's enough."

"There is some new information." Jed related to Dutch what had happened yesterday with the visit to Laila's niche.

"Hmm. Well, I just wanted to let you know what happened with the Feds yesterday. Take care of yourself," Dutch said and ended the call.

Jed started pacing. He was sick of living under a cloud. He had done nothing but find a baby next to a dead body and now his life was turned upside down. Monica entered the kitchen and threw her arms around him. "Who were you talking to?"

"Dutch. He wanted to let me know what the visit from Schultz and Kelly had unearthed."

"What do you mean?"

Just then Aja woke up and cried out. "I'll get her." Jed rushed out of the kitchen, glad to have a moment to decide if he wanted to worry Monica by repeating Dutch's account.

But he didn't have that moment since Monica followed him and asked, "What was unearthed?"

"It doesn't matter now after what happened at the columbarium yesterday."

"It does matter or you wouldn't be pacing. What did Dutch tell them?"

"Just that he reiterated what I had told Goodman about Laila being a drug runner. And he told them he didn't know the name of the trimmer."

"Isn't he afraid to be open about his farm operation?"

"He said the agents don't care because he sweetens the pot with some free samples. He said he's always done that."

"Well, that's good. Maybe free samples will make them forget ever considering you a suspect."

Jed shot her a look. "Yeah right. Can you take over? I'd like to return the other calls."

"From who?"

"Tony and Malcolm."

"Sure." Monica took Aja from him.

Jed started to leave the room but then turned around. "Oh, Malcolm asked in his voicemail if you had any more information for Homer."

"Yes, I do. I can email him the names of some places up in the northern California coast area. But they are rather expensive and the public ones are only for people already living in those counties."

"Oh. Homer has no money."

"Is he a vet?"

"I don't know."

"Actually, the ones for vets are full also. I'm not sure what help I can be."

Jed sighed. "Well, at least I need to let Malcolm know so he can maybe find some place down there."

"I'm sorry. He really wanted to be in northern California, didn't he?"

Jed nodded and went to the kitchen to pour some coffee before calling everyone back. He told Tony that he wouldn't need him but he was certainly welcome to come visit his goddaughter. He tried Malcolm's phone, but it went to voice mail. Jed finally hung up and looked at the time and realized he had better get a move on if he was going to get to work on time.

He opened up and got Aja situated in her stroller. Then he set up for a small memorial that was happening that day, but he was interrupted. Schultz and Kelly entered with a couple of other people. "Oh great!" Jed sighed a little too loudly.

"I knew you'd be happy to see us," Schultz replied grimly.

"I have work to do."

"We won't be long. No questions right now. We want to fingerprint Laila's niche door. Would you mind showing it to these nice technicians?"

Jed took Aja out of her stroller and brought the group upstairs to Laila's niche and left them there, happy to go back to unfolding chairs. The group left shortly after and Schultz called out as he walked out the door, "We'll be in touch." Jed ignored him but breathed a sigh of relief.

After the memorial service was over and Jed was putting away the chairs, he let his mind wander back to Dutch and the farm and what it might be like to live a peaceful existence miles away from town. Tony arrived just as he was finishing up. "Go get some lunch, Jed. I'll watch this beautiful little lady and this magnificent building."

Jed realized he had forgotten to eat breakfast. "Thanks. I think I will. Can I bring you back something?"

"Nah, I ate."

Jed walked to a deli a couple of blocks away. It was far different from Abe's Jewish deli where he had spent so many hours kibitzing with Sam, Abe and Irving. This one served Vietnamese sandwiches, also delicious, but quite different from the pastrami and pickles on rye that had been popular at Abe's. He brought the sandwich back and ate it quickly while relating the latest update to Tony.

"So what do you think is the connection between Laila and those two mobsters?" Tony asked.

"I don't know for sure that they're mobsters, but they do look like they're straight out of Hollywood casting."

"Do you think they're involved in all this?" Tony asked.

"Well they certainly look the part."

Tony started to leave and turned back around. "Keep your nose out of it as much as you can, Jed. The plot thickens, as they say but you ought to try and stay off the characters' list."

Jed had a busy day giving tours and signing up new occupants. Many people hadn't known about the columbarium before the news reports on the murder, so there was a spike in interest. The afternoon was over and he locked up quickly before members of any law enforcement agency could disrupt his evening. After dinner and Aja was asleep, Jed and Monica sat down to ponder their next move.

"What do you think about living in the country?" he asked, trying to sound casual. "Dutch seems pretty happy living off the grid, so to speak."

"Now you want to be a pot grower?"

Jed laughed. "No. It's enticing, though, to be away from the hubbub of the city and the problems associated with having a job dealing with the public. You know, retire and live off the land."

Monica laughed. "I don't think I'm cut out for that life."

"I know. I was kidding, sort of."

"Oh, that reminds me. I did some more searching for Homer, but I can't find any places in northern California that would be suitable. His Parkinson's diagnosis limits his choices even more. I'm sorry. He might be stuck in Los Angeles. Maybe you should let Malcolm know, so they can find an appropriate placement for him."

"Homer ought to be able to live out his last days where he wants. He's not a city guy, I guess. I better call Malcolm and let him know. Can I borrow your phone?"

"I think it's time for you to get your own phone again." Monica took hers out of her pocket and handed it to him. "You can't live under this cloud, always worrying that you're going to get arrested."

"I'll go to the phone store tomorrow." He dialed Malcolm. "Hey man, it's Jed."

"What's happening?"

Jed told him every detail of the last couple of days. "But the bad news is that Monica was unable to find a place for Homer."

"If he has to stay in the Los Angeles area, at least he'll have people here looking out for him," Malcolm said.

"How did he wind up in Los Angeles anyway if he's a country boy?"

"He had been a carney. He was working at the Santa Monica pier and decided he liked living by a beach with a warm climate."

"Will you be able to find a place for him?" Jed asked. "Maybe he needs to be in an assisted living place now."

"I hope so. By the way, Savali read somewhere how some Parkinson's sufferers have responded to certain strains of pot. Maybe Dutch can hook him up with a supply. Let me know the next time you want to go up to Garberville and I'll bring Homer along for the ride. He can pick up a stash."

"I'm sure you can find him some at Dr. Kush's on the boardwalk."

Malcolm laughed. "Yeah, there are plenty of dispensaries down here, but they're kind of expensive. I guess Homer will just have to keep playing music and dancing."

"So what's next?" Monica asked as Jed hung up.

"You mean for me?"

"Yes, dear. I'm sure Homer is a nice man but really I'm most concerned about you and Aja."

"Have you heard anything more from Elizabeth?"

"No. I can stave things off for a while, but you and I both know that she's only part of the problems facing us."

"I don't think there's anything more I can do except just deal with things as they come up. I will get a new phone tomorrow. That's one thing I can do."

"Are you seriously going to be able to continue taking Aja to work with you?"

"Yes. It really isn't that hard to have her. She's an easy baby and Tony comes almost every day to spell me a bit."

"He's a great friend."

"Yes. He is."

"And the other elephant in the room?"

"What? The FBI? I'll wait to see what turns up with the fingerprints on Laila's door. At least it's keeping the heat off me for now."

Monica smiled and took his hand. "Let's go to bed."

"Good idea."

29

THE NEXT SEVERAL DAYS WERE UNEVENTFUL. Tony stopped by most days to take Aja for a walk, and thankfully there was no word from Goodman or Schultz. And there were no visits from 1488 or the mobster duo. Jed was able to get a lot of work done. He had not been able to repair all of the damage that had happened the night of the murder and he felt badly about it. He had gotten a new phone and given his number to Tony, Malcolm, Finn, Dutch and Juniper. He debated about giving it to Goodman, Schultz et al, and relented when he realized that it wasn't fair to Monica to put her in the middle. So far, though, no one other than Tony had contacted him. He was enjoying the peace and quiet.

Goodman stopped in one morning. "They finally got a fingerprint identification back from the lab. You know that guy you fingered in the mug shot book? It's a match."

"Really? So do you know how to find him?"

"Yeah, he's been known to us for some time."

"What about the other guy? Were there any other fingerprints?"

"Afraid not. But it's a definite lead and it's more than anything else we have right now." He smiled. "And it'll keep Schultz off you for a short while anyway. I'd like to take a look at Laila's niche again. Care to join me?"

"I guess." Jed led him up the stairs. Goodman took a pair of gloves out of his pocket and opened the door to Laila's niche.

"Most urns can't be opened easily can they?" Goodman asked.

"No, most can't. Obviously ones that people keep ashes in to scatter are easy to open. And of course as you can see in our columbarium, many people use creative and unusual receptacles. Many of those are easy to open."

"Well, let's see about Laila's." Goodman reached out and found the top. It came off easily. "So is this one of those usually used for scattering?"

"Probably, if it came off that easily."

Goodman peered inside. "Hmm. Just as I suspected."

Jed looked inside. "Well, that's certainly interesting."

"I had a hunch."

"You knew it would be empty? What made you think that?" Jed asked.

"The guy you identified has an arrest record for some petty drug stuff and Laila being a drug runner."

"So what are you saying?" Jed asked.

"That there was a connection between them."

"I was thinking the same thing. But where are Laila's ashes?"

"That part I can't answer. I'd like to get the technician back here to lift some prints directly off the urn."

"It's probably just going to be prints of people from the funeral home."

"That may be so, but if our friend also opened the urn, we may have more to go on. Also, can you give me information about the funeral home this came from?"

"Sure. It's in the office."

Goodman put the top back on and closed the door to the niche. "Let's go," he said as he put his gloves in a plastic bag and back in his pocket.

Jed unlocked the door to the office and looked up Laila's file. "The Golden Crescent Mortuary in Santa Rosa." He showed him the file and Goodman copied down the address.

"Thanks." Goodman left before Jed had a chance to ask what he would be doing with the information. Aja started to fuss at that point, so his attention went back to her. He did wonder, however, as he was changing her diaper, if there were other empty urns in the columbarium. He had never thought to look.

He glanced at Laila's information again to see exactly when Dutch paid for her niche. It hadn't been that many days before Jed had discovered the body. But what was the connection with the murdered woman? Was she part of the drug ring too? He hugged Aja tightly, imagining the life that would have been in store for her if she had been brought up in that environment. And how did Dutch fit in? Did he really not know about Laila? And what about Juniper and Haji? Jed was positive that Haji knew more than he was letting on. He wasn't sure about Juniper.

A group of people arrived asking about memorial services and apartment prices, so Jed had to turn his attention away from obsessing over the investigation. Several old friends stopped in to visit their loved ones and Jed talked to all of them. The morning went quickly.

Malcolm called to report that Homer was antsy about getting out of Los Angeles. "He thinks he can handle going north and finding his own living situation," Malcolm groaned.

"Wishful thinking?" Jed asked.

"Yes. At least Savali and I think so. We would never let him go on his own. We aren't sure what to do. It's not like we have any jurisdiction over him. He hasn't assigned us power of attorney or anything."

"So he can just walk out of your house if he wants and there's nothing you can do. Does he have any money?"

"He has a social security check every month, but that's it."

"Does he have enough to rent an apartment?"

"I doubt it, but I don't really know. He does have enough to get on a bus and go, though."

"But where would he go?"

"Maybe to San Francisco and then get a bus further north."

"I have the feeling you're leading up to something, Malcolm." Jed smiled.

"I don't know. Homer won't say anything because he doesn't want us to go out of our way for him. He already feels indebted to us and he's an independent guy and a humble, sweet guy who doesn't like to rely on others. That's a lot of the problem. He has no choice but to rely on others, I'm afraid. He can't live totally on his own."

"I'll be happy to do what I can, but I don't know what that is."

"I don't either. Now that the residence is closed, I really need to work as much as I can at the restaurant. Savali offered to drive him north, but he won't have it. He said she's done more than enough already."

"Well, just let me know what happens and I'll do what I can."

"Thanks, Jed. I appreciate it."

"No problem."

30

AFTER DINNER THAT EVENING JED'S PHONE RANG. It was Malcolm. "Homer's on a bus headed for San Francisco. He left us a note while we were out. We're worried sick. We checked and the bus gets in to San Francisco tonight at about nine. Could you head him off and bring him to your house? We'll try to get up there as soon as we can."

"Sure, but Homer doesn't know me."

"I left a message on his voicemail to call me, but he hasn't yet. I'll leave another one letting him know that you'll pick him up."

"Okay. I'll find him, I guess."

"You can't miss him. He has a long scraggly gray beard and a ponytail to match. And he's just a whisper of a guy. It looks like you could knock him over with a feather."

Jed laughed. "Sounds like a character."

"Oh yeah. Have him call me in the morning, would you?"

"Okay." Jed hung up, looked at Monica, shook his head and grinned. "Our household is expanding."

"What now?"

"That was Malcolm. Homer's on his way up here and Malcolm asked if I could bring Homer to our house until he can get here."

"Maybe I should drive. He may not be able to get on Muni easily."

"No. Don't wake up Aja. I'll bring him home in a cab."

"That's a better idea. What was he planning to do?"

"Malcolm thought he would try to get another bus going further north."

"That won't do," Monica groaned. "How will you know him?"

"From the way Malcolm described him, he'll be hard to miss." He kissed her. "Will you wait up?"

"Yes. He'll probably be hungry. I'll put something together for him."

Jed got his jacket and started to leave. "I love you. Just in case you needed to be reminded," he called out as he walked out the door.

Jed had an hour to get to the bus station so he decided to walk. He got there in plenty of time and went to the gate. Malcolm was correct. Homer was hard to miss, especially since the driver had to help him down the stairs of the bus. Jed was surprised that Homer had managed to get this far by himself. "Hello, Homer. I'm Jed. A friend of Malcolm's."

"Oh yes, I know all about you."

"Malcolm asked me to pick you up and bring you to my house until he can come. My wife and I are happy to have you stay with us."

"Oh no. I couldn't ask that. I'll get a hotel room."

"No need. She's got the bed all made up and food on the table." Jed took Homer's arm and they both thanked the bus driver who handed Homer's suitcase and walker to Jed. They moved slowly through the bus station, Homer leaning on his walker. Jed noticed a cane strapped to the top of his suitcase. "Do you also use the cane?"

"I try to use it most of the time, but it's easier to get around with the walker."

It was a quick ride in the cab and they were inside the house by nine-thirty. Monica and Aja were both awake and Homer enjoyed playing peek-a-boo as he ate the meal Monica had prepared. Much of the food fell off his trembling fork, but he managed to shovel enough in to sustain his slight build. "Nice house you have here. I always liked San Francisco. Spent quite a bit of time here when I was young."

"Did you ever live here?" Monica asked.

"Nope. I was a carney so I was on the road a lot. Born and raised in a tiny place called Honeydew. Ever been to the Lost Coast?"

Jed and Monica looked at each other. "Not me," Jed said.

"Nor me. Where exactly is it?" Monica asked.

"Couple of hours south of Eureka. About four hours north of here, I reckon."

"Is it just west of Garberville?" Jed asked.

"Yeah. It's maybe an hour or a little less from there. Honeydew's about fifteen miles east of the Pacific."

"I was just up there. In Garberville, that is. Nice area."

"That's where I want to go. I grew up on a farm. Like to end my life where I began it." Homer nodded and smiled. "Hoping I can find a little place for myself."

Monica and Jed glanced at each other, both thinking the same thing. There was no way Homer could live alone. Aja yawned and that was a good reminder to all that it was time to call it a night. "I made up the sofa for you. There are clean towels on the coffee table. I'll clean up here, Jed, if you'll put Aja to bed."

"Sure." Jed picked up Aja, handed Homer his cane and led him to the living room. He changed Aja while Homer was in the bathroom and they were all safe and sound in their respective beds by eleven.

Aja's crying and the low murmur of voices awakened Jed. He reached his arm to the other side of the bed but found it empty. He looked at the clock and it was just after seven. He got up and went to the living room to find Monica and Homer sitting on the sofa drinking coffee with Monica trying to soothe Aja. "Good morning," she smiled at Jed. "I think she's teething or maybe colicky. She woke Homer and me up an hour ago. I'm surprised you were able to sleep through the screaming."

"I didn't hear anything until just now." He reached for Aja and took her to the rocking chair. His magic worked within minutes.

"You never cease to amaze me, Jed," Monica laughed. She turned to Homer. "He has a special touch with babies."

"Lots of practice," Jed answered.

"From what Malcolm says, he has a special touch in a lot of ways," Homer added.

Monica beamed. "He does have that reputation."

"How did you sleep until Aja woke you up?" Jed asked.

"Like a baby." Homer laughed at his joke. "I really appreciate you taking me in. It's a real nice place."

"It's absolutely no trouble. Stay as long as you want," Monica answered. Aja stared at Homer and smiled at him. "Apparently Aja wants you to stay."

"It's nice being around a baby instead of a bunch of old fogies. That's why I don't want to go into one of them assisted living or nursing homes. I don't like just being around old people. It wasn't bad in Venice because we were on the boardwalk. I could go out and be around lots of young people and the ocean. I don't want to be someplace where you're locked in and there's no nature around."

Jed and Monica glanced at each other, not sure how to respond. Finally Monica spoke. "You know, I tried to find you a place, but you have to live in those cities or counties before they'll even put you on their waiting list. I looked up north, near where you want to go."

"Yeah, Malcolm told me. I'll just have to go up there myself and find a place. I'll be okay."

Monica looked at Jed and he shrugged. "Well, let's just see how things pan out."

Homer frowned. "I'll just get on another bus north."

Monica sighed and looked pleadingly at Jed to say something. Jed finally spoke. "Homer, you can't do that. I was a drifter for a lot of years and I wouldn't dream of doing it

now. And I'm younger than you are and I don't
need a walker to get around. I know you used to
do that when you were a carney, but you really
can't. We'll help you figure something out, right
Monica?" Jed looked at Monica and she
nodded. "You could just stay here, as long as
you don't mind possibly being woken by a
baby."

Homer grinned. "I love being woken by
a baby. I wish I could hold her, but I'm afraid I
might drop her." He exhaled. "I don't really
know what to do." He smiled at Monica. "I
guess I could stay here . . ."

"Why not call Malcolm and tell him that
you got here safely and that you can stay here a
bit longer." Monica said. "But right now both
of us need to get ready to go to work."

"Oh, thank you. I appreciate that. I
won't be any trouble. I'll just, uh, watch
television or something."

Jed looked at Monica. "You can come
to work with Aja and me, if you like."

"At that columbarium place? I'd like
that."

Monica quickly piped up. "I'll drive you
there on my way to work. But Jed, you had
better shower and get on your way with Aja."

Jed put Aja on Homer's lap. "I think
you can hold her while I get ready." He then
placed a pillow on either side of the baby and

gave Monica a knowing look that told her not to worry.

Homer put his trembling hands on Aja's body. He smiled while a tear escaped from his eye and rolled down his cheek.

31

JED WAS A LITTLE LATE OPENING THE GATE SO THERE WERE A FEW PEOPLE WAITING. One of the people at the gate was the Middle-Eastern man who had been nosing around. Jed thought that perhaps it was time to call Goodman about this man, but he didn't want to alarm Homer with a police presence. And truly, Jed was tired of the whole thing. He wished he had never gotten involved. He should have let the police do their own investigating.

He opened the gate and then the front door. He greeted everyone who was waiting and then turned to the Middle-Eastern man who stood off to the side. "So you're ready for the tour?" Jed asked.

The man responded with his own question. "So where did you discover that body? I saw on the news that it was outside."

Jed was a bit taken aback. "Oh, um, right over there." He pointed to the brush area.

The man walked over and squatted down. He took a stick and moved some dirt around. "I'm a police officer myself in my country. Always interested in how murder investigations are done in other places. Have they found out anything yet? Identified the body?"

"Not much," Jed answered. "They haven't identified the body. What country are you from?"

"Pakistan."

Bingo, Jed thought. He easily slipped back into detective mode. "Visiting San Francisco or have you moved here?"

"Just visiting. I think I'll come back for that tour. I haven't had any breakfast and I have a few other sites I want to get to this morning."

"I'm Jed Gibbons." He put his hand out to shake the man's and hopefully get him to respond with his own name.

"Nice to meet you, Jed," he answered with a handshake. He left before Jed could ask his name.

Jed opened up the office and took Aja out of the stroller. He put her in the Snugli and started to make his rounds of the columbarium, singing to the residents as well as chatting with their visitors. Monica arrived with Homer about an hour later. "Oh my!" Homer exclaimed as he emerged slowly from the passenger seat. "This is a beautiful place!"

"I'll pick you all up a little after five," Monica said as she took Homer's cane out of the back seat. "He didn't want the walker. Too bulky. I hope he'll manage alright with just the cane," she said quietly to Jed as Homer scanned the building as well as the landscaped grounds.

"He'll be fine. There's plenty to see and do here and plenty of chairs to sit on. I'll place them around strategically. Did he call Malcolm?"

"Yes. He and Savali can't come right away, but they'll try to figure out how to get him into some good living situation up north. And I'll work on it some more, too."

"You're a saint."

She smiled and kissed him. "You're not so bad yourself." She left and Jed took Homer inside.

"You don't worry about me. I'll just look around. Monica told me about the insides of these niches, how they are decorated. She even told me particular ones to look for."

"Okay Homer. But please call for me if you need help. I'll get some chairs and scatter them around so you'll have resting places."

"That'd be good. Didn't I see you have Aja in a stroller?"

"Yes. It's in the office. It's easier for me to get things done with her in this Snugli."

"Snugli? Haha. We used to put our young'uns in a blanket tightly wrapped around our chests. No need to spend money on that fancy contraption."

"That would probably be just as good. We didn't have time to think about it when we got Aja."

"Yeah. Monica told me the whole story this morning. I hope you find that poor woman's family." Jed nodded unenthusiastically. He guessed Monica didn't tell him that he hoped they didn't. "So if you get that stroller, I can push Aja around with me and give you some breathing room. If I have something to lean on like the stroller, I'm fine."

"That's a good idea. I'll get it." Jed went to the office and came back with the stroller. He put Aja in it and Homer started his rounds on the first floor. "Let me know when you're ready to go to another floor and I'll help you bring the stroller up."

"I think we'll have plenty to see down here for quite a while." Homer started pushing the stroller and Jed watched as he walked slowly from niche to niche, talking to Aja the whole way. Aja seemed to lap up every word of whatever he was saying.

Jed's phone rang and he looked at the screen. It was Juniper.

"Hi, Jed. I've got some news I think. Haji returned. He was here a couple of days and then asked for a ride into town again. He said he'd be gone for about a week. That's really weird. He's usually one of the regulars who stays through the whole harvest season. He's a good trimmer and makes good money. He seemed kind of scared to me."

"So what do you think is going on?"

"I don't know. He was nervous. He wouldn't say much, but his phone kept ringing. He would look at the screen but not answer it. All he'd tell me is that he'd be in the city for a few days and that he'd call when he was back up so I could give him a ride to the farm."

"Any ideas?" Jed asked.

"He's just been acting really different since he came back. Staying more to himself. I think he found out something that's got him spooked. I just thought you should know and that he was back in the city if you wanted to try and talk to him. I'm not supposed to do this, but Dutch always gets people's emergency contacts. We had a horrible thing happen once. A young kid died and we couldn't find his family for several days."

"You're going to give me Haji's emergency contact?"

"Yes. Do you have a pencil?"

"Hold on." Jed sprinted to the office and took out a pad and pen. "Okay. I'm ready."

After giving Jed the address and phone number of Haji's parents in San Francisco, she blurted out, "Dutch wants to get to the bottom of this. He now thinks that there was something suspicious about Laila's death. He might not admit it, but she meant a lot to him."

"I'll see what I can find out. Do you think Haji is in some kind of danger?"

"I don't know. Maybe."

"I'll call you as soon as I find out anything. By the way, does Dutch know you called me?"

"Yes. He does care about his workers, you know. He's been doing this a long time and his people keep coming back. He's kind of like family for a lot of us."

"I could see that when I was up there."

"You and Aja should come back and visit. You could bring your wife."

"Maybe we will. Thanks. I'll talk to you soon." Jed hung up and sat back in his office chair. Haji knew something and finding him could answer a lot of questions, providing he'd talk, of course.

When he got to the main building and he saw Homer and Aja laughing together, he thought of what Juniper had said about Dutch's farm being a family-like place. In a sense that's what the columbarium and his and Monica's home were becoming. He laughed thinking that if he was the grandpa, then Homer would be more like the great-grandpa. And Tony would be the great uncle. This little baby had acquired a nice family, even if a bit unusual.

But Haji again crowded out these warm, fuzzy thoughts. He had to figure out a way to talk to him. It was time to include Goodman as long as he could protect Haji. He dialed Goodman's number and updated him with what Juniper told him. "So what's the parents' address?" Goodman asked.

"Here's the thing. I really don't want to spook Haji. He's already really scared according to Juniper. If he knows the police are involved, he'll run. Can I call them first? His parents probably know absolutely nothing about his farm job. I can just pretend to be a friend of his here in the city."

"I tell you what, Jed. I'll pick you up and we'll go together. I'll stay in the car while you pay a visit to his parents."

"Couldn't I just call them?"

"Trust me, Jed. Surprise visits work much better. Can you get that pal of yours to come take care of things at the columbarium? I can pick you up in an hour."

Jed sighed. "I'll call Tony. But you'd better wait for my call in case he can't come."

Goodman hung up and Jed immediately dialed Tony who was happy to come by and babysit the building, Aja, and Homer. Jed went to find Homer to tell him that Tony was coming, but he didn't tell him the rest of the story.

An hour later Tony and Homer were chatting like old friends, Aja was asleep in the stroller, and Goodman and Jed were driving through Golden Gate Park and down 19th Avenue. Haji's family lived in a neighborhood that was home to many professors and students at San Francisco State. Goodman had done some homework and found that Haji's father was a professor there. He hoped they would be home in the middle of the day. "Can your pal stay awhile if they're not home and we need to go over to the college to find him?"

"Yes." Jed was nervous, but eager to get some information. He wanted to talk to Haji, even more than Goodman did. He was more and more certain that Haji was the key.

"Jed, just a little advice from someone who's done a lot of interviewing. Take your time. Let them warm up to you."

"I should have brought Aja. Everyone warms up to her."

"Abe always said you had that quality too."

Jed hoped Goodman was right. There was a good chance that Haji had finally reached a point where he was looking for a friend and might start looking in unexpected places. Not just Jed, but even Goodman. Haji was in way over his head.

32

GOODMAN PULLED UP IN FRONT OF A PINK STUCCO ROW HOUSE IN THE MERCED HEIGHTS DISTRICT. It was a neighborhood of small two story houses over one-car garages, similar to many from the pre and post World War II era. It looked like a typical middle-class area except that now these modest San Francisco houses were worth at least a million dollars. Jed got out of the car and walked up the stairs to the front door. He knocked and looked back at Goodman, sitting in the car. A woman wearing a hijab opened the door but she kept the chain on. "Yes? Can I help you?"

Jed smiled. "I'm Jed, a friend of Haji's. I was wondering if he is home."

"No. He doesn't live here now."

"Oh, do you know where I can find him?"

"If you're his friend, don't you have his phone number?"

Jed was afraid she'd ask that. "I lost my phone and it had all my contacts. We talked once about where we used to live and that we once lived close to each other. I remembered he said that his house was on the corner of Monticello Street and Holloway Avenue."

"Oh, I see. Well I can give you his number."

"Thanks so much." Jed took out his phone to put in the contact. "Is he here in the city now? I know he sometimes goes up north." He wanted to see what Haji's mother's reaction would be. Maybe she knows more than he thought.

"I don't know. I don't keep tabs on him. We don't talk so much. Here's the number."

Jed put the number in his phone. He knew he could have just gotten it from Juniper, but there was a chance that Haji could have been here. "Thanks very much." He left and got in the car and related what happened to Goodman.

"Well, go ahead and call him."

"Are you going to let me talk to him alone?"

"I don't know if that's a good idea."

"I don't think he'll open up to a cop," Jed said.

"You think he's more involved in the drug angle than he let on?"

"Yes." Jed shook his head. "I don't get it. Nice middle class family in a decent neighborhood. Father's a professor . . ."

"Crooks come in all different shapes and sizes."

"I'm trying to think of what to say so he won't hang up on me."

"Just tell him you got his number from his mother. That's all it'll take," Goodman replied. "Even the hardcore criminals want to protect their mothers."

"I'm not going to threaten his mother."

"It doesn't matter. You don't have to say a thing. He'll talk to you just because he won't want you to talk to his mother at all. Trust me."

Jed dialed Haji's number and pressed the speaker button. No answer. Jed glanced at Goodman, silently questioning if he should leave a message. Goodman nodded. "Haji, this is Jed. Juniper called and asked me to contact you. She and Dutch think you may be in some kind of danger. I got your number from your mother. I'm here in San Francisco. I can help you. Please call me back." He hung up and shrugged.

"That was good, Jed, saying you can help him and bringing up the people who care about him."

"I think he's real scared. I bet he's sorry he ever got involved in this part of Laila's life. So what now?"

"We wait for him to call and we both go back to work." Goodman drove back up 19th Avenue and through the park to the columbarium. He dropped off Jed at the gate. "I've got some things to do. Call me as soon as you've talked to him and I can be here in a matter of minutes. Can your pal stick around if you need to leave?"

"You mean Tony?"

"If that's his name."

"I don't know. Probably."

"Who's the guy with the jitters?" Goodman asked.

Jed shot Goodman a sharp look. "He's got Parkinson's. He's staying with me for a while."

"No offense intended." Goodman laughed. "Boy, Abe wasn't kidding. You are some kind of saint." Goodman took off as soon as Jed shut the passenger door.

Homer and Tony were chatting and laughing with some visitors to Sunny's apartment. Sunny had been a gregarious, well-loved, African-American musician with a large group of family and friends. Hardly a day went by that he didn't have company. And they were all friendly and warm, lively and fun. One of the visitors was Sunny's daughter, Harmony, who held Aja and danced the giggling baby around. "Jed!' Harmony rushed over to him and kissed him on the cheek. "What a doll! Tony told us what happened to this poor baby's mama."

Jed glanced at Tony who shrugged as if to say he hoped Jed didn't mind. Jed smiled in response. "She's a good baby. And how are all of you?" Jed asked.

"We're doing fine. You're just in time to sing with us. We thought we'd sing an old Nina Simone tune, 'I Wish I Knew How it Would Feel to be Free.' You know it?"

Jed shook his head. "No, but I'd like to learn it."

One of the visitors, a young man whose resemblance to Harmony made Jed think he was her son, took out his phone and went to his iTunes library. He found the song and turned it on. He and Harmony started singing along and Homer started to sway and move in time to the music. Jed started to move over to Homer, thinking he needed to hold his arm so he wouldn't fall. But instead Jed watched as Homer's tremors and shuffling gait turned into steady, smooth dance movements. Tony and Jed exchanged glances and smiles, both surprised and delighted.

"You learn those words, Jed, so you can sing with us next time. And look at you cut a rug!" Harmony exclaimed as she hugged a beaming Homer. "Gotta go, guys. See you soon." She handed Aja back to Jed and she and her entourage left, singing and dancing down the steps.

Tony turned to Homer. "Did you know that music and dancing had that effect?"

"Yeah. Malcolm discovered that and bought me an iPod. That and my piano playing have been my lifeline."

"You can play the piano?" Jed asked.

"Not well. But when I do play, my hands stop trembling."

"Really?" Tony and Jed said in unison.

Aja whimpered to remind them all that it was lunchtime. "Oh, I haven't given Aja her bottle," Tony exclaimed. "All this singing and dancing, she and I both forgot."

"I'll give it to her," Jed said.

"How about I take Homer out for lunch and we'll bring you back a sandwich."

Jed smiled and pointed at Tony. "You are something."

"No, you are!" Tony pointed back at Jed. Tony handed Homer his cane. "Let's go get something to eat. My car's in the parking lot."

Jed took Aja back to the office to change her and get her bottle while Tony and Homer shuffled down the stairs. As soon as Jed got back inside the main building his phone rang. He recognized the number and answered it quickly. "Thanks for calling back, Haji."

"I don't know what Juniper's talking about. I'm fine."

"You don't have to worry, Haji. The police are just trying to find out who murdered the woman for the sake of her baby. They don't care that you're trimming for Dutch or that you're friends with Laila. But Laila is the key and you're the only one who seems to know anything about her."

Haji was silent. He finally spoke. "What did you say to my mother? She asked me why you came to visit her and how I know you."

"I just said I was a friend of yours and that I'd lost my phone so I didn't have your number."

"That's all?"

"That's all," Jed replied. "Haji, do you know that Laila's urn is empty?"

"What do you mean?"

"There are no ashes in it."

"Nothing's in it?" Haji asked.

"That's what I said." Haji sighed. "What's going on?" Jed asked. Haji was quiet. Jed decided to ask another question. "Do you know why a Pakistani policeman has been hanging around the columbarium, especially around Laila's niche?"

"He is?"

"Do you know who I'm talking about?"

"I gotta go." Haji hung up.

Jed immediately called Goodman and relayed his conversation with Haji. "Damn," Goodman responded when Jed had finished. "Well, what we do know is that Haji has more to tell us. I'm going to have to take him in."

"He won't talk to you," Jed replied quickly. "I'm sure of that. You have to let me talk to him. You were right about his worrying about his mother finding out too much."

"Jed, you're getting way too involved. This guy who you fingered down at the station is a real thug. If Haji has anything to do with him and drugs coming in from Pakistan, you need to step away and let me take over. Stop protecting this kid because you have some relationship with those pot growers."

Jed sighed. Goodman was right. And the more he got involved, the more Schultz and Kelly would be on his tail. He had Monica and Aja to worry about. "Okay. Go ahead." He gave Goodman Haji's phone number and realized that at that moment, a weight had been lifted off his shoulders. Why had he felt the need to protect all these people, especially those that were involved in drug trafficking? But he knew why. Somehow he thought he was saving Aja from an unsavory life and he didn't trust social services to protect her like he would. He did not feel confident that Aja's family, if they were ever found, would give her what he and Monica would give her.

"Thanks Jed. I'll let you know how my conversation with Haji goes."

Tony and Homer arrived at that moment with sandwiches. They ate their lunch and swapped stories. Homer told of his travels around the country being a carney, Jed of his days homeless on the Venice Beach boardwalk, and Tony of his international travels bringing pot into the country from the Caribbean. They were quite an intriguing trio.

33

AFTER TONY LEFT, JED WENT ABOUT HIS USUAL ROUTINE WHILE HOMER PUSHED AJA IN THE STROLLER AND CHECKED OUT THE CONTENTS OF THE NICHES ON THE SECOND FLOOR. Just as Jed was getting used to the idea of leaving well enough alone and minding his own business, 1488 arrived. Jed noticed him scurry up the stairs and go to the same niche he had been to the last time. Jed was determined to talk to him and find out why he was there. This time he could race up the stairs since he didn't have Aja strapped to his chest or in a stroller. He got there only seconds after 1488. "Hey, can I help you? If you want to decorate a niche, you have to buy one."

1488 wheeled around and glowered at Jed. "How much?"

"There's paperwork that we have to go through. Do you want to come to the office and I can help you there?" Jed immediately regretted saying that. The idea of being alone in his office with this man felt risky.

"Can't you get the papers and bring them here?"

"I suppose, but that isn't usually how we do it," Jed hedged. When 1488 didn't respond, he asked, "Whose ashes are you interring?"

"A friend. So will you just go get the papers?"

"Okay," Jed mumbled, annoyed and anxious over this man's attitude. He went to his office and debated about calling Goodman but decided 1488 was just rude, not a criminal. He gathered the papers and returned. He handed the packet to 1488 and said, "Do you want to take this home and then come back when it's completed?"

"No. You got a pen?"

Jed handed him one. "Do you have a check or credit card? We need the deposit, at least."

1488 handed him a wad of cash and went back to filling out the papers. Jed counted the money. "This is more than enough." He handed 1488 back some of it just as 1488 finished writing.

"So can I put the stuff inside now?"

"Yes. Do you want some help?"

"No." 1488 gave Jed a dismissive glare making it very clear that he wanted to be left alone.

Jed went back to his office to file the paperwork and put it into the computer. He took note of the name of the person's ashes to make a plaque for the apartment. Spencer Dickson. He then peeked at the name 1488 had written down as his own. John Smith. Hmmm. After he filed the paperwork, he went back to the main building and up the stairs. 1488 or John Smith was gone, but Jed gasped when he looked at Spencer's apartment. Across the back was a Nazi flag. The urn was shaped like a Ku Klux Klan hood with the triangular KKK symbol on the front.

Jed felt sick to his stomach. They had never tried to institute any rules about what people could and could not put in their apartments and condos. But no one had ever put anything so full of hate inside one. If he allowed Goldie to have a Jewish mezuzah outside the door of her apartment, he couldn't censor someone else's freedom of expression. Just then he heard Homer calling him from the second floor. "Jed? You up there?"

Jed exhaled. "Yes, I'll be right down." He went down a flight and found Homer sitting on a chair and Aja fussing in the stroller. "Are you okay?" Jed asked Homer as he took Aja out of the stroller to soothe her.

"Yeah, yeah. I just didn't want to try to pick her up. In case . . . you know . . . anyway

I'll just sit a spell. Maybe I'll do the third floor another day."

"It's almost closing time anyway. Just a little while until Monica will be here to take us home. I'm going to the office to get Aja's bag and lock up in there. You okay staying here?"

"I'm fine, Jed. You don't worry about me. I'll put my ear buds in and listen to some music."

Jed got everything closed up and was ready to leave as soon as Monica showed up. They piled into her car and stopped briefly to pick up a pizza for dinner, all of them too tired to think about cooking. Jed took Aja into the bedroom to change her while Monica set the table and got Aja's bottle ready. Homer sat patiently at the table, enjoying the warmth of having people around. "Can I get you a beer, Homer? Or some wine?"

"What are you having?"

"I was going to open a bottle of wine."

"That's good for me too, then."

"Please feel free to have whatever you want. Mi casa es su casa."

Homer looked at her with a puzzled expression. "Just Spanish for make yourself at home. My house is your house."

Homer smiled and Monica watched as his eyes watered. "You people are so special.

You don't even know me and you welcome me into your house."

Monica put her arm around Homer's shoulders. "Malcolm is family to Jed. Any friend of his is a friend of ours."

Jed walked in with Aja wrapped in a towel. "I want to give her a quick bath. She was, uh, pretty messy, shall we say. You go ahead and eat and then Monica can feed Aja while I eat. I like cold pizza. Lived on the stuff for a lot of years." He grinned and went into the kitchen to use the sink.

Homer turned to Monica. "He sure knows his way around babies. He must have had a lot of kids."

Monica smiled wistfully. "He spent many hours rocking babies, but no, he doesn't have a lot of kids." She left it at that. She poured the wine and took a piece of pizza out of the box and put it on a plate for Homer. She took another one for herself and sat down across from Homer. "I spent the afternoon searching for a place up north. They are pretty impacted and only taking county residents for the waiting list. I'm trying to pull some strings, but there just aren't many openings, anyway. Is there anywhere else I can look? Maybe someplace not as popular? The Central Valley?"

"You mean like Stockton?"

"Yes or Bakersfield? Maybe Modesto or Fresno? They might have openings."

Homer scrunched up his face. "So hot."

Monica nodded. "Yes, there is that."

"I'll just find a little studio apartment up north. Don't you worry about me."

Jed walked in with Aja and Monica reached her arms out to take the baby. Jed poured his wine, took his slice, and joined the group. Monica turned to him and repeated what she had told Homer. "He seems to think that he can find a place to live for himself."

"You mean not in assisted living?" Jed asked.

"I can do it," Homer interjected.

"Homer, you need to be realistic," Monica said. "You may not need a lot of help now, but you need to be someplace where there are people around you could call on. We'll figure something out." She put the bottle into Aja's mouth and started cooing at her as she drank.

Jed ate his pizza slice and then emptied the wine bottle into the three glasses. "I'd like to ask you two your take on something. That man with the 1488 tattooed on his hair was by again today." He turned to Homer. "This guy is a white supremacist. 1488 is some kind of symbol for that."

"Yeah, I know about them. Worked with some when I was a carney. Lots of them rednecks are into that." He shook his head. "Very sad. They are unhappy, mean-spirited people."

"Yes they are. He bought an apartment for a guy and decorated it with a Nazi flag and an urn made to look like the Ku Klux Klan hood."

Monica gasped and Homer frowned. "That's awful!" Monica exclaimed.

"I'm not sure what to do. This is the first time anything like this has happened. And I don't know if we have the right to censor what goes into someone's niche. I mean we allow religious symbols and fraternal organizations like the Elks or the Shriners to have their stuff in them."

"This is for the board to decide, not you," Monica said. "There's no policy already?"

Jed shook his head. "I know there's nothing written down. I thought I should have an opinion before I talk to them and I'm not sure what my opinion is. That's why I wanted yours."

"What do you mean you don't know what your opinion is? You certainly don't condone it," Monica exclaimed.

"Of course not. But on the other hand, I do respect freedom of expression. It's like the

ACLU supporting and defending individuals that have the right to espouse an opinion or way of life that I'm sure they don't agree with."

"This is a tough one, Jed," Homer sighed. "My gut feeling? I don't think you can deny this man putting what one presumes the dead person requested into his niche."

"I guess you two are right," Monica said slowly. "But it feels like the desecration of that beautiful building."

Jed's phone rang and he looked at the screen. "It's Goodman. Excuse me." He walked into the kitchen. "Hello, did you talk to Haji?"

"Can't find him here in the city. But I've shared everything with Kelly and Schultz and they are back on their way up to Garberville."

"Oh man. I hate that Dutch has to deal with all this."

"You need to stop worrying about Dutch. He's a big boy who's already been involved in something not so Kosher. He might be aboveboard now, but he's been growing a long time, way before it was legal. And the Feds are not interested in busting him. This thing Haji is involved with is big. The FBI has been working with Interpol. They don't care about some hippie pot farm."

"Well, thanks for calling and letting me know."

"Any new visitors at the columbarium?"

"As a matter of fact, 1488 was back. He bought a niche and decorated it with a Nazi flag and an urn shaped like a Ku Klux Klan hood."

"So that's all he wanted?"

"I guess." Jed thought for a minute. "Can I ask you something?"

"Shoot."

"I'm wrestling with the fact that he's got those items in the niche. But I don't think I have the right to censor. What's your opinion?"

"It's not illegal to express your views, last time I checked."

"Yeah."

"But don't be surprised if you get complaints. Or worse."

"What do you mean, worse?"

"Who knows? People like to cause trouble. I'll be in touch."

Jed started to walk back into the living room but then turned around and went back to the kitchen and made a phone call. "Hey Dutch, it's Jed. I just want to give you a heads up."

34

JED RETURNED TO THE DINING ROOM AND FOUND IT EMPTY. Homer was in the bathroom and Monica was putting Aja to bed. Jed cleared the table and was in the kitchen when Monica appeared behind him. She put her arms around his waist as he stood at the sink, washing the dishes. "What did Goodman say?"

Jed told her everything that had happened that day. "And now Kelly and Schultz are on their way up to see Dutch. I called and warned him."

"Well, at least you're out of it for now."

"I wish I'd never gotten into it."

"Me too. Homer's tired so I think we should leave him to rest. Meet you in bed?"

Jed kissed her. "See you soon."

Monica got Homer situated for the night and got ready for bed. Jed arrived half an hour later and climbed in next to her. "It's nice to have you alone," he said as he pulled her to him.

"Life has certainly gotten chaotic these last few weeks," she replied.

Jed laughed and kissed her. After they made love, Jed got up. "I need to call Malcolm."

"Now? It's kind of late." Jed shrugged and dialed Malcolm's number, but it went to voicemail. He left a message that he'd call back tomorrow and went back to bed.

The next morning was a repeat of the day before. Jed walked to work and Monica said she'd drop off Homer and Aja in an hour or so. Jed called Malcolm on the way. He repeated the whole story. "So do you think I should just let the Nazi flag and KKK stuff be?"

"Yeah, as much as I hate it."

"That seems to be the consensus."

"I just hope no one creates a major issue. It could get ugly."

"Goodman alluded to that. Like what?"

"I don't know. There are people who demonstrate over less than that."

"Demonstrate?"

Malcolm laughed. "Where were you in the sixties?"

"I'm not that old, Malcolm. I was too young to partake of all that sixties stuff."

"Didn't you hear about that rally in Charlottesville?" Malcolm asked.

"You mean when the far-right opposed the statue of Robert E. Lee being removed?"

"Yes, "Malcolm answered. "A woman was killed when some guy rammed his car into a group who were protesting the protesters."

Jed sighed. "Yeah, but that was a highly visible, public object of long standing. How many people would even know about this niche? I'm at work, so I gotta go. Talk to you soon, Malcolm." Jed hung up and unlocked the gate. He walked up the path but before he got inside the front door he noticed 1488. His duffel bag was slung over his shoulder. 1488 brushed past him and took the stairs up to the apartment he had decorated for Spencer Dickson. Jed followed and watched him open the duffle and take out some pictures and objects. There was a small statue of Robert E. Lee and a little confederate flag. There was a milk carton and a frog pin. Jed had a vague recollection that this frog and milk were symbols of the alt-right movement from his initial research into 1488.

1488 noticed Jed watching him and sneered at him, "Whatcha' lookin' at?"

Jed turned away and walked down the stairs. He didn't want to confront him. He took some deep breaths and greeted some visitors, but realized he had to inform the board of the situation.

1488 left just as Jed's phone rang. It was Goodman. "Schultz and Kelly found Haji."

"What are they going to do with him?"

"Make him an offer. They'll go easy on him if he gives up names."

"So it's in their hands now?"

"I'm still on the murder case. They're handling the drug angle."

"Aren't they connected? Isn't Laila the key to both?" Jed asked.

"Looks that way. Anyway, I'm giving you a heads up. Schultz and Kelly will be calling you."

"Why? I don't know anything about the drugs."

"They think you might get information out of Haji."

"I tried. Remember?"

"Yeah, but now he's scared because he's in custody. You have a good shot at it."

"I really don't want to be involved anymore."

"What I told you before still holds. You're protected. I guarantee you that. But you are involved. They are trying to identify the ring leader and it might be the man you saw with the bodyguard you fingered."

"I've already given the description. What else is there?"

"Just cooperate with them. Call me after you've talked to them." Goodman hung up.

Monica, Homer and Aja arrived at that moment and Jed filled them in on what had happened. "I just want it all to go back to the way it was," Jed sighed.

"That's not going to happen," Monica replied. "Are you going to call Tony to come in?"

"I'm going to ask Schultz to bring Haji here."

Monica nodded, kissed Jed and Aja, and gave Homer a hug. "I'll pick you up a little after five." She left.

"Aja and I have the third floor to do today," Homer said.

"I'll bring the stroller up there. Do you want to join me in my rounds? I have some people to sing to."

"Sure. What songs are they?"

"'Give my Regards to Broadway', 'Happy Trails', 'When the Saints Go Marching In', 'Summertime' and one you probably don't know called 'Let it Go' from a recent children's movie."

"Well, I know all the others. I could sing 'Happy Trails' in my sleep."

The two men and Aja started walking and their voices rang out. Jed watched Homer's gait change from what looked like a drunken stagger to a smooth stride as he sang along. Aja bellowed with them in her own version of joining in. When they were finished, Homer pushed Aja around the third floor so he could look at the apartments and condos he hadn't seen the day before. Jed went downstairs and was approached by two young hipster men. They wore T-shirts imprinted with a fist and the words *No Pasarán* written above it. Jed had seen a few people wearing shirts like that before, but didn't know what the words meant. "Are you looking for anyone in particular?" Jed asked them.

"Spencer Dickson," one of the men answered.

Jed stiffened. These two did not look like the white supremacist type. "Third floor. What does that mean?" Jed asked as he pointed to their shirts, hoping to find out if they were sympathizers.

"They shall not pass," the other man replied.

That didn't help Jed much in deciding which side they were on. "Does it have a political context?"

"Yes. Against fascism."

"*Nicaragua: No Pasarán* was the title of a documentary about the rise to power of the Sandinistas," the other man added.

Jed didn't know what to say. He wanted to ask the men to please not do anything rash to the niche or the building, but he didn't want to make any assumptions. "It's upstairs on the right, about halfway down the hallway."

"I'm sure we'll find it easily," one of the men said with a smile.

Jed watched them climb the stairs and remembered that Homer and Aja were on the third floor. He grabbed a dust rag and followed up the stairs, dusting the doors of apartments and condos as he walked. He stopped a few niches down from Spencer Dickson's and opened the door to another one, pretending to inspect the hinges. The men saw that Jed was nearby so all they did was take pictures with their phones. They finished quickly and walked down the stairs, nodding politely to Jed as they passed him. One of them stopped and turned to Jed, "Do you know who Spencer Dickson was?"

"I assume a white supremacist."

"Yeah, but more than that, he was an Internet troll. He liked to expose and bully people whose views differed from his."

"What do you mean expose?" Jed asked.

"Have you heard of Antifas?"

"Not really."

"You will." And at that, the two men left.

Jed searched for Homer on the third floor and found him singing 'Happy Trails' to a niche with a pair of tiny, metal cowboy boots in the corner. He smiled as he watched Homer push Aja's stroller back and forth in time to the music and waited for the song to finish. "Hey Homer, do you know who the Antifas are?"

"No, can't say I do."

"I'll ask Malcolm." He dialed Malcolm's number. "Hey, it's Jed. Do you know about Antifa?" Jed's demeanor immediately changed. He frowned. "Okay. Thanks." He looked at Homer. "They are an anti-fascist movement that uses violence. They are like the leftist version of the KKK."

"Why do you ask?"

"Two guys were just here asking about that white supremacist guy's niche and they wore T-shirts with the saying *No Pasarán* on them. I asked them what it meant and they asked me if I knew about Antifas."

Homer raised his eyebrows. "You think they're going to vandalize it?"

"I don't know. I hope not but it's entirely possible if they are what Malcolm says. We've been vandalized before. But it was coming from the other side. It was always against the Blacks, or the Jews . . . or a drug dealer."

"A drug dealer?"

"Yeah, Goldie over there was a pot dealer and hers was vandalized I think by people looking for something specific in her apartment."

"This place has a fascinating history," Homer said.

"Oh!" Jed suddenly exclaimed.

"What?" Homer asked.

"I need to make a phone call. I'll be right back." Jed headed to Laila's niche, dialing his phone as he walked.

35

FIFTEEN MINUTES AFTER JED MADE THE CALL, KELLY AND SCHULTZ ARRIVED WITH HAJI. Goodman had gotten there just a minute or so before them. Jed brought them up to Laila's niche where Homer and Aja were waiting. Aja was starting to fuss so Jed took her out of the stroller and rocked her as he talked. He looked straight at Haji. "Is this urn being filled with drugs instead of ashes?"

Haji shrugged. He glanced at Schultz who was staring at him and then his eyes darted to Goodman who nodded slightly as if to say it was okay to answer, but Haji stayed silent.

"Hey, Schultz and Kelly," Goodman said suddenly. "Come with me for a minute. Jed, where's that Nazi guy?"

Jed immediately caught on to what Goodman was doing. "It's up there." Jed pointed to Spencer Dickson's apartment. As soon as the three left, Jed looked back at Haji. "Tell me what's going on, Haji. Goodman told me you would be taken care of. They want to find out who the drug lord is. They're not after you or Dutch or Juniper."

"I really don't know much. I was just doing Laila a favor. She's done a lot for me."

"Just tell me what you do know. Then, hopefully, they'll let you go and you can go back to Garberville."

Haji glanced at Homer. "Who's he?"

"He's my friend. A good guy."

"Why's he shaking like that?"

"I have Parkinson's Disease," Homer answered.

"Oh, sorry. I thought you were drunk or stoned or something."

"It's okay," Homer shrugged. "A lot of people think that."

Aja decided rocking wasn't good enough and started whimpering. "Haji, tell me now before the Feds decide to press charges against you," Jed said as he tried a new routine on Aja. "Where are Laila's ashes?" Haji was silent. "Give up the name of the boss and the FBI will take him in and leave you alone."

"But what about Laila?"

"What are you worried about Laila for? She's dead."

"No she's not."

"What do you mean? Dutch paid for this niche for her."

"Yeah, but she's not dead."

Jed and Homer looked at each other. "I think I get what Haji's saying," Homer said to Jed.

"Yes. I think I do too. So Haji, is this urn a drug pick-up?"

"Only one time that I know about. And I didn't do it. I wasn't part of that. You gotta believe me. There's a funeral home in Santa Rosa. That's who you need to talk to."

"Okay. But where's Laila?"

"I don't know, man. Honestly. I wish I did. I'm really scared."

"Have you told me everything you know about Yasmin?"

"Yasmin?" Haji shook his head. "I don't know anything about this Yasmin woman. Just that she called me to find Laila."

Just then Goodman, Schultz and Kelly showed up. "Such tasteful décor!" Schultz gushed sarcastically. "You know some see the Nazi flag as treasonous. In fact, several European countries ban the use of them. But the United States is too hitched to the first amendment. So did Haji have anything to share?" Schultz asked.

"Yeah. Let me go to my office and I'll get you the name and address of the Santa Rosa funeral home that may be the real center of this drug ring. And Laila's urn is empty because she isn't dead."

Schultz, Kelly and Goodman exchanged glances. "What about your boss, Haji?" Schultz asked.

"Who? Dutch?"

"No," Schultz scoffed. "Dutch is small potatoes."

"I don't have no other boss."

"Who are you running drugs for?" Schultz asked. He drew his body closer to Haji who shrunk toward Jed.

"I just helped Laila a little. I'm not a drug runner."

"So where's Laila?" Kelly asked.

"I don't know. Honest. I don't know. And I don't know who she works for."

Jed decided he needed to step in. "You guys can come with me to my office and I'll give you the name and address of the funeral home. I'm sure that's how you'll find who you're really looking for."

"Go ahead. I'll stay here with Haji," Goodman said.

Schultz and Kelly nodded at each other and followed Jed to his office. Left alone, Homer squinted at Goodman. "Haji here is innocent and an idiot." He glanced at Haji. "No offense. I only say idiot because you got yourself involved in something way over your head. What do they say now — one's brain is not fully developed until twenty-something?"

Goodman laughed. "Homer, what's your connection to all this anyway?"

"None. I'm a friend of Jed's. I'm staying with him until I can get up north."

"Oregon? Washington?"

"No. I grew up in northern California and want to get back there."

"Garberville's nice," Haji said.

"Yeah, I know. I grew up northwest of there, closer to the coast."

"You wanna get back there soon, Haji?" Goodman asked. "Then tell me everything and I'll take you back myself."

"I told Jed everything I know." Just then Jed came back with Schultz and Kelly and Aja sucking from a bottle.

"Jed, Haji here says he told you everything he knows. You think that's true?" Goodman winked at Jed.

"Haji, tell them what you told me," Jed said.

"They used Laila's urn here one time that I know of to hide the drugs. But I wasn't part of that." Haji's voice ran up with fear. "It was the guy from Pakistan."

"What man from Pakistan?" Schultz asked.

"The guy she was getting the drugs from over there. But I don't know his name or anything. And I don't know the guy here who was buying them. I only know Laila. I only helped her out a little." Haji's voice was cracking and his eyes welled up.

"You know about this Pakistani guy?" Schultz asked Jed.

"There was a Pakistani guy here a couple of times recently," Jed answered.

"And you don't know his name?" Schultz asked Haji.

Haji shook his head. "It was Laila's connection. It was where she got the drugs in Pakistan. I think he's a policeman."

"The Pakistani police are totally corrupt," Kelly said. "Interpol's been onto this for a long time."

"Haji, this is important," Goodman interjected. He cast his eyes toward Schultz and Kelly. "I think I speak for the San Francisco Police Department and the FBI that you don't have to worry. Just give us names and tell us everything you know and we can help you." Schultz and Kelly nodded in agreement. "Think about it. Who is the guy here in the states Laila works for?"

"I'm telling you the truth. I really don't know his name. And I don't know the Pakistani's policeman's name. And I don't know where Laila is. I would just deliver some stuff for Laila to certain places. That's all. And she would pay me out of her own take. It was just when she didn't want to be seen or something. That's all I know."

"Are you sure you know nothing about Yasmin?" Jed asked.

"Who's Yasmin?" Kelly asked.

"I think that's the name of the woman who was murdered," Jed answered.

"Only that Yasmin might have been the name of the woman who called me to find Laila. But that was a long time ago."

"How long?"

Haji shrugged. "A month, or maybe more."

Schultz nodded at Kelly and then turned to Haji. "Go on back to Garberville but don't go anywhere else. We need to find you easily."

Haji exhaled loudly. "I can leave?"

Goodman rolled his eyes. "Yeah, you can leave."

Haji almost broke into a run before Jed called out, "Hey, wait a minute, Haji." He looked back over his shoulder to the Feds. "Can I get back to work now too?"

"Sure," said Kelly as he and Schultz turned to walk away.

Goodman brushed a hand across Jed's shoulder as he followed the men out. "We need to talk more about the Pakistani policeman." Jed nodded and turned to Haji who was dancing about impatiently.

"What do you want?" Haji asked.

"How are you going to get to Garberville?"

"I don't know, man. I just want to get the hell out of here. Maybe the bus."

"How about a ride instead?" Jed turned to Homer. "How about a road trip?"

"Up north?"

Jed nodded. "I'll need to make some calls. I don't have a driver's license, but I have some ideas." He turned back to Haji. "I'll call you tonight. Okay?"

"Yeah."

"Are you going to your parents' house now?"

"No. I have a place to stay."

"Where?"

"The Haight. Can I go now?"

"Yeah, but keep your phone on and don't let me down."

Haji left and Homer grinned at Jed. "Can I take Aja for a song-and-dance walk down the halls?"

Jed put Aja in the stroller and swung the handles around toward Homer. "Be my guest."

36

JED CALLED TONY TO SEE IF HE COULD WORK FOR THE NEXT COUPLE OF DAYS. After that he dialed Dutch.

"The FBI just left, Dutch. They had Haji and got some information out of him, so they're willing to leave him alone for now. He wants to go back to the farm. I've been assured that you're not under any suspicion, but they may want to speak to you again. If he cooperates by returning here for questioning, they have no reason to return to your farm."

"Okay. I'll kick his butt right back down there if he's called. Is he coming on the bus?"

"I'm going to bring him up. I have a friend who needs an assisted living place and wants to look for one up north. Do you know of any?"

Dutch laughed. "No. I'm not that far gone yet."

His next call was to Monica. "Well, things have gotten even more interesting." Jed told her about the latest developments. "So now I will also be bringing Haji."

"And have you figured out how you're all going to get there?"

"Not yet. Any ideas?"

"Yep. I need a vacation."

"You mean you'll take us?"

"That's what I'm saying."

"Are you sure you want to use up your vacation days? You might need them . . ." his voice trailed off.

"I am not going to let this disease run my life. Where's your carpe diem spirit?"

"Can you just take off work like that?" Jed asked.

"I can do whatever I damn well please. When do you want to leave?"

"Tomorrow morning?"

"This will be fun," Monica answered.

"Our first family outing with Aja," Jed replied.

Monica laughed. "Some family. More like a motley crew!"

Jed hung up and called Haji to get his address. "How early will we leave?" Haji asked. "The guys I'm staying with like to party late."

"Haji," Jed replied darkly. "Do you want a ride or not?"

"Okay. Okay. Text me to wake me up."

Jed sighed. "Better me than the FBI."

"What?"

"Get your priorities straight while you get some sleep tonight."

"I'll be ready."

Jed hung up and went to find Homer and Aja. "Monica is going to take off work and she will drive us up north. We can drop off Haji in Garberville and then look around at some places for you."

"Really? I thought she said that they didn't have any room."

"Monica thinks we'll have better luck if we're there in person," Jed replied.

"It'll be nice to go back up north, even if it's just for a couple of days. We gonna stay in a motel? I'm a little short until the beginning of the month."

"Don't worry about it, Homer. We can bunk together and put Monica and Aja in another room."

"Back in Venice, George used to spend the night in my apartment sometimes when my Parkinson's acted up and he said I snored. I don't want to keep you awake."

"Well, I haven't heard you snore in my living room. We'll manage. I won't mind."

"George minded everything." Homer laughed. "He could be awfully grouchy sometimes."

Jed laughed. "He couldn't have been too bad, helping you out like that. But that's how cranks can be. Like Finn."

"Ah, Finn and George are nothing compared to Nick."

"Nick?"

"He's another guy who used to live at the senior residence in Venice."

"Oh yeah. Nick's the one who came up here with Finn, Malcolm and Savali to visit his mother and then disappeared, right?"

"Yeah. That's him."

"So he's another one huh?"

"Another what? Drug dealer?" Homer asked.

"Well, I meant another cranky old man, but was he a drug dealer?"

"He got out of it a while ago, but his family continued the tradition."

Jed's wheels began turning. "Was his last name Balducci?"

Homer shrugged. "I don't know. He changed it when he left the drug-dealing business. I knew him as Nick Bailey."

"I wonder if there's a connection."

"What do you mean?" Homer asked.

"Between Laila and Francesca Balducci. Both of them are in the drug trade."

Homer laughed. "They are probably not the only drug dealers buried here."

"Well, Francesca had visitors recently and the same men also paid a visit to Laila. And one of the men is a known criminal to the police. I need to call Goodman and Schultz." Jed was about to leave Homer with Aja again when he saw that the tremors were getting worse. "Hey Homer, do you need a break?"

"I could use a sit-down. Yeah."

"Let me get a chair." Jed brought over a chair and helped Homer into it. "I'm going to make those calls. Is there anything else you need?"

"I-I-I'll be f-f-fine."

Jed hadn't noticed Homer stuttering before. He had noticed some slurred words. He hoped Homer wasn't getting worse. "Do you have any medication that helps?"

"The doctor g-g-gave me some stuff, s-s-s-synthetic d-d-dopamine. But it makes me n-n-nauseous."

"Do you want to go home? I could call a cab."

"No."

Jed nodded and left Homer in the chair. He greeted some visitors and took Aja to the office. He took care of her needs and then called Goodman to share his thoughts on Laila and Francesca Balducci. "That's an interesting theory. I'll call Schultz and fill him in."

"Thanks. I appreciate not having to talk to him." Jed hung up and realized the only person in his recent circle he hadn't updated was Malcolm. He called and left a voicemail, thankful he didn't pick up.

The afternoon went quickly and they piled into Monica's car, eager to get home and prepare for the trip north. They discussed the logistics over dinner and agreed that they should go to bed early. Jed wanted to make sure they had enough time to look around for a place for Homer. All the travel and excitement of the last week surely didn't help his condition, but the severe tremors Homer had that afternoon made Jed doubly conscious that he needed assisted living.

Malcolm called just as Jed and Monica got into bed. "Sorry," Jed grinned sheepishly, "but I want to update him."

""Just hurry back. I've been spending a few too many nights alone in this bed lately. You and your friends and pot farm visits!" She winked.

Jed flashed her a big smile and went into the kitchen to talk to Malcolm. "Monica is going to drive you?" Malcolm asked. "That's wonderful."

"I'll call you from up north and let you know how we're doing with Homer. Monica has a list of places for us to visit up there. Maybe we can work some magic in person."

"Good luck."

Jed went back to bed but alas he was too late. Monica was snoring softly. Jed smiled, kissed her gently, and climbed into bed.

37

JED SLEPT SOUNDLY. The last few weeks had been so full and busy that exhaustion took over. Aja started to sleep through the night and that was a pleasant turn of events. He glanced at Monica who was still snoring softly. He tiptoed into the kitchen because Homer, too, was out cold. He got the coffee started and checked the clock. It was a little after four. He'd get his shower over with so the bathroom would be available for the others and they could hopefully be on the road to Garberville by six. He would start texting Haji at five because he was sure it would take several texts to get him up.

By the time Aja started stirring, Jed was showered, dressed and packed. Aja had found her voice recently and enjoyed hearing herself bellow. It was her wake-up call and there was no sleeping through it. They got through their morning routines quickly and were all out of the house before six. Even Haji was waiting outside when they got there to pick him up. "This is my wife, Monica," Jed said as Haji got in.

Haji was still half asleep so all he could muster was a grunt. He got in, leaned against the window and nodded off. Jed frowned. He certainly wasn't going to find out much more from him on the ride up. "Let him sleep," Monica said. "Homer, did you look at the list I gave Jed of the assisted living places? There are several in the Eureka area."

"What about senior residences like where I lived in Venice?"

"I don't know if you can handle that now, Homer. There's no help there like at the assisted living ones."

"I don't need that much and there were always people willing to help when I needed it."

"I know, Homer, but you can't count on that. When you do need assistance there might not be a Malcolm or Savali to help you. You'd just be sucked into the medical system with no voice in the matter."

Jed glanced at Homer's face to see how he was reacting to what Monica was saying. He didn't know if anyone had been that blunt with him before. "Maybe he can just find a place temporarily and then move into assisted living when he needs it," Jed added.

"Yeah!" Homer agreed.

Monica gave Jed a withering glance and then shrugged. Homer diverted his attention to something more pleasant. Aja was sitting in her seat next to him and started to kick Haji. Homer laughed. "What's funny?" Jed asked.

"Aja's trying to wake up Haji and she knows what she's doing. You should see the look on her face."

"She's an imp," Jed said with a bit of pride. He also noticed that Homer's speech pattern was close to normal. He was having a good day.

"There's a Starbucks," Monica said as she pulled off the freeway and into the parking lot. "Better wake up sleeping beauty. We still have a two-hour drive ahead of us, so let's hit the restroom and get a cup of coffee and maybe something to eat."

Homer shook Haji's shoulders while Monica took Aja out of her car seat. Jed took Homer's arm. "Let me help you and we can leave the walker and cane in the car." Haji finally stumbled out of the car and followed them into the store as if he was sleepwalking.

They piled into the Starbucks. "I'll take Aja into the restroom and change her," Monica said.

"I'll get us some coffee and a pastry," added Jed. "What do you want, Homer? You too, Haji."

Jed took the orders and went to the counter while everyone else went to the restroom. After about ten minutes everyone was ready to go.

When they got to the car, Jed told Homer to get in the front with Monica. "I may need to deal with Aja during the trip."

Monica took off and said, "I think we should drive to Eureka this afternoon. It's nice and cool there, Homer. Nothing like the central valley."

"I really appreciate all you're doing for me, Monica," Homer said, "but I really don't want assisted living."

"We'll see," Monica replied wearily.

"I'm not ready to go out to pasture!"

"Calm down, old man," Haji blurted out. It was the first time he spoke that morning.

"Watch yourself, Haji," Monica reprimanded. She reached for the radio as a distraction. A push of the scan button did not please her. "Dammit, where's NPR?"

"You keep your eyes on the road. I'll do it," Homer said as he raised a shaky finger to the button. He seemed to have the magic touch. A music station came on playing classic rock and blues. "How about this?" Homer asked.

"You know the guy who owns the farm we're going to is an old musician from the sixties?" Jed said. "His name is Dutch Bogart. You may not have heard of him, but he played with some famous bands and wrote a lot of songs."

"What does he play?" Homer asked.

"Guitar."

"He plays other instruments too," Haji added.

"I didn't know that," Jed replied. "I only saw him with a guitar."

"Well, he does," Haji said and then leaned against the window and closed his eyes again.

"Maybe he's got a piano," Homer mused. "I could practice a little when we get there. It's been a long time since I practiced."

"I bet he has one," Jed answered.

"How long are we planning to stay at this pot farm?" Homer asked. "You're doing a lot of driving, Monica. Aren't you going to want a break?"

"Don't worry about me," Monica answered. "I don't mind driving."

Jed decided to change the subject. "How's the gas situation?"

"We have enough. I filled up yesterday." Monica glanced at Homer who was obviously enjoying the music, smiling as he swayed and tapped his fingers rhythmically.

They drove in silence for a while and then Aja started to get restless. Jed didn't want to stop the car so he tried to amuse her. They had just passed Leggett and Jed knew from his past trips that they were now only about a half hour away from the farm. Jed hoped Haji would direct them once they got off the freeway because he hadn't paid close attention when Juniper drove him to the farm. He looked over and saw that Haji's eyes were open and he was looking out the window. Jed felt sorry for him. He had gotten himself into a big mess and Jed thought about what would happen if his parents ever found out.

"So here's the Garberville exit. Where do I go now?" Monica asked.

"Haji, can you guide Monica to the farm?" Haji gave directions as Homer snored and Aja fretted. "Should I call Dutch or Juniper for the code to the gate or is it always the same?"

Haji shrugged. "I don't know."

"You never used it?"

"I never came alone. Juniper or Laila always picked me up in town."

"Well, I'll try." Jed remembered the code from last time and got out to punch it in. The gate opened. He got back in and they drove up to the house. Jed took Aja out of the car seat but noticed that Homer had still not woken up. "Haji, could you wake up Homer and see if he's okay?"

Haji shook Homer's shoulders, but he didn't open his eyes. "Hey, man," Haji said shaking Homer harder. Haji looked at Monica with alarm. "Nothing's happening!"

Jed had already reached the door of the house and was knocking when Monica called out to him. "Jed, Homer won't wake up."

Jed walked back to the car and felt for a pulse. "It's okay. He'll probably wake up soon." He was reluctant to leave Homer alone, but he also had a squirming Aja. "Haji, would you find Dutch or Juniper?"

Haji returned with Juniper. Jed introduced Monica and pointed out the sleeping Homer. "I'm not sure what to do about Homer."

"Just leave him in the car. He'll be all right. Nobody's going to bother him. I have to find Dutch. He's probably got his headphones on so he can't hear anything." She went into the house and Jed followed with Monica and Aja.

Juniper was right. Dutch was listening to music with his headphones, smoking a joint. He stood, smiled and removed his headphones. "Hey Jed. Good to see you."

"This is my wife, Monica," Jed smiled back.

"Great to meet you," Monica said.

"Likewise," Dutch replied.

Juniper took Aja from Jed's arms. "She looks like she's grown."

Jed was surprised at Juniper's interest. "Yes. She's lifting her head and trying to roll over, too. Not with any success. I guess it's a little early."

"How old is she?"

"We don't know."

Juniper looked at him incredulously. "You don't know how old your baby is?"

"She's our foster child."

"Oh." Juniper didn't seem to need to know more. "I'll give her a bottle if you want."

"Thanks. She also needs to be changed." He handed Juniper the diaper bag. "We were hoping to use the computer to look for senior housing."

Juniper stared at Jed, bewildered. "Not for me, for Homer, the guy in the car. I need to go check on him. Monica, you stay here and take a break. You've done all the driving."

"I could start the computer search if it's okay with everyone," Monica replied.

"Follow me." Dutch took Monica to his computer.

Jed hurried back to the car and found Homer trying to get out. He was quite unsteady on his feet. Jed had never seen him so bad. "I'm o-o-okay," Homer said as he held onto Jed and stumbled into the house. Juniper met them in the front hall with a contented Aja sucking on her bottle.

"Come on in here," Jed said guiding Homer into Dutch's music room.

"Oh b-b-boy. This is f-f-fantastic!" Homer exclaimed as he saw all the instruments and the production equipment. "Music helps me c-c-control my t-t-tremors. Play, will you?"

Dutch picked up his guitar and started strumming. Homer started swaying to the music and then dancing around the room. "That's remarkable," Dutch said. "You have Parkinson's?" Homer nodded.

"Homer plays the piano," Jed jumped in. "That helps stop his tremors, too."

Dutch was curious. "Would you like to play for us?"

"I can't play well, I'm just learning. Nothing like you."

"I hate to rush you," Monica interrupted, "but if we're going to Eureka to look at those places, we'd better get going. I found a few places to check out."

"I want to see the farm, though," Homer protested.

"Let me show him around before you leave," Dutch said.

Jed hadn't ever seen the whole farm, only the house and the trimming rooms. "We can wait a little while," Jed said looking at Monica. She nodded.

Dutch took Homer's arm. Monica followed and Jed went to get Aja. "Thanks," Jed said as he took her out of Juniper's arms. "She's happy to see you again."

"Yeah. I think so," Juniper replied and then turned away.

Jed caught up to Monica and they all listened to Dutch give them a synopsis on the cultivation of marijuana. Homer was mesmerized and asked many questions. "Are these just medicinal varieties?"

"I stick mostly to medicinal. It keeps the Feds away." Dutch looked at Jed. "Well, sometimes."

"So do you think any of these would work for my Parkinson's without making me high?"

"If you don't want to get high, you want something higher in CBD and less THC. But you want it sativa-dominant."

Homer shook his head. "I'm confused."

"Yeah, it takes a little while to get it. But I do grow something I think would help you, but it's potent."

"What is it?"

"Amnesia Haze. Usually it's a very strong high, but I've been growing a variety higher in CBD, so it won't make you feel so stoned. Do you want to try it?"

Jed and Monica looked at each other. "Should you talk to a doctor, Homer, and make sure it doesn't interfere with the medication you're already taking?" Jed asked.

"That stuff is awful. I hardly ever take it." Homer turned to Dutch. "I would like to, but I'd like to finish the tour of the farm. I've always been interested in gardening. Used to be quite good at it when I was a kid. Hell, we had to be or starve to death!" Homer laughed. "But this growing marijuana is new to me. Do I have to smoke it? I gave up smoking many years ago."

"You can use a vaporizer." Dutch never let go of Homer's arm while finishing the farm tour. They were deep in conversation as they walked. The fact that Homer had been an electrician before the Parkinson's had set in was great news for Dutch who wanted to go off the grid and needed advice. When they returned to the house, Dutch took Homer to a couch in the music room. "Wait here." Dutch left and returned with a plastic bag and a vaporizer. Jed and Monica watched as he showed Homer how to inhale it. "Okay. Now lie down and let it do its thing."

Homer lay down, his hands shaking and his head moving rapidly from side to side, and closed his eyes. His body relaxed within minutes. "Wow. It works well," he grinned.

"It should peak in about half an hour."

"How long does it last?" Jed asked.

"Depends on the person and the amount. I didn't want to give Homer too much for the first time. It should last at least two or three hours."

Homer stood and walked over to the piano. He did an elementary rendition of "I've Been Working on the Railroad." After he finished, Dutch sat down and played "Sweet Georgia Brown" and Homer sang along. Jed bounced Aja in time to the music. When Dutch finished, they all applauded. "That was wonderful!" Monica said. "But we really need to go."

"Just what kind of assistance does Homer need?" Dutch asked no one in particular.

"I never know," Homer shrugged. "Like today, it comes on suddenly when I have a bad day or something. But it doesn't usually last long."

"But I mean, you don't need a nurse or anything?"

"No, no. I still got all my faculties and stuff. And if I buy this stuff from you, I'll be just fine."

"He shouldn't live alone," Monica interjected. "Where he used to live, there'd be people around to help him if he needed it. They could watch out for him and make him dinner or help get him to bed."

"I don't want to go into no home!" Homer yelled. Aja startled and started to whimper. Homer went over and patted Aja's back. "I'm sorry baby. I didn't mean to scare you." Aja stuck out her lower lip, stifled a sniffle, and then managed a smile.

"Well," Dutch said slowly, "go ahead and take a look at some places and then come on back and sleep here tonight."

Jed and Monica looked at each other, shrugged, and smiled. "Sounds good to me," Monica replied.

"Oh yes. I'd like that!" Homer exclaimed. "This place is like heaven to me. Just like where I grew up in Honeydew."

"You were raised in Honeydew? That's only about thirty miles from here," Dutch said.

"Okay," Jed said. "Let's get going so we can be back tonight before it's dark."

"Wait a minute," Dutch said. "I had a thought. Why don't you stay at the farm for now, Homer? I'm here, Juniper's here, and there are always young people like Haji around. You can help us."

"How can I help?" Homer asked.

"You seem to know a lot about gardening. You could let those young kids do the work. It would help me out not having to supervise as much. And there's plenty of music around and a piano to play."

Homer looked at Jed and Monica, his eyes bulging. "Wow."

They smiled at him and shrugged. Homer choked up. "I don't know what to say."

"How about yes?" Dutch grinned.

Jed and Monica looked at each other, and then Monica, always the social worker, turned to Dutch. "You understand that he needs to be taken to doctors' appointments and there might be an emergency? How quickly can an ambulance get here?"

"Juniper or I can get him to any appointments and there's a hospital in Garberville." Dutch smiled at Monica. "You city folk think this is the sticks, but it really isn't."

"What do you think, Homer? Sound like a good idea?" Monica asked.

"Hell yeah!" Then, a bit sheepishly, he turned to Dutch. "I could give you some money each month from my social security check."

Dutch raised his hand. "Not necessary. I'll show you a nice bedroom you can have." He turned to Jed and Monica. "Now that you don't have to go to Eureka, you two want to stay here tonight, also?"

Monica and Jed looked at each other. "Sure. Why not?" Monica said.

Jed couldn't wait to tell Malcolm.

38

THEY SPENT THE REST OF THE
AFTERNOON MEANDERING AROUND
THE FARM. Besides the gardens of marijuana
plants, there were meadows, trees and creeks. It
was a bucolic paradise. Jed and Monica strolled
hand-in-hand with Aja strapped to Jed's chest.
Homer and Dutch were inseparable, walking
arm-in-arm and talking nonstop. Dutch was
fascinated with Homer's life as a carney and
Homer was likewise fascinated with Dutch's life
as a touring musician.

The day was warm and clear, and it
made for a relaxing afternoon, something
everyone desperately needed after the last few
weeks.

They got back to the house and Juniper
was in the kitchen preparing dinner. Dutch took
the group into his music room and offered
them beer. He put on some Miles Davis and the
atmosphere was mellow, everyone lost in their
own world. Dutch took a few hits from a joint
and gave Homer the vaporizer. He offered the
joint to Jed and Monica, but they declined.

"Dinner's ready but you'll have to serve yourselves in the kitchen. I have to weigh the day's take from the trimmers," Juniper said, popping her head into the room.

They piled into the kitchen, all of their appetites whetted by their bodies' intakes of the last hour. There was a large pile of food on the counter. "She made enough for an army!" Homer exclaimed.

"She's feeding more people than just us," Jed answered. "She has to feed Haji and the other trimmers, too."

"Just like a lumber camp!" laughed Homer.

Jed made a bottle for Aja before getting his plate of food and joining the group back in the music room. He guessed that the trimmers ate at the kitchen table and Dutch liked it that way. Jed glanced at Homer, wondering if he had been able to serve himself and carry his plate. Jed's curiosity was soon satisfied when Homer said, "I think the stuff is working, Dutch. I haven't been able to eat with my right hand this well for a long time."

Dutch grinned. "I've got some other strains we can try too." He then turned to Jed. "So, I paid for an urn that's being used for a drug exchange? And Laila's alive?"

"That's what Haji told us."

"Do you know where Laila is?" Dutch asked.

"Not yet. That's what the Feds want to know too."

"She's in a shit pile of trouble, I guess," Dutch sighed. "I don't understand why she would turn to smuggling drugs into the country. She didn't have expensive tastes and she made enough here to keep her going for the rest of the year."

"Maybe she owed someone money," Homer interjected.

"That could be," Dutch said. "Or maybe she was helping someone in Pakistan. She definitely had some stories about how crappy life was there."

Jed also had a hard time imagining the whole thing. From what he had heard about Laila, she didn't fit the stereotype of a drug mule. It's one thing to deal some pot, but quite another to take heroin across the ocean. And if Yasmin was Aja's mother, how and why would she have involved herself in this with a baby in tow? She really must have been desperate. Homer woke Jed out of his daydream when he tried to get out of his chair. "Oh dear, the legs just don't want to move and I need to go to the bathroom."

Before Jed or Monica could come to Homer's rescue, Dutch was out of his chair and by Homer's side. "Let me help," Dutch said in a gentle voice. Dutch continued to show different sides from the first time Jed saw him, holding a rifle and looking like a gruff redneck guarding his home.

"It'll pass. It usually does. So far it has, anyway."

"Why not lean on me and I'll help you to the bathroom. I'll get some more of that weed for you. It's probably worn off. And then you'll just have to keep making music and dancing," Dutch added.

Homer smiled. "Guess I came to the right place for that."

Dutch helped Homer out the door as Aja let out a big yawn. "We need to get her to sleep," Monica said. "Do you want to leave early tomorrow, Jed?"

"Let's play it by ear." Jed took his wife's hand. Dutch had told him earlier to use the same room with the futon on the floor for Aja's sake.

As soon as Jed got Aja changed and onto the futon, the baby fell fast asleep. Jed wasn't sure if it was the fresh country air or the wafts of marijuana drifting throughout the house. He took out his phone and Monica rolled her eyes and finished undressing. He dialed Goodman's number. "Any news about the Santa Rosa funeral home?"

"The funeral home is closed. And that apparently happened right after Dutch paid for Laila's urn. We're trying to locate the owners."

"I think that Pakistani policeman may know something about that."

"Schultz told me that they're in contact with Interpol and Transparency International to see if there's a connection."

"Transparency International?"

"They're a watchdog group that looks at corruption around the world."

"Dutch doesn't think Laila's the type to do this. I'm thinking maybe she owes somebody something and had to."

"Yeah, Jed. That's what everyone says."

Jed hung up, ready for a good night's sleep. He hoped Aja's new sleeping hours would continue as he glanced lovingly at his sleeping wife.

39

HOMER AND DUTCH WERE ALREADY UP, CUPS OF COFFEE IN HAND, WHEN JED AND MONICA WANDERED INTO THE MUSIC ROOM. "Breakfast's ready in the kitchen," Dutch said. "Go get yourselves some food and coffee and join us. Homer and I have already eaten."

Jed glanced over at the clock on the wall. "How long have you both been up?"

"Last night Homer asked me to get him up early so he could see the sun rise."

"This is like the garden of Eden to me," Homer said.

"It sounds like a perfect situation for you, Homer," Monica said as she hugged him.

"This is more than I ever hoped for. And you and Jed have been . . ." Homer choked up.

Jed gave Homer a big hug and then turned to Monica. "Let's get some breakfast and be on our way."

Jed and Monica were on the road by eleven after assuring Homer that they would be back to visit soon. Monica also told him that she would handle having his social security and Medicare records changed to his new address. "I hope it isn't too much for Dutch," she said to Jed as they drove off. "I'm not sure he knew what he was getting into."

"Dutch seems as happy about it as Homer," Jed replied. "And there are other people there to help. I'm glad the marijuana is helping so much, but that's not going to take care of everything. He'll need medical support too."

Monica started laughing. "Have you noticed how much of our life is about drugs these days?"

Aja was restless so they stopped often. They had all day to get home so they decided to do a little sightseeing. A sign for Lake Mendocino came up near Ukiah and they found a nice place to get out and enjoy the scenery. They took Aja for a half hour walk and then got back on 101 South. After about an hour they were approaching Santa Rosa. "Do you mind if we stop? I'd like to look for that funeral home."

Monica gave Jed a quizzical look and shook her head. "If you want, but I thought you were giving up on being a detective."

"It won't take long."

"Where is it?" she asked.

"I don't know. I have to look it up."

"Do you know the address?"

"I'll find out." Jed called Tony at the columbarium and asked him to go into the office and look up the address.

"Where will I find it?" Tony asked.

"Look up Laila Aziz. The information will be there."

"Okay. I'll call you back when I get it."

"Thanks, Tony." Jed hung up and turned to Monica. "He's going to call back with the address."

"Yeah, but where should I get off? There are a bunch of exits for Santa Rosa."

"I'll look at the map on the smartphone after Tony calls back."

"When did you learn how to use a smartphone?"

"I'll figure it out." Jed looked at his phone. Tony called back with the address and Jed put it in the phone. The directions came up immediately. "This is simple. Is this Route 12?"

"I saw a sign for Route 12. It's a couple more exits."

"Okay. Get off there." He gave Monica directions and in fifteen minutes they were in front of the place. But as Goodman had said, it was closed. What was weird, though, was that it didn't look like it had been open anytime in the recent past. Hadn't Goodman said that it closed right after Dutch had paid for Laila's niche?

That wasn't that long ago, yet the place looked desolate and not at all like the funeral homes Jed had seen. They were usually comfortable, serene places with lots of carpet and nice furniture. Jed peeked in a window and saw worn linoleum and lots of dirt and debris.

"So," Monica sighed. "Here we are and what exactly have you learned?"

"Well, I know for sure that this place is a sham. Let's go."

Monica made a U turn and they were soon back on 101 south. Aja slept all the way home and Jed and Monica were quiet as well. They were both ready to be back home with just each other and Aja.

Jed was eager to call Goodman and tell him about the funeral home. The building seemed much more suited as a front for drug trafficking than for mourning or celebrations of life. Dutch was completely believable in his shock over Laila's other life, but that didn't jive with choosing such a disreputable looking funeral home. Unless he was simply following some anonymous directive.

As soon as they walked in the door, Jed sat down with his phone. "Goodman? I was just at that funeral home in Santa Rosa. We were driving by on our way back from Dutch's so we took a detour. It looks like it hasn't been in use for years, not weeks."

"Hmm. Schultz called and said that it is registered and has a business license, but that's pretty interesting. Maybe Laila was their only customer. Well, let me look into it some more. Why don't you check your records and see if you ever received any other ashes from them."

"Okay."

Monica appeared with Aja just as Jed hung up. "I'll make dinner if you deal with her. And there's something we need to talk about."

"What's up?"

Monica sighed. "I wanted to wait until we got home."

"What's going on?"

"I'm hungry. Let's wait until after dinner."

"Come on, tell me."

"Okay. Okay. Elizabeth called. Our emergency foster care permit is running out. Something has to happen quickly or they will place Aja in a more permanent foster situation."

"Can't we get a permanent foster care permit ourselves?" Jed asked.

"It takes time. It won't happen fast enough."

"Well, can't she pull some strings?"

"Jed, if she could do anything, she would."

"So what are we going to do?"

"If we could guarantee that there are no family members who want her, I think we can try to adopt her. But she may still have to go into another foster home first."

"No!" Jed shouted. His outburst surprised them both. Aja, too, was startled and started to cry. Jed went to comfort her. "I'm sorry. I didn't mean to yell," he said glancing apologetically at Monica.

Monica shrugged. "That's just how it is."

"Maybe Goodman can do something?" Jed asked.

"I doubt it. More likely one of the columbarium board members would have better connections and pull."

"Then I'll ask them. So if we could identify the body, and be sure there are no relatives, we could start the adoption process?"

"I guess."

"You don't sound very enthusiastic."

"Jed, you know my feelings. I'm just not sure."

"Well, how about this. We start the process to adopt and then decide."

"I suppose," she sighed. "I'll pull together the necessary paperwork and you can talk to some board members and see if they can help with the fostering issue."

Jed nodded and stared out the window. Even he started to feel uncertain. What if Monica's HIV status advanced to full-blown AIDS and she died before Aja was able to be self-sufficient? Jed wasn't sure he could handle it alone, or if that was truly best for Aja.

Jed got Aja ready for bed and tucked her in. He took out a bottle of wine and brought it into the living room. Neither of them felt like making dinner, so they made a couple of grilled cheese sandwiches and a salad and finished the bottle. Their conversation was trivial. Monica half-heartedly shared a few work-related stories about some of the children in the Glide Church shelter who had been successful in their own searches for homes. They went to bed, but their lovemaking felt both forced and distracted.

40

AJA MUST HAVE PICKED UP ON THEIR MOODS BECAUSE SHE SLEPT FITFULLY, CRYING OFF AND ON ALL NIGHT LONG. Everyone was pretty cranky the next morning and Jed was not in the mood to talk to board members. Hopefully a bit of breakfast and coffee would brighten up his mood, but Aja was the most uncooperative she had ever been during their morning routine. Jed vowed no more long car trips for a while.

As soon as he got to work, Jed went to the office to see if there had been any other ashes from the Golden Crescent Funeral Home. There were none. Laila was the first and only. A glance at the clock reminded him to unlock the door into the columbarium. When he swung open the door, he found a very unpleasant looking crowd in front of him. Several of them were dressed all in black, including black ski masks covering their faces. They held signs like *Make Racists Afraid Again*. One sign had the Nazi symbol with a red circle and a line through it. The word *Resist* was written under the symbol. There were several signs saying *No Hate*. Jed's heart started pounding as he stepped forward and shut the door behind him. Two men apparently leading the protesters wore T-shirts saying *No Pasarán* and Jed thought they were probably the same men who had told him about the Antifa movement. Jed tightened his arms around Aja and approached the two, hoping to talk to them before there was any violence. Tony came rushing over to Jed and steered him away. "Jed!" Tony yelled. "Give me Aja!"

"Oh thank goodness you're here!"

"I wasn't sure if you were back yet!" Tony replied breathlessly as he grabbed Aja. He started to run, yelling over his shoulder, "Call the Police!"

Jed took out his cell phone and dialed Goodman. Once told of the situation, Goodman said he'd call SWAT and that he'd come along with a squad from SFPD. The protesters milled about the courtyard, chanting slogans. Jed lost track of the two *No Pasarán* men as more and more Antifas showed up. They took turns by twos and threes, banging on the front door. With Aja now in safe hands, Jed felt a strange resolve that he would not unlock the door. If they were going to do damage, at least he could keep it outside.

Jed waited at the gate, eyeing the group but also looking out for the police. The media had started arriving, probably tipped off by the Antifas. Then he noticed the crowd running toward him and shouting, with reporters tagging along, holding up cameras and microphones. Suddenly 1488 broke away from the crowd just a few feet from where Jed stood.

Three of the protesters jumped on 1488 and started beating him. "Stop!" Jed shouted, but they paid no attention. 1488 fell to the ground, holding his arms over his head. Without thought of the consequences, Jed found himself trying to pull the Antifas off 1488. The scuffle continued with the three men trying to push Jed away while pummeling 1488. Jed received a few blows, but it didn't deter him. Distraction arrived in the form of the police who were soon on the melee with batons and twists of arms. They pushed everyone to the ground, holding their hands together to cuff them. Jed tried to explain who he was, but it was no use until higher authority in the form of Goodman showed up. He barked angrily at them to take the cuffs off Jed.

"You okay, Jed?" Goodman asked as he helped him up.

"I'm fine. What about 1488?"

Goodman shook his head. "What do you care?"

Jed ignored him and walked over to 1488, sitting on the ground, his head covered with blood and his clothes ripped. There was a policeman talking to him. "Did you call an ambulance?" Jed asked.

"Yeah, there's one on the way."

Jed's attention was diverted to the chanting and shoving between the protesters and the police who were trying to keep them away from 1488. Jed flashed back to that TV news scene from the nineties when Reginald Denny was beaten by a group of Blacks protesting the Rodney King verdict. The jury had acquitted the policemen who had beaten Rodney King and it sparked awful riots in Los Angeles. Hate has a way of feeding on itself. Jed agreed with what this Antifa movement stood for, but their violent tactics were ultimately self-destructive.

News reporters and photographers surrounded Jed, shoving microphones in his face and bombarding him with questions. Goodman elbowed his way through and grabbed Jed's arm and pulled him away. "Come on." He shoved Jed inside a squad car and sat in the back with him. "You'd better stay out of the way. They won't like that you tried to save that Nazi, even if you are Black."

Jed exhaled loudly and leaned back, realizing now what he had done. It had all happened so fast. It hadn't even registered that he had put himself into any danger until now. "They could have killed him."

"Yeah. You probably saved his life."

"Thank God Tony came and got Aja out of here."

"1488 had the bad luck to show up at the same time as the protesters," Goodman mused as he looked out the squad car window. "It looks like enough cops are here now to break it up."

"I hope they didn't do anything to the building."

"That's probably what they had in mind before 1488 showed up."

"This poor building has had its share of vandalism."

Goodman shook his head. "It's a beautiful place. It's a shame." He chuckled. "But protecting it is job security for you."

Jed's phone rang and he looked to see that Monica was calling. "Oh God! I heard the news!" she cried. "Are you —?"

"I'm fine, I'm fine," Jed cut in. "Tony took Aja away. I'll call you back later." He hung up and realized that Tony needed to know what was going on too, so he called him to update. Tony said he would keep Aja until he heard that all was back to normal.

Goodman was on his own phone, so Jed sat back and waited for the police to clear everyone out. He realized that he had indeed been hurt a little, but he could ignore the pain for now. His back had been beaten on and his shoulders ached, but that may have been from the police pulling his arms behind him to put on the handcuffs. Finally, the crowd was disbursed and Goodman got off the phone. "I think you can go inside now. I'm going to meet with Schultz and Kelly."

Jed got out of the police car and did a walk around the building to make sure there was no damage. Besides many trampled plants, nothing had happened to the building. Jed sighed with relief and unlocked the front door. He went inside and visited some of his old friends to sing and commiserate. He glanced at Spencer Dickson's apartment as he walked by and realized the situation had publicly and loudly landed in the board's lap.

He called Tony who said he'd be by in about an hour. He had taken Aja to the de Young Museum and she was enjoying the art. "This baby is going to be quite cultured by the time you're finished with her. Antique shops, art museums. When are you taking her to the opera?" Jed laughed. It hurt his back and shoulders, but he needed to laugh.

But things were not back to normal. Once the police and protesters left, Jed assumed the news media would leave too, but they stuck around. They wanted to discuss Jed's rescue of 1488. Jed was not interested in being lauded as a hero, and certainly not in this context. He brushed them off on his afternoon rounds and ignored them altogether by locking himself in his office. Their incessant knocking finally got to him and he yelled out, "I have nothing to say!" He heard a titter, some shuffling, and a few muffled questions. Eventually they grew tired and deadlines pressed. The hall outside grew silent.

Jed called Tony again with the latest news. Tony said he would bring Aja, Advil and a sandwich. "I bought some liquid formula for Aja. I didn't have a bottle, but she did quite well with an eyedropper and a spoon. It took a while, but it worked. I also bought some diapers. I'll keep them at my house just in case."

Jed smiled when he hung up, thinking what a good "uncle" Tony was. Tony came soon after they hung up and stayed while Jed ate his sandwich. By the time Tony left, the Advil had kicked in and Jed felt like he would be able to manage the pain without having to share any of it with Monica. Aja slept in the Snugli for the rest of the afternoon. The museum had done her in. They got home before Monica. Jed cooked some chicken he found in the fridge along with rice and made a salad. It was a regular home-cooked dinner in the house he owned with a family he adored. He never took for granted the fortunate turn his life had taken.

41

IT DIDN'T TAKE LONG FOR THE MEDIA TO CATCH UP WITH JED AGAIN. His phone started ringing just as he was squinting in disbelief at his exploited heroism on the evening news. He shut off his phone and the television and then turned to Monica, wondering how he was going to work the next day. Surely the columbarium would be overrun with reporters and the curious. She stopped swiping on her own phone and looked up. "You think the TV news is overhyped? You should see social media!"

"No thanks!"

Soon there was a loud knocking at the door and Monica peeked out from behind the curtains, scared that it was journalists looking for an exclusive interview. "It's Goodman." She sighed as she went to the door.

"I guess you're the man of the hour," Goodman bellowed as he came into the living room. Jed grimaced. "Well, I have some news that might cheer you up a bit. Schultz and Kelly have identified the Pakistani policeman.

Interpol has been watching him and he entered the country just a couple of days before you found the victim."

"Are you linking him to the murder?"

"We can't make that connection just yet, but they do have this guy's fingerprints on file. In Pakistan you have to be fingerprinted to get a cell phone. It's kind of a strange thing. Anyway, Interpol's been observing him because he is apparently part of some angle in the drug trade. He may be connected to Laila and the Balduccis."

"But you still don't know who the victim is?"

"They're doing a DNA investigation. That should be ready soon."

"Can you get reliable DNA from a dead person?" Monica asked.

"Oh, sure. It's amazing how far forensics has come. They will need to take some DNA from the baby, though. Has Schultz called you about that yet?"

"No." Jed felt very protective all of a sudden. He knew he had to let them if they were ever going to find out about Aja's family. He couldn't go further with the adoption process if they didn't do that first, but he was afraid to find out. "How will they take the DNA?"

"It's not easy to get it from a baby. Their saliva doesn't always have enough DNA in it and unless you can get her to spit, they may have to use a syringe or something."

"Oh man. That doesn't sound good."

"I'm sure it's not that invasive," Goodman said. "Anyway, I thought you'd like to hear this. Things are moving, Jed. Hang in there. The media blitz will die down soon. But be prepared for a couple more days of it until somebody shoots up a school or blows up a building."

"Nice," Jed muttered.

Goodman left and Jed put his arm around Monica and pulled her close. "I know all this heroism bullshit makes you uncomfortable, but you do make me proud," she said as she snuggled into his arms. "Why did you put yourself in harm's way for a man like 1488?"

"Because he's a human being and I'm a human being and I am going to do what I know is right."

"I don't think I would have done it."

"Maybe you're just smarter than me. You have other things to consider — your strength, your health. Anyway, it doesn't matter." He kissed her. "I don't think any less of you for not wanting to jump in and get beaten on."

"Well, that's good." She smiled at him. "I was thinking," Monica continued. "Maybe Tony could work for you tomorrow so you could avoid all the reporters."

"No, I've asked him for so much lately. I'm not going to let them get to me. I'm going to do my job."

"It was just a thought."

"Well, thanks for the suggestion, but I'll be fine. Now, let's get to bed before Aja wakes up. I could use some shuteye."

"Maybe you should check your voicemail and recent calls, just to make sure there isn't something important," Monica added.

Jed took out his phone and turned it on. He frowned at the number of voicemails. "How do they find my number so quickly? This may take a while. I guess I'll meet you in there." Monica went to bed and Jed scrolled through the recent calls and listened to the voicemails. There was only one call he needed to return. "This is Jed."

"Yeah, I need to get a DNA sample as well as fingerprints from Aja," Schultz answered.

Jed took a deep breath. "Does a baby have usable fingerprints?"

"At about three months. We don't know how old she is, but we're going to try. We'll be there tomorrow."

"What time?" Jed hoped they would come in the morning. The presence of the FBI might distract the reporters from bothering him and turn the questioning to Schultz.

"I don't know. It's up to the technician." Jed hung up and sat for a few minutes before joining Monica in bed.

There was a mob of reporters waiting for him at the gate the next morning. He remembered watching how those people did it on the news: just walk by and say no comment. So that's what he did. The reporters followed him inside. He turned around abruptly and said, "This is a quiet place where people come to visit loved ones who have died. Please respect that. I am not going to answer your questions and you are frightening my baby so please leave." Jed was surprised how effective his little speech was. The cacophony of questions died down, camera lights started going dark. A few lingered but ended up leaving when they saw that Jed meant what he said. Although his statement wasn't sensational, it was still something: it had decency they could profit from.

Schultz showed up toward noon and he and Jed went into the office with a technician to swab and prick Aja. She cried, but not for long. It was pretty quick. "You'll call me as soon as you get any information?" Jed asked.

"Yeah. Sure. And you call me right away if Ahmad shows up again."

"Ahmad?"

"Yeah, the Pakistani policeman. Ahmad Tahir. He's a real gem. Drug dealer, violent, one of the most corrupt."

The mention of drug dealer gave Jed an idea. "Hey, did you think to check that bag I found in the bathroom for his prints?"

"You telling me how to do my job, Jed? Don't you think we already did that?""

"Well, were his on the bag?"

"No. But nice try." Schultz glared at him and left.

Jed realized that the FBI was much more interested in catching an international drug dealer than a murderer. Now he understood why Goodman wanted to be in on everything and he was glad that he had kept Goodman in the loop. He wanted to call the board members to see if a decision had been made about Spencer Dickson's niche and more importantly, if they could help speed up Aja's foster/adoption process. He scrolled through all the names and found the person he thought would be most sympathetic and called her. She said she and the other board members were still debating about the decorations adorning the niche, but she would see what she could do about Family and Children Services. Jed hung up feeling hopeful.

He went back to the main building and made his rounds. Monica called to say she had received the paperwork and they could do it tonight. He told her what had happened with Aja and Schultz and how he had managed to keep the reporters away.

"Good blocking," she replied.

"Thanks," Jed chuckled.

"I'll pick up groceries on the way home so I'll be a little late," Monica added.

"By the way, I've been thinking. I want to get a driver's license again."

Monica laughed. "You want to visit all your newfound friends up in Garberville?"

"I want to take some pressure off you." He didn't want to tell her the real reason: that she might get too ill. They hung up and Jed and Aja passed the afternoon in a fairly quiet columbarium with only grieving visitors and a few tourists who had come to marvel at the architectural masterpiece. The looky-loos remained outside where the riot had been televised.

The next few days were problem-free and quiet, much to Jed's surprise and pleasure. That all changed by Monday of the following week when Goodman, Diaz, Kelly and Schultz arrived at the columbarium en masse. "Can we go to the office?" Goodman asked.

"Sure." Jed took the group back and waited for them to talk, wondering who was going to show themselves to be the leader of the pack. It was Goodman who spoke before Schultz could get a word in. "We got a real break in the murder case from Aja's DNA. She and Ahmad are related."

"What?" Jed stood and started pacing.

"The Feds and Interpol are still working on it, but our best guess is that the woman who was murdered was definitely Aja's mother and possibly Ahmad's sister-in-law. We've found Ahmad's father and brother in Pakistan. Rasul, the brother, had a wife who was pregnant when she went missing." He stopped and looked into Jed's eyes. "Her name was Yasmin."

Jed's eyes widened. "Really?"

"We're waiting for more information from Interpol. They are still in the process of interviewing Ahmad's family," Schultz chimed in.

"Are they part of the drug business also?" Jed asked.

"Doesn't look that way. It seems that Ahmad was working the drug angle in his position in the police department."

"Jed," Goodman said as he took his arm gently. "They are doing a DNA test on Rasul to see if the match is there for sure."

Jed took a deep breath. "What did the test show with Ahmad? I mean . . . does the test show a strong connection like —"

"Very strong. Yes, Jed," Goodman interrupted.

Jed was crestfallen and his face showed it. Goodman picked up on that and nodded to the others that they should leave. "We'll be in touch," Schultz said with unusual empathy.

Jed took Aja in his arms and held her tight. His phone rang. "Hello," he answered quickly. It was the board member he had called earlier.

"Hi Jed. I've checked our bylaws. We don't have anything specific written about what is allowed in niches, so we're going to have to write up a resolution on the matter. I have a call in to Family and Child services, but at this point I don't know how much influence I can pull there."

"Okay, thanks." Jed sat silently for a few minutes, not sure if he should call Monica or wait until he got home. His phone made the decision for him by revealing that Monica was behind the ring. "Hi," he said, trying to muster up some cheerfulness.

"What's wrong?" she asked.

"What do you mean?"

"Come on, Jed. You sound awful." Jed was silent. "What's going on? Are they hounding you again?"

"No."

"Is Aja alright?"

"Yes. She's fine. Can it wait until we get home? I really need to get back to work."

"If that's what you want."

"Why did you call?"

"Oh. I got the paperwork mostly done and I think I found a loophole making it easier for us to apply quickly." Jed didn't answer. "Hey, that's good news," Monica added.

"Yeah. Good news. I really have to go. See you later." Jed hung up and put Aja back in the stroller.

The columbarium had a lot of visitors the rest of the afternoon and that kept his mind off things and made the time go quickly. At five he locked up, changed Aja, and started the walk home. Monica was already home when he got there.

"I thought maybe we should go out for dinner to celebrate. I think we can sail through the process as soon as they clear it that she has no family," Monica called from the bedroom. She walked into the living room when Jed didn't answer and found Aja babbling on a blanket on the floor and Jed staring out the window.

"What is going on with you?" she asked as she rubbed his back.

"Goodman and Schultz came by with the results of Aja's DNA test. Apparently she's related to that Pakistan policeman who's been coming by. Interpol is interviewing his family and his sister-in-law has been missing. She was pregnant when she ran away. And her name was Yasmin."

"Oh no! So does that mean Aja would go back to Pakistan to the family? And don't they also have to show that the murdered woman is her mother?"

"That's pretty much a given, but yes."

Monica put her arms around Jed. "I know I've been ambivalent, but the idea was really growing on me and I saw how happy it made you."

"Well, maybe it's best for Aja. She really should be with a younger family." Jed looked over at Aja, playing with her fingers.

"Let's just appreciate the time we have with her." Monica kissed his cheek.

"But I don't feel like going out to eat. I'm sorry if you were looking forward to it," Jed said, kissing her on the forehead.

"It's fine. Eggs and a salad?"

"Sure."

"And a bottle of wine?"

"Absolutely," he said and kissed her again. He picked up Aja and held her close to his chest as Monica went into the kitchen to prepare dinner. Malcolm called while she was gone and Jed filled him in on all the latest news.

"Oh man, that's quite a story. I'm sorry. How do you feel about it? Last we talked you weren't sure about whether you wanted to adopt her if her family wasn't found."

Jed decided it was time to put his mind in acceptance mode. "It's probably best all around. It would be hard to take her to work with me everyday when she started crawling or walking and Monica could never take her. And we never know the long-term prognosis of Monica's HIV." He hoped that by telling Malcolm all that, he could believe it.

"I get what you're saying," Malcolm replied.

"So what's happening with you and Savali?"

"I'm doing some film work here and there and waiting tables at night. Savali's found some part time work."

"Oh yeah? What's she doing?"

"Some LGBT agencies have hired her to do some writing and speaking. It pays well and she gets to work from home." Malcolm laughed. "Now we just have to get used to both of us being home during the day and not getting into each other's hair."

Monica came in with the wine. "Sounds like things are going well," Jed said. "I need to go. I'll let you know what's happening."

"Same here. Love to Monica and Aja." Malcolm hung up.

"That was Malcolm."

"Everything good there?" Monica asked.

"Yes, everything's good there."

42

JED WOKE UP AND LAY IN BED, FEELING MORE RELAXED THAN HE HAD IN AGES. He was confident that no matter what happened, Aja would be loved and cared for, even in Pakistan. She would have extended family there, something she wouldn't have here in America. Jed thought about all the people Aja met in the few short weeks she was here: Tony, Malcolm, Homer, Dutch, Juniper, Haji, and even Goodman . . . what a motley crew that would be at the Thanksgiving table. He laughed out loud, waking up Monica. "I'm sorry," Jed said.

"It's good to hear you laugh." Monica kissed him. She then slipped out of bed as his laughter had caused Aja to stir.

Jed's phone rang immediately and he saw it was Goodman. "Hello?"

"Thanks for answering this time. I have some interesting news for you. Apparently the brother in Pakistan is not the father of Aja."

"What do you mean? Isn't he Yasmin's husband?"

Goodman laughed. "Jeez, Jed, did you just fall off the turnip truck?"

"Okay, I get it. Yasmin had an affair or something. But then how did Ahmad's DNA match up if his brother's didn't?"

"Jed, are you awake?"

"Oh! Ahmad's Aja's father?"

"It's looking that way."

"Oh no! Does the family know where Ahmad is?"

"No. But they were not too pleased, as you can imagine, when I told them about the DNA matching up with Ahmad and not with Rasul."

"That must be an awful thing to hear."

"As bad as it might be for you or me, in their culture it's the kiss of death, literally."

"What do you mean?"

"You never heard of honor killings?"

Jed gasped. "Oh."

"If she wasn't killed here, she would have been killed there."

"Killed by her own family?"

"It's happened before. In that culture it's all about not disgracing the family."

"That's awful. Any leads on where Ahmad is?" Jed asked.

"No. But we have a lead on Laila."

"Really? Is she here in San Francisco?"

"We think so. A woman called our department asking about the murdered woman at the columbarium. She had called earlier, soon after it happened, but we hadn't put it together because we were getting so many similar calls at the time. We always do in a case like this. I had a trace put on her phone and we have some uniforms going out to the neighborhood where we think she is."

Jed glanced at the clock. "I have to go to work. Please let me know when you find her."

Jed rushed into the kitchen to tell Monica and then hurried into the shower. He and Aja were a few minutes late, but luckily no one was there waiting. He did his singing and visiting and decided to call Garberville to let them know the latest. He wasn't sure who to call and decided on Juniper. She would care most about finding Laila and would also be the one to tell him honestly how Homer was doing. "Hello, Juniper? It's Jed."

"Hi, Jed."

"The police may have found Laila. And they are quite sure that it is Yasmin who was murdered."

"Wow. Big news. I'm not sure how well it's going to go over here, though. Dutch was pretty upset that she let herself get involved with that drug ring."

"I know. How's Homer doing?"

"Great. He's happy and so is Dutch. Homer has a lot of knowledge about stuff that Dutch needs help with. Homer jokes that his family was organic before organic was cool. And he knows the local conditions."

"So it's working out well for both of them."

"Yeah. Even the kids, the trimmers, are enjoying Homer's stories about his carney life."

"Say hello to everyone for me and tell Haji about Laila."

"Okay. I'll tell him. Hey, Jed?"

"Yes?"

"You know that guy, Malcolm, you came up here with the first time?"

"Yeah?"

"The one who wanted to make a documentary? I looked him up and found that he'd made one on transgenders. I watched it on Netflix. It was really good. Could you give me his number? I'm planning a trip to Los Angeles and would like to talk to him."

Jed was surprised. "Uh, sure." What was this all about? Was Juniper considering a change? He gave her Malcolm's number.

"Thanks. Let me know when they find Laila. I'll tell Dutch and Haji."

Jed hung up, a little perplexed, but then so much of the last few weeks have been a mass of confusion. He shrugged and thought he'd take more advantage of the lack of visitors and call Tony to update him as well.

He got through the morning fixing some niche doors, giving a tour to a few visitors, and signing up a new guest. But his mind was elsewhere. He kept checking his phone, thinking he may be missing Goodman or Schultz with news they had found Laila. He took Aja across Golden Gate Park to a Pakistani restaurant and brought a couple of orders of Samosas back to the columbarium for lunch. He thought he should be introducing Aja to Pakistani food, even though she couldn't eat it yet. At least Jed would know what it tasted like so he could tell her about it. They sat down for lunch and he tried to describe the flavor and the texture and how spicy it was, but Aja wasn't too interested. He thought he might go to the library and see if there were any Pakistani children's books he could read to her.

Jed's immersion of Aja into Pakistan culture was interrupted by the arrival of Schultz and Kelly. Goodman was not with them. "We didn't find Laila but we know where she lives and Goodman's set up a stake out. No sign of Ahmad, I take it?" Schultz asked.

"No," Jed answered.

"We may have to pick up Haji again and question him. He knows more than he's saying."

"But you're still going to give him immunity?"

"Jed, we never said we would give him immunity. We just said we would do everything we could to help him out."

Jed frowned. "He's a good kid. He didn't know the extent of what he was getting into."

Kelly laughed loudly. "Yeah, that's what they all are. Good kids."

Jed shot Kelly a piercing look and turned back to Schultz. "Do you have any leads on Ahmad?"

"Interpol does. They think he's still in San Francisco. No record of him getting on any flights yet."

"So Jed, they say you're quite the hero," Kelly said. "A regular peacemaker."

Jed ignored Kelly again and said to Schultz, "Thanks for letting me know what's happening." He took Aja, put her in the stroller, and walked away.

He was leaning into a niche, cleaning an apartment for a guest who would be moving in tomorrow when he was tapped on the shoulder. He took his head out and looked into the eyes of 1488. His head was bandaged and he was dressed in sweatpants, a sweatshirt and a baseball cap. He looked more like a slacker college student than a Nazi activist. "Hello," he said quietly.

"Hello," Jed answered warily.

"I, uh, want to thank you."

"That's okay."

"You saved my life."

"Well, I'm not sure if those protesters would have gone that far."

"I just wanted to tell you thanks. And to let you know that, I . . . " He exhaled and looked at the floor.

"No need," Jed replied quickly.

1488 glanced around and then looked again into Jed's eyes. "I'm getting out of this. Nothing good is going to come of it. You helped me see that." 1488 turned around abruptly and limped away.

Jed watched him leave and then squatted down to Aja's level in the stroller and smiled at her. "Charles Bukowski said that you can save the world by saving one person at a time. I hope he's right." Jed kissed Aja and she gurgled back at him with a huge toothless grin, kicking her feet and waving her arms.

He decided to go upstairs and check out Spencer Dickson's apartment. Sure enough, the flag was gone and the KKK urn had been replaced with a more generic one. There were still a few items with a Nazi or KKK bent, but the display was far more subtle than before. Jed thought that was a good compromise.

Monica called to say she'd be a little late getting home. "There's a steak marinating in the fridge and I think there are some frozen vegetables. Maybe you could pick up a loaf of French bread on your way home?" she asked.

"Sure." He decided to wait until they were eating dinner to tell her all the latest news. It was coming fast and furious now. Goodman called on his way home to inform him that Rasul's family did not want any part of the baby. "Yasmin has brought shame to the family by her affair with Ahmad. It wouldn't surprise me if Yasmin ran away knowing that she might be killed by her own husband and father-in-law."

"But what about Ahmad? Doesn't he shoulder some of the blame?"

"He's a man. The rules are different for men and for women in that culture. Ahmad probably thought no one would ever find out — — until this happened. He'd know sooner or later a DNA test would be involved. But Yasmin either knew, or was afraid for her life if they ever did find out. That's why she ran."

"How did you get Ahmad's DNA?"
"Interpol had it."

"What about Yasmin's family? Do they know about the baby?"

"According to Rasul, her family died in a suicide bombing. That's when his family took her in and he married her. They knew her from the village."

"So Aja is free to be adopted here?" Jed couldn't help but grin.

"Looks that way, Jed. I hope it works out for you."

"But what about Ahmad? Does he have any rights if he's caught? I mean could he stand in the way?"

Goodman laughed. "Jed, do you really think Ahmad wants her?"

"I guess not. Thanks."

"You're welcome." They hung up and Jed took Aja and hugged her.

On his way home he bought a bottle of champagne to go with the French bread and had Aja changed and fed by the time Monica walked in. "What's this?" she said when she saw the champagne chilling with a couple of flute glasses.

"Take off your coat and sit down."

"Okay, give me a minute to change my clothes." She went in the bedroom and came back in, picked up Aja and gave her a kiss, and snuggled into the sofa next to Jed.

Jed told her the news about Aja as they toasted each other. Monica smiled and kissed him, but he knew that her heart wasn't in it. "I know there's still decisions to make, but at least we have a shot at it and we can help choose what's truly best for Aja."

Monica just nodded and finished her glass of champagne. "I'm starved. Let me go put the steaks in the broiler." She got up and went into the kitchen. This was not exactly the celebration Jed had hoped for. Jed took a deep breath, trying to recapture how he felt when he awoke that morning — relaxed and confident. He had to trust the best situation for Aja was forthcoming.

43

A WEEK WENT BY WITHOUT ANY NEW INFORMATION ON LAILA OR AHMAD. Malcolm called to ask if he and Savali could stay overnight. "Savali has some meetings and talks at the GSA Network in San Francisco on Monday and Tuesday next week. We thought we would drive up early Monday morning and I could hang out at the columbarium with you and Aja while Savali does her thing. Then we'd like to take you and Monica out to dinner. Savali should be done by noon on Tuesday so we plan to leave that afternoon. Will that work?"

"Of course!" Jed answered. "You know you can stay longer if you want."

"I'm afraid we need to get back. Savali's got a lot going on. And don't worry about a place to sleep. We can drag in the futon from the van."

"That would probably work better than both of you on the sofa." Jed laughed and went on to tell Malcolm all the news about Yasmin and Ahmad and Aja's family.

"That's wonderful news! Now you can adopt her?"

"Well, we still have to be accepted . . . and . . ." Jed hesitated.

"And?"

"Nothing. Anyway, look forward to seeing you two. What's the GSA Network?"

"Gay Straight Alliance. It's a wonderful organization that teaches students how to start LGBTQ programs in their schools."

"LGBTQ? Is that the politically correct acronym? I didn't know there was a Q."

"Q is for queer. Some people use it without the Q, some like it with. There are even some that use LGBTQIAP or even more letters."

"So what's the I, A, and P?" Jed asked.

"Intersexual, asexual, and polygamous."

"Isn't the point of an acronym to make it easy to remember? That many letters hardly make it easier."

Malcolm laughed. "I know. I also have a hard time with using 'they' instead of 'he' or 'she' when people want to be referred that way. I mean, why did we bother to learn all those grammar rules if we're just going to throw them out the window?"

Jed laughed. "True. By the way, remember Juniper from Dutch's farm?"

"Yeah, of course."

"I hope it's okay that I gave her your number. She's going to Los Angeles and wants to get in touch with you. She didn't say why, just that she saw your film and wants to talk to you. Maybe she's curious about transgenders or maybe she just wants to talk to you about making documentaries. I'm not sure."

"I'm happy to talk to her. Did she say when she was coming?"

"No."

"Okay. We'll leave early Monday so I'll see you at the columbarium about noon."

"Great. See you then."

Goodman called with the news that they had located Laila. "Schultz and Kelly talked to Haji again. He finally gave up some places where Laila hangs out when she's in San Francisco. They picked her up and are questioning her now. She's not saying much yet."

"Is she arrested?"

"No. There's no evidence connecting her to anything. There are only the statements made by Haji."

"Can they keep her in custody?"

"For twenty-four hours at least. But they can usually find a way to extend that to seventy-two or ninety-six."

"Do you think they'll be able to get anything from her?" Jed asked.

"She's smart but she's also scared. Somebody or something has her spooked."

"You know, from what Dutch and Juniper said, Laila doesn't sound like a drug smuggler. I know Schultz and Kelly don't believe that, but I do."

"Those assholes always think they're right 'til they're wrong," Goodman sniffed. "I think she's doing it because she has no choice and that's why she's afraid. The Feds just need to make her more afraid of them."

"Do you think it's her connection here in the states who's intimidating her?"

"Could be. Balducci or Ahmad."

"What can Ahmad do to her now, though?" Jed asked. "He's on the run."

"Never underestimate the power of those who are vindictive, Jed." Goodman ended the call.

That evening, Jed relayed the news to Monica of Malcolm and Savali coming and then told her that Laila had been picked up for questioning. "Goodman thinks Schultz and Kelly will break her, but I'm not so sure." Jed decided to broach the adoption subject again. "Did you file the papers yet?"

"Of course I did," she snapped. "I said I would."

"I know, but we kind of left things dangling as far as what we wanted to do."

"Jed, I want you to have Aja. I know it's important to you. I'll get over my misgivings. Since Family and Child Services can now dismiss the possibility of her family wanting her, it should go relatively quickly."

Jed nodded, not sure how to respond. They pretended that everything was fine through the evening and the next day, but there was undeniable tension in the air. He called Goodman the following afternoon. He wanted to know if they had been able to keep Laila in custody. "Has she said anything at all? Does it seem like she might open up?" he asked.

"A little. They are good interrogators and their interpretation is that it's Balducci she's afraid of. They told her they knew that Yasmin was a friend of hers. That reminder seemed to have angered her. Hopefully she'll let that fact override her need to protect anyone else."

"I wish I could talk to her."

"Why?"

"Maybe if I bring Aja and talk to her about Dutch, she'd open up to me."

"I doubt they'd let you while she's in custody. Maybe if they release her, you could meet her."

"Where do they have her?"

"At 450."

"450?"

"450 Golden Gate Avenue. The civic center, you know, on Van Ness."

"Should I call Schultz?" Jed asked.

"Go ahead and try. It can't hurt."

Jed hung up and called Schultz's cell phone. It went to voice mail so Jed left a message. Schultz finally called back later that afternoon. "She's already been released, but she won't go far. She knows better than that. She's under surveillance and she knows she'd be in deep shit with both us and Balducci."

"So you think that she's protecting Balducci because he's threatened her?"

"Absolutely. She doesn't have to worry about Ahmad and anyway, she wouldn't care about protecting him. She hates him. She would definitely turn him in if she knew where he was."

"So she's back at — wherever she's staying?"

"Yes. We have some agents there, protecting her from Balducci as much as making sure she doesn't run."

"Could you give me the address? I'd like to try and bring Aja. Maybe seeing the baby will open her up somehow."

"Angling for her maternal side, Jed the detective? Can't hurt, I guess. She's over in the Haight. 1850 Page. I'll call ahead to the agents and let them know you're coming."

"Thanks." Jed hung up and turned to Monica. "Schultz agrees. I'm going to take Aja over to Laila's and try to talk to her."

"Is that safe for Aja?" Monica asked.

"There are FBI agents guarding her house. I doubt it could get much safer than that."

"I'll drive you."

"You don't need to. It's not far from here."

"Maybe you should just show her Aja and then I can take her home."

"I don't know . . ."

"Jed, who knows what those criminals are capable of. I don't want Aja to be put in those circumstances. Or you, for that matter."

"Why don't you drive me there and we'll play it by ear. Maybe Aja will be the icebreaker, so I don't want to jeopardize that. Just park down the street and I'll text you after I've gotten inside."

Monica frowned. "You're banking a lot on Aja's mediation skills, but I can see you're set on this crazy idea."

Jed kissed her. "Maybe this will break the case open and we can put it all behind us."

Monica nodded and smiled half-heartedly.

44

TWENTY MINUTES LATER MONICA PULLED UP IN FRONT OF LAILA'S APARTMENT AND JED GOT OUT OF THE CAR. He was getting Aja out of her car seat when a man came up behind him. "Jed?"

"Yes?" Jed said as he pulled his head out of the car.

"We want you to wear a wire."

"Oh, I . . ." Jed wasn't sure how to react.

"She won't know."

Jed looked at Monica. "Do it, Jed. You want to get this over with as soon as possible, don't you?" Monica said.

Jed turned back to the agent and nodded. The agent put the wire on and brought Jed and Aja into Laila's building. Jed knocked on the door and Laila answered. She was a beautiful, exotic-looking woman who looked much younger than Jed expected. "Yes?" she said, giving the agent a puzzled look.

"My name is Jed. I am the caretaker of the columbarium. I am a friend of Dutch and

Juniper and Haji. And this is Aja. She is Yasmin's daughter. I found her lying next to Yasmin's body at the columbarium. May I come in?"

Laila was dumbstruck for a moment and froze. Aja reached out to her and smiled and Laila had to smile back. She started to reach out to Aja but caught herself and dropped her hands. "I guess so," she replied, casting a pained expression aside. She opened the door wider and the agent left as Jed entered. Laila led Jed into the living room and motioned him to sit down. She hesitated, seemingly at a loss for words. Finally she said, "So how're things up at the farm?"

"Good. Dutch has taken a friend of mine under his wing. Homer has Parkinson's and Dutch is letting him live there."

Laila smiled faintly. "Dutch is a good guy."

"Yes he is." Laila fell silent, so Jed decided to explain why he was there. "My wife and I have been fostering Aja. Family and Child Services are releasing her for adoption because Yasmin's family doesn't want her." He was about to add that they were thinking of adopting her, but decided against it. Things were too up in the air.

"Poor Yasmin," she sighed, rubbing her hands.

"You knew Yasmin in Pakistan?"

"Yes. I helped her get here."

"You did?"

"I hooked her up with a family who she could stay with and they were able to get her here. I'm not sure how they did it. I didn't ask."

"Do you know that Ahmad is the father of Aja?"

Laila stared hard at Jed. "What?" She shook her head slowly. "When I saw her last in Pakistan she was still pregnant. She didn't tell me who the father was. She just said it wasn't Rasul and she was afraid that the family would kill her if they found out."

"So Yasmin ran for good reason," Jed said, more to himself.

Laila gasped loudly. "That bastard killed her!" Her outburst startled Aja and she started to cry. Laila instinctively went over to Jed and took her from his arms. "I'm sorry," she soothed. "I didn't mean to startle you." Aja settled into Laila's arms and Laila held her tight.

Jed stood up to be closer to Aja. "Who killed her?" he asked softly.

"Ahmad. I'm sure." Laila sniffed.

"But how did he know how to find her?"

"Oh God!" Laila's eyes teared up. She handed Aja to Jed and ran out of the room.

Aja started whimpering and threatened to cry again over all the commotion. Jed rocked and walked her around the room until she quieted down. It was several minutes before Laila returned and leaned against the wall, lifting her red and tear-stained face to the ceiling. "Are you okay?" Jed asked.

"It's all my fault," she said brokenly.

"What is?"

"I was supposed to meet her at Cup and Cake Café, you know that place on Geary?"

"The one just a few blocks from the columbarium?"

"Right. I told her to meet me there at six," she took a deep breath "the night she died."

"So she knew you were alive? She knew about all the drugs?"

"All she knew is that I wanted to meet her there. She didn't know anything about the drugs."

"How did you know where to contact her?"

"She was staying with the family that had brought her here. I told her to call Haji when she arrived and that he would know how to contact me."

"But if she was supposed to meet you at that café, what was she doing at the columbarium?"

"I'm not sure. I told her I needed to go there first to pay my respects to someone and that's why I was going to meet her at that café. She probably got to the café early and thought she'd meet me at the columbarium. She didn't know anything about what I was doing there. God, it's like I killed her!"

"No it isn't." Jed paused before asking, "What were you going to do at the columbarium?"

Laila stared out the window for a while before finally answering, "We were using my urn as the drop off place."

"Drop off what?"

"It's where we were going to exchange drugs for money."

"Inside the urn?" She nodded. Jed frowned, knowing he had to be careful in getting her to speak for the wire. "How long had you been doing that?"

"That was the first and only time."

"How did you make the exchange before that?"

Laila looked at him suspiciously. "Why are you asking me all these questions?"

"For Aja. My wife and I are thinking of adopting her. We want to know everything we can about her."

Laila wiped her eyes and walked to the window. Jed played peek-a-boo with Aja, hoping her giggles would soften Laila enough to talk to him. It worked. After a few minutes she came back and sat down. "We used to put the drugs in the casket going to a sham funeral home in Santa Rosa."

"Why didn't you keep using the funeral home?"

"They were onto Ahmad and found out about it."

"The funeral home?" Jed asked, trying to play dumb.

Laila sighed. "No. Interpol."

"So you needed to come up with a different scenario?"

"Yes."

"And Ahmad was your drug connection in Pakistan?"

"Yes. He killed Yasmin. I'm sure of it."

Jed sat back and tried to process everything Laila had told him. Now if he could just get Laila to verify that Anthony Balducci is the American side of this drug ring, the Feds could concentrate on finding Ahmad and Anthony Balducci and he would be out of it. "But how did Ahmad know Yasmin would be at the columbarium? Had you told Ahmad you were meeting her afterward?"

"No. I was supposed to get the drugs that he left in the urn that day. He wasn't supposed to come and get the money until the next morning."

Now Jed realized why Ahmad had been at the columbarium those times he had seen him. He was looking for the money. Laila wouldn't have been able to get in the day after the murder because of all the police presence. They weren't letting anyone in. Ahmad must have seen Yasmin at the columbarium when he left the drugs. "So it was just a terrible coincidence that Ahmad saw Yasmin."

"Now I see why he was so angry when he found out she was pregnant. He's a violent man and Yasmin was afraid of him. If he knew that baby was his, who knows what he would have done."

Jed sighed. The story made sense now. "You need to tell the police all this."

Laila started to cry again. "I'll go to prison for good. I am as much to blame for Yasmin's death as Ahmad."

"No you're not. You didn't put them together again. That was just a freak coincidence. If you tell the Feds all this and who the American kingpin is, they'll let you off easily. Is it Anthony Balducci?"

Laila looked into Jed's eyes and nodded. "I'm . . ." her voice trailed off into more sobs.

"Why are you doing this? No one seems to think you're the type to get involved in a drug ring."

She closed her eyes and sighed. When she opened them again she found Aja studying her intently. Laila smiled in spite of herself, and Aja smiled back. Laila went over to Aja, picked her up and held her close. "I have a son who was doing this. He fled with some of the drugs. Anthony had already paid him, thinking it was all accounted for."

"So he ran away with both the drugs and the money?" Jed asked incredulously.

"That's what I was told. The only way I could get Anthony not to kill my son was to reimburse him. So I started doing it just to pay Anthony back."

Jed was flabbergasted, but he understood why Laila did it. "Where's your son now? Is he safe?"

"I don't know where he is. I haven't heard from him at all since. I was contacted by Anthony and told about it."

"Did you know your son was doing this?"

"My son is mentally ill. He left home at eighteen and I would only hear from him once in a while. When I tried to get him help, he got angry and wouldn't speak to me."

"I'm sorry, Laila. Shall I call the FBI? You need to tell them."

She nodded and squeezed Aja tightly again as she gazed out the window at the sunset colors reflecting off the buildings. Jed quietly made the call. When he finished she turned to him with sorrowful eyes. "I guess I'm glad to get all this over with."

"Were you close to paying Anthony back all that your son owed him?"

"I don't know. That's what makes it even worse. I never knew exactly how much he was owed." She shrugged. "He could have strung me along after I had already met the amount and I wouldn't know."

"Would you like to call Dutch and talk to him?" Jed asked.

"I don't want to talk to Dutch."

"May I tell him?"

She shrugged again. "I don't care. I don't care about much of anything . . ." She gently rocked Aja.

"Why didn't the family Yasmin was staying with contact the police? Didn't they wonder when she didn't come home?"

"They're illegals. They would never contact the police. And Yasmin may have told them that she was going to stay with me."

At that moment, Schultz and Kelly walked in to the living room with a couple of other agents. Laila handed Aja over to Jed without a word and followed them out. Jed trailed behind, shutting the door behind him.

Schultz, Laila, and the two agents got into a black van and drove off. Kelly turned to Jed and said, "Would you mind coming with me. I need to get a recording of what you two talked about."

"Why? She said she would tell all."

"C'mon Jed. You'd think by now you'd get the picture. They don't always do what they say. And your testimony can help a lot."

Jed took the wire off and handed it to Kelly. "It's all here."

"Yes, but there may be some more questions and clarifications."

Jed sighed. "Can I bring Aja to my wife so she doesn't have to go too?"

"Is that your wife in that car?" Kelly pointed.

"Yes."

"I'll wait for you."

Jed nodded. "Can you give Laila a break? You heard her story."

"She just gave up two drug lords. That will go a long way for her."

Jed took Aja to Monica and then got into Kelly's car and went to FBI headquarters. "Is Goodman going to meet us there?" Jed asked as they drove down Oak Street.

"Yeah, he and Diaz will be there."

"Good. I don't want to have to tell this story more than once."

They got to 450 Golden Gate and went inside. Jed was there for three hours and by the time he got home, Aja was asleep and Monica was reading in the living room. A cold dinner awaited him on the table. Monica closed her book and joined him at the table to hear the story while he ate. "You must be starving. Eat first and then talk."

"Thanks." Jed finished and they went back to the living room. Monica sat next to him on the sofa with her head on his shoulder and listened while he told her the whole story.

45

THERE WAS A COUPLE WAITING AT THE GATE WHEN JED ARRIVED AT THE COLUMBARIUM THE NEXT MORNING. He went to the office to get forms for them to fill out and then helped them with the business end of setting up an apartment for their loved ones' ashes. He watched them empty out a shopping bag. He hated that he now had to monitor what people brought to decorate their niches, but he had to make sure there was nothing offensive. His phone rang and when he saw it was Schultz he answered right away. "Hello?"

"Laila spilled everything."

"Good. Will you be able to cut her some slack?"

"If all works out as we hope."

"And Haji?"

"Oh, he's nothing. Nobody really cares about going after either one of them."

"What about Ahmad and Balducci?"

"That's why I'm calling. We had Laila call her contact to tell Ahmad that the money's in the urn now. We'll be waiting for him."

"So Ahmad will be here some time today?" Jed asked, starting to feel nervous.

"You won't be involved except to give us a signal when Ahmad has arrived. There will be agents waiting outside."

"Call you?"

"Just text me."

"Okay. What about Balducci?"

"We have another plan for him. We can get to him through his bodyguard. Neither you nor the columbarium will be involved with that."

"Thanks. Ahmad is about all the excitement I can stand right now."

Schultz chuckled softly. "You're right to feel that way. Thanks for your cooperation, Jed."

Jed heard a familiar voice calling from behind just as he ended the call. "Hey, Jed!"

Jed spun around. "Malcolm!" They hugged. "You're early."

"We woke up at four so we figured why not just leave and get here early."

"Where's Savali?"

"She'll meet us later. She went straight to the GSA headquarters. Let me see this beautiful young lady." Malcolm stooped down and kissed Aja. "You know, I haven't seen this place before. Can I push Aja around and take a look? Give you time to —"

Just then Jed saw Ahmad enter the building and rush upstairs. "Malcolm, just take her outside and walk around the block, okay?" he said in a low voice. Malcolm gave him a strange look. "I'll explain later," he added as he texted Schultz. "But go now!"

Malcolm took the stroller and walked briskly out the door. Schultz came in right after Malcolm left, leading two other FBI agents. Jed pointed upstairs and Schultz nodded. They clamored up the stairs and soon there was a scuffle and shouts. Jed ran to the couple decorating their niche and brought them inside one of the alcoves. Luckily they were on the first floor, quite removed from the action. They huddled together as Jed briefly explained that an arrest was in progress and how sorry he was for the scare and inconvenience. They listened to the yelling and scuffling on the floor above and Jed tried to reassure them, but he was also concerned. They heard a thud and some glass break and then the sound of running footsteps. The couple turned toward Jed with frightened looks. Did Ahmad get away? They heard one of the agents shout, "He's cuffed!" Jed peeked from the alcove as Schultz and the agents shoved Ahmad down the stairs and out the door. After heading the shaken couple back to their niche, he made it to the door just in time to watch a combative Ahmad get pushed into a black van. Jed sighed and texted Malcolm to return with Aja and then called Monica to give her a quick run down.

"What's going on, Jed?" Malcolm asked as he approached with Aja.

"So much, you're not going to believe it. But let me finish helping these people and then I can tell you during lunch. Take a look around and hopefully Aja will fall asleep and you won't have to worry about her."

"She's fine. And I'm fine. I have had a lot of experience with babies, you know." Malcolm started walking around the rotunda while Jed went back to the couple.

Malcolm took Aja out to get some sandwiches and they were finally able to sit down together in the office and catch up. "Wow! That's incredible!" Malcolm exclaimed after Jed had finished his story.

"Thanks for taking Aja this morning. By the way, did you talk to Juniper?"

"Yes. She was just interested in filmmaking. Hey, let me take Aja this afternoon. I could even bring her home if you want to give me the key."

"Really? That would be great for her and for me."

"I'd love to spend more time with her."

Jed handed Malcolm the key to the house. "I'll be home a little after five."

"Okay. Savali should be there about five thirty."

Malcolm took the diaper bag and the stroller with Aja inside and left. Jed went up to check on Laila's niche to see if any damage had been done, and then realized that it shouldn't really be there. Laila wasn't dead and they certainly weren't going to be using it as a drug receptacle anymore. He decided to empty it out and ask Dutch what he wanted to do. Jed was quite willing to make sure Dutch got a refund for the niche. He wanted all traces of the situation to be erased, and that would be the easiest way to do it.

Jed and Monica arrived home at the same time and Savali came a few minutes later. Malcolm had Aja changed and dressed and was on a blanket on the floor with her. After the introductions and hugging, Aja became the center of attention when she started grinning and gurgling at Savali. Savali responded in kind. Before long, Savali was on the floor too and both were playing with her while Jed and Monica looked on. "Have you heard about the adoption yet?" Malcolm asked.

"Not yet," Monica answered. "Elizabeth is working on it and trying to push it through."

Savali looked over at Malcolm. "Maybe she can help us to adopt?"

"But we don't live in San Francisco."

"I know, but it sounds like she understands unusual situations and she was more than willing to go out of her way to help Monica and Jed adopt."

Malcolm beamed at Savali. "So you're ready?"

Savali kissed Aja and then grinned at Malcolm. "Yeah. I think I am. So what do you think Monica? Could you talk to Elizabeth?"

"Um, yeah." She looked at Jed whose curious look slowly aligned with her thoughts. "Sure," she added definitively.

"So where are we going to dinner?" Jed grinned.

"It's our treat," Savali said. "You pick the place."

"Let's go to Zazie's," Jed said. "All of our important and momentous occasions have happened there."

"Hey," Malcolm said. "It's great to see you and all, but momentous?"

Jed cast a loving look at Monica and said, "I think it will be turning into one. Do you have the same thought, Monica?"

"Absolutely. I always wanted to be a grandmother."

Savali looked up at them in wonder. "I didn't know you already had children." She shot a critical look at Malcolm. "At least Malcolm never mentioned it to me."

Malcolm winked at Jed. "She'll catch on eventually." He looked at Monica. "Do you think it can work?"

"I'll call Elizabeth right now." Monica left the room, scrolling through her frequently contacted numbers.

"Would somebody please clue me in?" Savali asked.

Malcolm picked Aja up and put her in Savali's arms. "Aja, say hello to your mama."

Savali looked at Malcolm and then Jed. "You mean . . . <u>we</u> adopt Aja?"

Malcolm hugged and kissed Savali and looked lovingly into the baby's eyes. "What do you think, Aja?"

Aja gurgled and smiled up at Savali and Malcolm.

Acknowledgments

As always, I want to thank Tin Roof Café for providing me a place to write with my endless cups of Earl Grey tea and my community of wonderful friends who also spend their mornings there: Margie, Earl and Marilyn, Judy and Richard, Skye, Mark. . . to name just a few as well as all the delightful baristas who come and go.

Glenn Tucker for all my audio and technology assistance.

Rafiki Webster and David Gallo for being sounding boards and giving many helpful suggestions.

Chris Saur and Daniel Nauman for their invaluable, superb editing.

An excerpt from Emily Gallo's next novel *The Last Resort*

PROLOGUE

It was July 1998 and Luther was waiting to start college in September. He finished dinner and decided to go down to the playground and see if he could join in a pick up basketball game. There were several people playing, some of whom he had seen before but no one he knew personally. When it got too dark to see, they asked if he wanted to join them for a beer. Luther didn't have a car so a couple of them offered to give him a ride. They stopped at a convenience store to pick up a couple of six packs. Luther stayed in the car while the other two went inside. Two shots rang out and then one of the guys ran out the door and down the street. Luther got out of the car and ran inside. Two people lay on the floor. One was the driver of his car and the other was a middle-aged woman, both of them holding guns. Two teenage girls, crying hysterically, sat against a cooler. And that's when his life changed irrevocably. He never made it to college. In fact, he never made it home that night. In a matter of minutes he was sitting in the back of a patrol car charged with murder.

1

LUTHER WALKED TENTATIVELY INTO THE CAFÉ. He was tired of answering questions. He wasn't interested in a book deal or another lawsuit. He just wanted to get as far away as possible from the place he had lived for thirty years. He wanted to forget everyone connected with it. He wanted to bask in his exoneration and freedom. This wasn't even about a fresh start. It was about leaving behind the memories and the scars that had been etched into his mind and body. He had lied to the lawyers and the warden when he told them that he had a nephew who lived in San Francisco's Richmond District. That's where the bus dropped him off. But there was no nephew. He had been disowned and forgotten by his whole family other than his mother, and she had died several years ago. He had won the lawsuit and would get some money eventually, but now he had two hundred dollars and a small duffle bag.

He read what was written on the chalkboard and was bewildered by the café menu and shocked at the prices, but aware that after thirty years in San Quentin, there would be a lot to get used to. Chai? Café Macchiato? What were they? "Do you have plain old coffee?" he asked the waif of a barista who poured him a cup without responding. "How much?"

"Three dollars," she answered.

"Three dollars for a cup of coffee?"

She stared at him and sighed. "That's what I said."

Luther put three dollars on the counter and went to one of the tiny tables to contemplate his next move. He checked out the other customers. They were mostly singles, reading or working on laptops. A couple of them were talking to each other across the tables. As Luther sipped his coffee, he noticed them sprawled out as if they had been here a while and were not leaving anytime soon.

He glanced at the clock on the wall and saw it was after one. He knew what he had to do before looking for a place to sleep. He threw his cup away and walked out, took a left and started walking east on Geary. He had studied the map and knew exactly where he was going. He took a right on Arguello, then a left on Anza, and looked up at the magnificent building when he got to Lorraine Court. The sign said San Francisco Columbarium. He had come to the right place. He took a deep breath and walked through the door and was greeted warmly by an older African-American man. "Hello, may I help you?"

"I'm looking for someone," Luther answered.

"What's the name of the person you're looking for?"

"Isabel Banks."

"Follow me. My name is Jed."

"Luther."

Jed took him to a computer terminal on a table. He punched a few keys and then said, "Here's the list. You can scroll down to find her."

Luther looked at him and shrugged. "I don't know how to do this."

"Oh, okay. No problem. I can show you."

"Uh, could you just find it for me?"

"Sure." Jed sat down at the table and scrolled through as Luther watched him, mystified. "Here it is. Second floor. C'mon. I'll show you."

"Thanks." Luther followed Jed up the stairs.

"Let me know if I can help in any way. I'll be downstairs." Jed left Luther standing in front of a glass door.

Luther took out a paper napkin from the café and wiped his eyes. "Hello Mama." He peered into the niche at a picture of an elderly Black woman next to a brass urn. There was a bouquet of artificial flowers in a sconce perched right outside the glass door. He stayed for several minutes and then turned around and walked back downstairs.

"Is there anything else you need?" Jed asked as Luther started out the door.

Luther turned around and looked into eyes that made you feel like you could tell him your darkest secrets. Jed was the other end of the spectrum from the waif at the café. "Yes."

Jed led Luther to a couple of chairs and said, "Let's sit down over here. Now . . . how can I help?"

Emily Gallo was born and raised in New York City and now lives on two and a half acres in northern California and in 750 square feet on the beach in southern California with her husband David, their Schiller hound Gracie and their rescued cat Savali.